# A Love Divided by Time

## Richard McMaster

ISBN: 979-8-218-76395-4

# Acknowledgements

I am grateful for the support of my editor, Susan Pohlman, who possessed multiple layers of talent in helping to deliver this story, and others, and for her lovingly tactful honest ways of not offending me. Over the years I learned I can be straightforward with people, hope for the same, and work best with caring people who are smarter than me—she was perfectly that.

https://www.susanpohlman.com

# Reviews

In his profoundly moving new novel, *A Love Divided by Time*, Richard McMaster explores the power of enduring love, the potential for evil to destroy, and our ability to overcome.

What stands out is the author's belief in his characters' courage and resilience. Through it all, he reminds us of the power of enduring love, the forces of good and evil, and the strength of the human spirit. A Love Divided by Time is a journey not to be missed.

Dr. Kixx Goldman, Psychologist, Coach

Author: Speak from Your and be Heard

https://www.drkixxgoldman.com

"If you're looking for a book that will take you on an emotional journey, A Love Divided by Time is it. The story of Forrest and Allie is both heartbreaking and inspiring, and the way the author explores the idea of past lives is truly fascinating."

- Lorena Wilkins

"A Love Divided by Time is a stunning novel that will leave you breathless. The story of Forrest and Allie is tragic and beautiful, and the way the author weaves their past and present lives is truly remarkable. This book is a must-read for anyone who loves a good love story with a twist."

- Rogelio Wilkerson

"This book is simply amazing. A Love Divided by Time is a timeless story that will leave you breathless. The author's attention to detail and vivid imagery makes the story come to life, and the characters are so real that you can't help but feel invested in their journey. I loved every page of this book and would recommend it to anyone looking for a great read."

- Juana Chandler

"McMaster's novel is a masterpiece. The way he writes is so immersive, and the story itself is a true gem. A Love Divided by Time will take you on a journey of love, loss, and self-discovery that will stay with you long after you finish reading."

- Cecil McGuire

"A Love Divided by Time is a beautifully written novel that captivates the reader. The author uses words that draw you into the story and make you feel like you are right there with the characters. I loved how the author intertwined the past and presented it to create a timeless love story that inspires you. The story arc of Forrest and Allie is beyond comparison.

- Carol Coleman

# 1

*Does life ever follow a straight and intended path?*

*Allie and I married in a summer wedding in Minnesota on the shore of Lake Bemidji. We vowed to have and to hold from that day forward, for better, for worse, for richer, for poorer, in sickness and in health, until death did us part, as two lovestruck loons floating up to the shoreline bore witness that Alexandra Wellington became Alexandra Nelthorpe.*

*Who would have guessed, Allie, the New York City girl, and me, the son of a lumberjack, were meant to be together? Before we met, I thought I'd play hockey for the University of Minnesota, then move on to the National Hockey League. In high school, I was first-team all-state in Minnesota and led the state in goals scored two years in a row, even though I was injured at the end of my senior year.*

*The first time I saw Allie it felt as if our now and forever love had formed in previous lives and being born again a game of hide and seek to find each other in plain sight, seeking our other halves, united and whole. When I close my eyes, I am always with her. I think of all our days together— when we met, our first kiss, the miracle cabin, and white puffy clouds.*

*I remember the day when I thought I lost her. I was horrified to think what it would be like living without her. How could I go on? Whenever we talked about it, she always smiled, tilted her head slightly in an all-knowing, keeper-of-secrets way, and flashed her green eyes, "We'll find each other again."*

*It's why I believe in miracles.*

*Miracles. Scientists don't believe in them, so they refer to them with asterisks. Science doesn't understand love is like a miracle, as powerful a force as gravity. Can science determine when you love someone or who? In the ways of love, there must be miracles, and I will always be with Allie.*

*I remember the surreal moment when I first saw her in college ethics class. It was like yesterday.*

# 2

Usually, the first student to arrive, Forrest removed his stocking cap and coat, tossed them to his feet and took a seat in the third row. He wore a navy-blue heavy Pendleton sweater, his sandy short cropped hair combed up like the bristles of a brush, not cut as short as his customary summer crew cut.

Iowa winter classes at 6:00 am were as much a matter of determination as a duty.

The surviving half of the students who attended the first-semester ethics class, all twenty-five, were wearily strung out in a lecture hall that could easily hold 150, slouched in their seats, some rested their heads on their hands—gloves, scarves, and coats were strewn over chairs and at their feet.

On the blackboard at the front of the room written in cursive:

Department of Philosophy

Ethics

Professor Smithson

Professor Max Smithson entered through a side door, ambled up the lectern steps, leaned out over his elbows on the lectern, and peered over the top of his tortoise reading glasses. "I recognize a few of you." Looking back to his notes, loud enough to be heard, "Back for more."

Professor Smithson, the legendary reputed authority on ethics, author of five books, owner of seven advanced degrees, and chair of the philosophy department, played the professorial role masterfully. Today, he dressed in blue jeans, a denim shirt, a brown tweed sport coat, and a dark flannel tie—the same one he wore every day of class last semester. A professional student, like others in his field, he searched for something beyond reach, the elusive unraveling of the universe of mind and spirit, right in the palm of his hand but not quite.

Pulling off his glasses and twirling them in his hand, he continued, "Okay, it's time to wake up—literally and metaphorically. This semester we're going to explore ethics on a more personal level. Last semester we explored the best way for people to live and what actions are right or wrong in particular circumstances. Does anyone recall the three major areas of study within ethics recognized today?" With a wave of his hand, he invited answers.

A student in the back row blurted out, "Meta-ethics." Another student yelled out "Normative." Three others called out, "Applied."

The professor raised his eyebrows. "There is hope for this class. This semester we'll start with a survey of famous philosophers: Aristotle, Plato, Kant, Nietzsche, Buddha, Confucius, and Averroes. We will explore more deeply these great philosopher's contributions and the consequences of ethical breaches in everyday life."

A familiar voice in the back row yelled out, "How about politicians?"

Recognizing the voice, Forrest turned to locate Woody, his roommate, sitting in the back row. Woody loved to sleep in and usually arrived last to his early morning classes.

Hockey teammates and best friends, James Woodruff, Woody, the top defenseman in Minnesota, was best in the country according to Forrest. His kind freckled face resembled more an Irish priest than a rough and tumble hockey player. Still, he would have been a goon in professional hockey since he never turned down a hockey fight. When Woody got into a fight, hockey players from both teams leaned back and said in unison, "Ooh."

Forrest played forward. They played well together, seemingly attached by an invisible string. Hockey fights were inevitable, so when Forrest saw a fight coming on, he always threw the first punch and made it count. Then inevitably, the two hockey fighters came together as figure-eight skaters staring each other down, until sometimes the referee called out, "Let 'em fight."

"We'll take that up, too." Smithson paused and looked out over the top of his glasses, hunting for the face behind the voice. Finding it, he smiled and nodded, and moved out from behind the lectern and wandered across the stage. "Politicians? Let's explore that. What role does a belief system play in ethical breaches and consequences for politicians?" Then with a wave of his hand, he dismissed the question, "We'll save it for another day. Politicians are too easy a target. I'll save it for a lecture on psychopathy."

He returned to the lectern and continued, "So how important is our daily ethical behavior? Do you think our actions affect us? Others? How are we affected by the unethical actions of those around us? Is it the grand design, the glue of energy that holds us together—actions ripple and cause reactions, some small, some large, but always consequences? For every action, there is an equal and opposite reaction."

"It's called Karma," another familiar voice interrupted. Forrest had only recently met Arjun Dewar, who roomed across the hall, a black-haired wisp of a boy, who introduced himself as RJ. Forrest turned to see RJ standing in the row opposite him. His hair down over his shoulders. He waved his hands like an orchestra conductor. "Call it Karma, the great law of cause and effect—action and reaction, which controls the destiny of all living entities. Consequences are woven into the fabric of life and come in many shapes and sizes. You disrupt the natural flow when you step outside your everyday values."

With a raise of his eyebrows, Professor Smithson turned his gaze to RJ, "I remember you Mr. Dewar. Glad you're back. Thank you for sharing your wisdom."

As Forrest watched the professor stroll back and forth, his gaze was interrupted by the vision of a girl in the front row. Unable to shift his gaze from the back of her head, he willed her to turn, even a small twist so he could see her.

Her gaze followed the professor but never at an angle to allow scant tantalizing temptations of what she looked like. He was fascinated by her image, an image only in his mind since he could only see her back. He shook his head and looked back to the professor as his voice reentered Forrest's consciousness.

Professor Smithson continued, "By next class read Aristotle's moral theories found in the ten books of Nicomachean Ethics." He liked to throw a curve to students on the first day, knowing there were only two hard-to-find versions of the ten books in the library.

As the mystery girl departed, Forrest caught his first view of her. She had stunning green eyes, and her smile looked to be carved onto her unblemished, wintery cheeks, her fair olive skin like a Greek goddess. He had never seen green eyes like that—the color of Lake Louise.

Making her way out of the lecture hall, she hesitated and looked toward him, but somewhere over his head, searching for something, an unexplainable response to the mysterious urge to turn, as if someone had called out her name.

He turned to see what she was looking at and found no one behind him, only beige painted walls. Had she looked directly at him, she would have seen a man with his mouth open, not lacking in confidence or at a loss for words.

He watched her every step out of the lecture hall before he exhaled. What is it about a simple place and time?

***

The next time the ethics class met was Friday. This would be his last chance to connect with her on a campus of over twenty thousand students until next week. How could he find her in this mass of students?

Forrest was mildly interested in the subject—ethics. He fell somewhere between the fifty percent of the students who thought ethics boring and were fulfilling graduation requirements and had little expectation the subject matter would ever land them a high paying job, and the few dedicated students.

The lecture hall was located across the river from the main campus, across the Burlington Street bridge over the Iowa River, the coldest place in Iowa on most winter days, especially at 6:00 am, as the frigid howling wind turned the quick feet of students sideways against it. When he arrived, the hot lecture hall was a potion for sleep.

Looking out at a sea of bleary-eyed yawning students, with a smirk, Professor Smithson began. "Good morning, lovers of Aristotle," he boomed loud enough to rouse the sleepy-eyed students. Looking out, he saw heavy coats draped over empty seats, on the floor or in the aisles, and many drooping heads, some resting on their desks. "It is good to see so much enthusiasm. By now, Aristotle must be your favorite philosopher. So, what did we learn? What did Aristotle believe to be our highest virtue?"

As he surveyed the hall looking for a student to call on, many shifted from side to side, looking skyward or down to their desks, pretending to be taking notes.

"Nobody has an answer? Somebody can surely tell me what Aristotle believed the highest virtue man seeks." Professor Smithson paused and smiled. "Okay, by man, I mean women too. Is it knowledge?"

No student raised their hand. Forrest, sitting in the third row, watched the female student in the first row. Today her hair was pulled back in a long ponytail, tied with a yellow ribbon. He had planned to be early to sit near her, but he had arrived after the other students had taken their seats. Professor Smithson pressed further, "Was it Aristotle who said knowledge was power?"

Suddenly, as if Forrest willed it, the female student in the first row turned toward him and smiled. She wore blue jeans and a brown, bulky turtleneck sweater dotted with snowflakes. Forrest smiled. She looked away quickly.

"Ah-ha," professor Smithson blurted out. "I think Mr. Nelthorpe has the answer."

Still looking at the female student, Forrest blurted out. "Happiness."

"Very good. You did your homework. So, was it Aristotle who said knowledge is power?"

"Bacon." Forrest blurted out again. "It was Sir Francis Bacon who said knowledge was power. He also said, 'he that thinks himself the happiest man is really so.'"

Professor Smithson beamed. "And?"

"'But he that thinks himself the wisest is generally the greatest fool.'" Forrest smiled broadly and looked down at the girl in the first row looking back to him, smiling.

"So, Mr. Nelthorpe, I can see by the smile on your face you are quite happy yourself. What is it that makes you happy?"

Waving his hand toward the girl in the first row, "I'm thinking how happy I'd be if the girl in the front row would go out with me."

Laughter broke out and brought a smile to Smithson's face. Looking at the female student who had turned away, blushing, he continued, "I am sure that would be a happiness of which Aristotle would approve."

When class ended, and students rushed to leave, she turned and left him staring at the back of her head as she exited. When he finally escaped the hot lecture hall, he spied her down the hallway standing before the bulletin board. As he approached, she turned and walked away.

# 3

After the football game Saturday, Forrest made his way to the library. Eighteen credit hours were more of a challenge than he expected. Holding a book open and taking notes, he saw the girl from his ethics class in the distance. He watched as she weaved her way between the tables toward him. When she arrived, she dropped her books on the table and sat down, as casually as meeting someone on the street said, "Hi."

Forrest looked toward her uncomfortably. He wasn't sure she recognized him from class. Speaking in his library voice, "Hello, I'm in your ethics class."

She arranged her books on the table without looking at him and retrieved a pen from her bag. Barely above a whisper, she responded. "Oh, sure. I remember you. The happy one. Is that class boring or what? Aristotle must have been a pretty boring guy. Did he sit around dreaming this stuff up?"

"Yeah. Yiata, yiati, yiata." Reaching out his hand. "My name is Forrest."

"Yiata? What is that?"

"The Greek word for why. Aristotle spoke with a lisp. Probably the first *Yada. Yada. Yada.*"

"How do you know all that stuff?"

Pointing his finger to his head he answered. "Filled with trivia. Not sure why I remember things like that." With a puzzled expression, he said, "Forrest. I'm Forrest."

"Hello, Mr. Forrest."

"You are?"

Hesitating, her expression turned serious. "Alexandra."

"That's a lot of name."

Looking around uncomfortably at the other students with their heads bent low, studying, she explained, shrugging her shoulders apologetically, "My grandfather was a history professor at Penn. He did his doctoral thesis on Nicholas II. Alexandra, the last empress of Russia."

"Your grandfather?"

"Not sure how my grandfather got involved in naming me." Shrugging her shoulders, she added, "When I was only a bulge in my mom's belly, Father always called me his little princess, I guess."

The silence was unnerving. In a soft voice, Forrest said, "That certainly explains the name." He repeated her name reverently, as if he was wrapping his arms around it, "Alexandra."

"Strangers call me Alexandra. But if I let them in, they call me Allie."

"I guess I need to go to work on the getting close part. How does a guy do that?"

Allie opened one of her books and flipped open her notebook, leaving Forrest waiting for an answer. "Forrest? That's a nice name."

"Father is in the wood business. No long line of Forrests here. No kings or revolutionary heroes. Just an occupational thing."

"Like a lumber company?"

"No, more like lumberjacking. My father cut down trees for a living. He took 'em down, and I put 'em up." Forrest worked for the U.S Forest Service planting trees in the summers, but there was never any danger of him following in his father's footsteps. His father, Francis, loved to talk about the old days, the day of big cuts, skidding logs with mules or oxen, and swinging the big logs onto trains by derricks or into the river. Always quick to stress logging was a hard way of life, "It'll wear you out early and can kill you." More fortunate than most logging men of his generation, his father became a whistle punker at a young age, an important job for a responsible man. "Father now works in a sawmill. I'm from Bemidji, Minnesota. Me and Paul."

"Paul?"

"Paul Bunyan. Obviously, you haven't been to Bemidji?"

Born and raised in Bemidji, Minnesota, Forrest lived in a modest home not far from the lake and close to what they believed was the Mississippi River's source. His grandmother, a schoolteacher, moved to the area when his father was a boy after his grandfather died in an iron range explosion. His father met his mother Ethyl in a remote tent camp, a sister of a fellow lumberjack's wife.

Forrest inherited his strong back and his crew haircuts from his father. Even when home on college breaks, the two would make Saturday morning trips to the barber. And also, from his Dad, the rough-and-tumble, get-knocked-down-and-get-up and-skate attitude that served him well in hockey and in life. From his mother, he inherited the grace of a figure skater and a cheeky smile.

The murmuring sounds of students interrupted the silence. Forrest followed Alexandra's gaze to the far side of the room. Straining to see what the whispering was about, they glimpsed Tommy Horn breaking away from a group of fans and making his way toward them. Along the way, he stopped and talked to three female students. Allie raised her hand to get his attention. Tommy nodded and broke away.

When he arrived at their table, Alexandra stood, and Tommy gave her a shoulder hug. He looked over to Forrest then back to her. "Sorry I'm late. Coach wanted to see me after the game. Big game, huh?"

Alexandra interrupted and put her fingers to her lips. "Shhh."

"Oops. Sorry." With a crooked, toothy smile, he nodded to Forrest. "Not in the library much."

Looking over to Forrest, Alexandra said, "This is Forrest Nelthorpe. He's in my ethics class."

Forrest rose out of his chair, shook his hand, and congratulated him, "Good day for the Hawkeyes."

"Nelthorpe, huh?"

As Forrest collected his books and papers, Tommy asked Alexandra if she had seen the game. Her expression said she hadn't. "Big game," she responded dispassionately. "I didn't get to see the whole thing. But we laid it on 'em. Congratulations."

Forrest flung his book bag over his shoulder. Stocking cap and gloves in hand, he looked to Alexandra and softly muttered, "I'll leave you guys to your studying. See you in class."

***

Monday morning ethics class convened on time. Alexandra sat in her usual spot in the first row, and the other students were strewn around the lecture hall, heads in their hands, resisting the requirement they had to wake up in a class they found boring.

When Professor Smithson entered, he didn't take his position behind the lectern but stationed himself in front of it and surveyed the class, shaking his head. The door at the top of the hall burst open, and Forrest hurriedly rushed down the stairs and took a seat near the front, next to Woody, a few rows behind Alexandra.

"Enter the late, but happy, Mr. Nelthorpe." The professor let Forrest take his seat. "So, Mr. Nelthorpe, are you still happy?" As Forrest tossed his coat aside and flung his gloves and hat to his feet, the professor continued, "Did you ever get a date with Miss Wellington?"

"No, and he's not so happy anymore." Woody blurted out. The hall erupted with laughter.

Looking over to Alexandra, "Well, Miss Wellington, is it true?"

Turning her head back to Forrest, she answered, "That's true. But he never asked."

**4**

College daze felt like a penny poker game to Forrest who didn't have a care in the world—waiting on reality, living in the purgatory between childhood and manhood. He knew it all and nothing at the same time. Confidently insecure and playfully serious, he began plotting how to date the wonderful Miss Wellington—the famous history professor's granddaughter, the namesake of the last empress of Russia, and, to his way of thinking, about to become his princess.

Forrest had little dating experience. Before now, he hadn't had a serious date, ever. When it was necessary to have a high school date, he got one, but with no one in particular—it wasn't his time for dating, and pickings were slim in his small Bemidji High School. A date with Alexandra was different as if mortally wounded by the cherub's quill.

Before he met Alexandra, when he first arrived on campus and going through rush, he met a girl named Brandi Lynn and was rudely introduced to the new world. He was a freshman, and she a sophomore Alpha Chi Omega sorority sister. By reputation, AXΩ girls were a little wilder than girls in the other sororities, and Brandi did little to dispel her reputation.

Brandi was a party girl. She called herself that. A petite brunette with puppy dog brown eyes, she bragged she could out drink any guy, entered all the chugging contests, and was an amorous drunk. A fraternity brother told Forrest, drunk one night, she stood on a bar table and stripped down to her bra and panties before the owner pulled the plug and ended her routine.

Forrest pledged to the Alpha Sigma Phi, $A\Sigma\Phi$, but lived in the dorm. For two weeks, she stuck to Forrest like flypaper, taking him to all the rush parties, showing him the ropes, tailgate parties, and football games.

He had never been serious about girls, and while she was fun and initially irresistible, he was always nervous around her, like dating a movie starlet. In the end, he stopped answering her calls, and when they finally did meet again, he awkwardly told her, "Not now. This is all so overwhelming. Let's be friends."

He got the "let's be friends" line from his roommate, Woody. "Are you out of your mind? Woody exclaimed. "You're tossing Brandi back for some other fisherman to catch." Every college boy dreamed of dating a beautiful popular girl. "Guys are tripping over themselves to be in the same room with her, and you want to get rid of her—a woman who wants the same thing as us guys? Are you sure you like girls?" he joked.

Clinching his jaw, wanting to end the back and forth once and for all, he said, "Woody, I can do better than that, and will. I have this feeling there is someone special or me."

Brandi became a memory, quickly put aside when Allie agreed to meet at the Memorial Union for a soda, which they thought would be equal distances between their residence halls— hers, Burge Hall, and his Quadrangle.

In the sixties, securing a room in the Quadrangle was like drawing aces. Vine covered brick towers, a center courtyard, a short-order grill, the best pecan rolls in the Big Ten, a barbershop, library, lounge, post office, and radio station, at one time the largest dormitory in the country. Originally, a barracks for the army training corps in World War I and then home to naval pre-flight cadets in the forties, famous residents included Nile Kinnick, John Glenn, and many of the 1943 national champ Iowa Seahawks preflight football players.

Woody told him Alexandra liked to bowl. He argued and cajoled, even asked him to trust him. It was questionable Woody even knew her, but sitting in the Memorial Union, uneasily drinking a cup of hot chocolate, trying to fill the spaces in their conversation, he asked if she wanted to go bowling.

Surprised at the question, thinking it was a curious first date invitation, she asked, thinking it must be important, "So, you're a bowler, huh?"

"I bowl," Forrest responded awkwardly. "Sure." Proud of his ability to communicate, but now he was tongue-tied and saying stupid things? Lies.

Alexandra told all her friends about a disastrous date in New York with a bowler. "I'll never go on a date again with a bowler," she proclaimed. His confident, mischievous smile suggested something fishy. Against earlier proclamations, having made up her mind she wanted to be with him, she agreed to go bowling. "You can call me Allie," she said as they parted.

***

When he picked her up, Forrest wore the same blue jeans he wore last summer, planting trees for the U.S. Forrest service—gray Bemidji High School sweatshirt with the Lumberjack logo, a hooded jacket, and mukluks. Allie wore designer jeans, the same snowflake sweater she was wearing in class, knee-high New York leather boots, and a fur-lined, hooded full-length coat.

The late afternoon sky looked more like evening. Iowa snowstorms come on like that, dark cloud cover so dense, days end early with spitting snow that builds to blizzard conditions. The forecast called for a foot of snow, but he was from Minnesota, and his black '57 four-door Bel Air had new snow tires. What was a little snow?

The Colonial Bowl was a few miles north up U.S. Highway 218. It smelled of beer, cigarettes, and fried food, and ten frames of bowling were enough for both. The number of gutter balls and open frames put their bowling abilities on full display. Neither broke a hundred. Afterward, they sat and watched the other bowlers. "I thought you were a bowler?" Allie chided.

Raising his eyebrows as he propped his feet on a chair, "I thought you were a bowler."

Allie bristled. "Me? What could have given you that idea?"

"You know Jim Woodruff? Woody?" Forrest inquired hesitantly. He could tell by the puzzled look on her face the answer was no. Embarrassed to be caught in a prank, he explained Woody had told him she liked to bowl. He should have known by the look on his face he didn't know her. And he called her Alexandra. What a giveaway. He changed the subject. "Love your shoes."

Holding one foot in the air to show off her faux suede rented bowling shoes, she said, "Pretty snazzy, huh?"

"Next time we go bowling, I'm gonna buy you a bowling shirt," Forrest chortled.

"Next time? So, who's Woody?"

"Woody's a friend of mine. Popular guy. Maybe you've heard of him. He and some guys reactivated KWAD, the Quadrangle radio station. It can only transmit twenty or thirty feet from the building, so maybe you haven't heard it. It's been kind of fun. Woody and I go way back." Forrest hesitated, then shook his head. "He told me you liked to bowl."

Allie began to laugh, a whisper of a laugh at first, then unexpectedly, a rainbow of flocking birds taking flight, drawing curious glances from the couple bowling two lanes away.

"What's so funny?"

"I get it. Somebody told Woody I went out on a date with a bowler. Bet he knows my roommate. It was a blind date." Allie stifled a smile. "I told Susan I'd find another roommate if she ever did that again. Tell me about Woody."

"I'm from Bemidji. Woody's from Walker just down the road, forty miles up and around Leech Lake. We roomed together on hockey all-star trips to Wisconsin, Michigan, and Boston. A fearless defenseman, he'd get down on his knees and block shots with his face." Forrest laughed. "He caught a puck in the face, and it put his eye out. So, remember when you meet him, look at his right eye. That's his good one."

A curious expression crossed her face. "So how did you guys end up here at Iowa, all the way from Minnesota?"

"Iowa didn't have much of a hockey program. It's a football school. Woody and I wanted nothing to do with the University of Minnesota after they pulled our scholarships. Shattered dreams. We wanted nothing to do with hockey."

"Why'd you lose your scholarship? Don't tell me you only have one eye too?"

"Right after Woody's ordeal, I broke my leg in two places and was told I couldn't play again. My kneecap never fit right after that. And that's how I ended up at Iowa. We came together. Hockey rejects. Too proud to go to the University of Minnesota."

Allie leaned back on the vinyl bench, removed her bowling shoes, and laid her white stocking feet across his lap. They paused and listened to the howling wind outside, and at the far end of Colonial Bowl, a ball spun along the waxed wood alley and crashed into the pins sending them scattering.

Several times he wanted to ask but didn't want to be too obvious. "So, how do you know the quarterback? He's a big man on campus."

A coy smile spread across her face. She had thought about letting him dangle but decided to be sympathetic with his uncomfortableness. "I tutor him and a couple of the other players."

Relieved, Forrest changed the subject. "So, how did you end up at Iowa from New York City?"

"I always wanted to be a writer. Not a journalist type, but a writer who inspires people, fiction stories about life. Hemingway said fiction writing is the toughest of all. 'You have the blank sheet of paper, the pencil, and the obligation to invent truer than things can be true. You have to take what is not palpable and make it completely palpable, and also have it seem normal, so it becomes a part of the experience of the person who reads it.' Sounds like fun, huh?"

Forrest studied how she encircled the words and caressed them as she released them like each as important as the other. He could see she was passionate about being an author.

She enthusiastically continued. "Camus said 'fiction is the lie through which we tell the truth.' I love the way my favorite authors do that by painting pictures with their words. You can read a whole chapter in a textbook that a fiction writer can sum up in one sentence or a word. I'm reading a book, *Crockett's Education.* It's a sports memoir. You'd like it. It's serious, at times funny, about a man raised by an abusive survivalist father who overcame his childhood, ran away to New York when he was fifteen, become a professional baseball player, and later a WWII spy. He had such a philosophical way of looking at his predicaments, like when he tells his readers he accepted his swings and misses and always goes to bat thinking about a home run. At one point, when things were at their worst, he wrote, 'Life pitched a shutout yesterday. Life one Me zero. At least life didn't score a lot of runs, and it wasn't the World Series.'"

"*Crockett's Education*, huh?"

The alley lights blinked off one by one as people finished bowling and left. It was getting colder, and snow was piling up, but he hoped she wasn't eager to go back to the dorm. Only one lane at the far end had its lights on.

"It wasn't easy. My father and I argued my whole senior year. My father is an attorney in Manhattan, and that's what he wanted for me."

"Once a city girl?" Forrest questioned.

"Once a country boy?" Allie threw the question back.

"Well, Minnesota's a different kind of country, not like this corn country. More like lots of trees and lakes country. More like water with dots of land where I live."

"Father wanted me to go to Georgetown, his alma mater," she continued. "I didn't have the heart to tell him I didn't want to end up in his law firm. Anyway, he loves a good negotiation. He wanted me to go to law school. I wanted to be a writer, so we compromised. He told me to try it out, take all the prerequisite courses, and then when law school comes around, if I don't feel it, I can be a writer.

"I agreed under the condition I could go to a good writing school. Father said the University of Iowa was the best, and they have a good law school too. He said the top lawyer in his firm was an Iowa law graduate. So, here I am, getting ready to be a lawyer hoping to write poetry or children's books. I think deep down, Father is a little jealous of my wanting to write. But if I end up becoming a lawyer someday, I'll have a library filled with the classics."

Allie grew quiet. Forrest wondered what she was thinking, maybe about home, New York City, or a library filled with classics. Did she regret being here? Could a city girl like her become a Minnesota girl? An Iowa girl? She was still, in an angelic pose, as peaceful as a sunny summer lake. Their gazes locked momentarily, and then she turned away.

They were the only people left. At eleven o'clock, Forrest went outside to check the conditions and found it worse than he imagined. Customarily the bitter cold didn't favor large accumulations, but this had turned into a blizzard. The snow had drifted halfway up the side of his car, and there were eight inches of snow neatly stacked on the roof. The parking lot lights were mere dots of light.

When he returned to the bowling alley, he wondered if they could stay until the plow cleared the roads, so he sought the proprietor. He found him in an office behind the counter, sitting at his desk. After explaining the situation, the owner, shrugged his shoulders and said, "Makes no difference. I'm not going anywhere."

Next, he asked Allie if she needed to go back to the dorm. No doubt, she never experienced weather like this. Allie called her dorm and told them she would be there when they plowed the streets.

The bowling alley was eerily quiet. Overhead, popular music continued to serenade racks of bowling balls and lonely darkened lanes. When they returned to their seats, Forrest leaned back and propped his feet on one of the wooden chairs. Allie laid her feet across his lap.

The room temperature alternated between open furnace, sleepy hot, and snow drift cold.

He took a moment to admire her.

There were questions on her lips, but her eyelids were heavy and struggling to stay open, resisting the comfort of sleep wanting to know more about the man in the Lumberjacks sweatshirt. Her lips moved slowly, ever so slightly. "I'm tired."

Forrest wondered what she was thinking, what to say, or whether to say anything and release her to blissful sleep. When the room turned cold, he reached for her coat and laid it over her. Her Mediterranean complexion looked soft and creamy.

They both fell asleep, but twenty minutes later, he opened his eyes. She was not a dream. Without opening her eyes, as if she could tell he was watching and waiting for her to wake, she softly wondered out loud, "Is this what Minnesota weather is like?"

"Our winters are colder and longer."

"You like that?"

"I love lakes and tall trees. Weather comes with it. It's not a desert. I figure life is what you make it wherever you are. Maybe life's more about being with people you like to be around. I figure you can spend your whole life chasing perfection, and the weather is not top of my list. Is New York where you want to end up?"

"Not really. Never thought I'd end up there." In a hushed voice, like at the end of a late-night pajama party conversation, Allie asked, "Tell me about Bemidji. Maybe I'll get to see it sometime."

Cautiously, her being from New York City, he worried not to make it sound too deep in the backwoods, keep it light. "You remember me mentioning Paul Bunyan?"

She smiled, rolling her eyes up toward the ceiling, "Paul Bunyan?"

"There is a Paul Bunyan statue there that stands eighteen-feet-tall and weighs seven and a half tons. Well, he was much bigger in real life. They say Paul and Babe the Blue Ox, his companion, created the lakes in Minnesota." He looked at her quizzically. "You heard of Paul?"

"Well yeah, but . . . ."

Interrupting, Forrest continued, "When Paul cleared out the forests, he made footprints in the earth, and rainwater filled 'em. That's how the lakes were formed. Seriously, if you look at a map of Lake Bemidji, you can see his footprint. One time two mosquitoes lighted on one of Paul Bunyan's oxen, killed it, ate it, cleaned the bones, so Paul sent to Australia for two special bumblebees to kill these mosquitoes."

Allie maintained a curious expression, holding her lips tight to suppress a smile. "And, they killed the mosquitoes?"

"Nope," Forrest continued eagerly. "The bees and the mosquitoes intermarried, and their children had stingers on both ends." Forrest paused, grinning.

"There's more?"

"Well, to get rid of them, Paul brought in a boatload of sorghum up from Louisiana, and while all the bee-mosquitoes were eating at the sweet sorghum he floated them down to the Gulf."

Allie laughed, shaking her head.

He noticed she had opened her eyes wide, like right before opening Christmas presents.

Feigning fascination, she said, "So maybe you'll introduce me to Paul. I wonder if he knows the New York Paul Bunyan, the one at Old Forge, that made the upper New York lakes. All these years I thought the real Paul lived in New York," she said sarcastically. "We used to go up there as a kid, my brother and me."

Pretending to be stunned by the revelation, opening his mouth and grabbing his chest, he said, "After all these years, I thought Paul was born in Bemidji. Must be like there's no Santa Clause."

Allie's whimsical smile suggested she had more to say about Paul Bunyan. "Robert Frost wrote, 'to drive Paul Bunyan out of any lumber camp all that was needed was to say to him, "How is the wife, Paul?" Then he'd disappear. Some said it was because he had no wife, hated to be twitted on the subject, or had been jilted by the love of his life. The truth be told Paul wouldn't be spoken to about a wife in any way the world knew how to speak in.'"

Forrest held his breath, then let out a heavy sigh in a broad smile that shaped the unspoken words, *I love this girl.* "He wrote that?"

Five o'clock in the morning, the first hint of the new day peeked through the front door. The wind had died down. The Colonial Bowl proprietor was asleep with his head on the counter.

Forrest looked back to the main entrance. "Shall we check it out?"

As Allie put on her boots, she looked at him. "Forrest."

Hesitating, he stiffened, anticipating she had something important to say. "Yes."

"Don't ever take me bowling again." Playfully, she hooked her arm in his, and they walked to the front door.

A confident young man, living in a black and white world, Forrest wondered how to hook the girl of his dreams—Miss Wellington, as Professor Smithson called her. Hooking her was the most important thing in his life right now.

Minnesota boys know how to fish and play hockey, having spent half their lives on any of a thousand lakes. Fishing was a lot about presentation, an attractive lure, enough to catch the fish's eye, a temptation at first, then irresistible. You had to know when the fish was on the hook, not too soon and never too late, or the fish would spit it out, swim away and never return. One chance. *This better work.*

Beyond his college years, Forrest knew what he wanted out of life. He wanted Allie. He wondered if it would be appropriate and decided what the heck. What better way to make his intentions clear? Like her fiction novels, one sentence could be more informative than a volume of textbooks, and the wrong string of words might not be adequate at this early stage of the relationship and maybe misunderstood. Words can be forgotten, blown away in the Iowa storm, or interpreted and reinterpreted for days.

She might think him impulsive, but all night long, he watched her wet her lips, seductive, always on the verge of breaking out in a smile and turn the howling wind into a summer breeze. All evening he wondered what it would be like to kiss her full lips. There were only two ways to interpret the kiss, he figured.

Forrest insisted she stay inside while he dug out the car. "This isn't for New York city girls," he said.

After digging out, he escorted her to the car and opened her door, and as she was about to enter, he pulled her back. Fluffy blowing snow caressed the fur lining on her hooded coat. She turned and faced him. She had a curious expression, wondering what would happen, what he was about to say. Their gazes locked. Courage rose in his chest and warmed his blood. They were so close their exhaled breaths turned into a vapor cloud engulfed them, her cheeks were rosy, and her eyes were green with flecks of gold.

A gust of wind blew snow through the open door onto the front seat. Fast-moving clouds were making a break for it, chased away by the sun poking in and out. Forrest felt his heart trying to beat its way out of his chest.

Shivering, she turned her face up to his as if delivered by fate. *Just right.* Their lips met in a full kiss as if they had practiced the moment, only briefly, long enough for a lasting memory before he eased away and said, "I like you." There wasn't a hint of anything nefarious, no ulterior naive motives. The kiss was as pure as the snow they were standing in. She smiled as he eased and into the warmth of the car.

# 5

Forrest and Allie married midway through graduate school in a simple summer ceremony on Lake Bemidji's shore. Allie insisted she wanted a simple wedding in her newly adopted home state of Minnesota.

Allie's folks flew in from New York with her brother, his wife, and family friends. They stayed in a rented house. They were disappointed in the wedding location but didn't show it. No doubt their feelings were overruled by her graduating with honors and acceptance to law school. Still her father hoped someday she would join his law firm, although her new husband, an ex-hockey player was heading for an advanced marketing degree and Alexandra had declared Minnesota was her new home.

He hoped she would tire of the cold and the damnable mosquitoes. He was worldly enough to know life was like aging wine, and time revealed what nature granted they year's grape. "You can't make a great wine with wishes," he stoically told his wife, Luciana. He never argued against her decision. He added, "Of course, there is always this chance she'll grow tired of the damnable mosquitoes."

Forrest and Allie stayed with his folks. They slept in separate bedrooms and kept warm under Hudson Bay blankets on deep mattress feathery log beds. Ethyl wouldn't have understood them sleeping together.

The night before the wedding, they cuddled before a roaring fire in the fire pit down by the lake. Before falling asleep under the stars, the last words of Allie were, "I love it here. I never knew there were so many stars. I want a cabin on a lake someday."

***

Allie's father, Kristopher Wellington, appeared to be a well-bred Englishman but was a second-generation American from the Upper East Side and the only one to wear a suit at the ceremony. Most of the time, he loosened up and wore a sport coat and an open-collared shirt.

Her mother, Luciana, Mr. Wellington called her Lucy, a descendant of José Sanjurjo,a general in the Spanish civil war. Her father emigrated from Spain and became wealthy in the textile industry. She carried herself as Spanish royalty, but, come wedding time, she cried as if her house had burned to ashes at the wedding.

At first, Kristopher and Luciana enjoyed the peaceful contrast to New York City, forests so thick they hid an unimaginable variety of wildlife, lakes everywhere, and the black nights, the stars. They soon missed the restaurant scene, the traffic and city noises, cars honking, and sirens. After three days, they hated the mosquitoes and couldn't wait to return to New York.

An unpredictable odd-couple tale that Francis and Kristopher hit it off so well. Francis loved to tell stories, and Kristopher loved history, an inheritance from his father, the famous Penn history professor. Ethyl and Luciana were of different breeding, but they both possessed old fashioned mothering sensibilities and basked in the satisfaction their only children had chosen so well.

Francis gave Kristopher a Bemidji Sawmill ball cap, which he wore with his blue blazer, and gray wool trousers to breakfast at the White Wolf café—a stuffed white wolf displayed in the window. They hiked into a tamarack bog and explored three-hundred-year-old pines, paid the obligatory tribute to the Paul Bunyan and Babe statue, reputed to be the second most photographed icon in the country, and toured the sawmill.

Francis, explained how his grandfather emigrated from England by way of Ontario, Canada, then died in an iron range explosion. He described the area's logging days history, and his marriage to Ethyl, how in the early years of their marriage, they rode horses to and from the camps where they lived in a tent when the weather was good. For three years they moved from camp to camp until they had enough money to buy the Bemidji house they lived in today—east of Lake Avenue, off the Blue Ox Trail, not far from where the Mississippi flowed from the lake. The house built at the turn of the century was updated twice, the last time by his father, who was not handy chopping down trees and making them into lumber, but fine at carpentry as well.

Wedding day morning broke like any other Northwoods summer day, an early sun, frogs croaking on the shore, ducks quacking, the bugle of an unseen Moose, a motorboat banging across the water carrying fishermen to their favorite fishing holes, and across the lake the distant sound of a chain saw.

Up at the crack of dawn, Forrest's ritual had always been to stand on the end of the dock with a mug of steaming coffee and watch the sun come up. Even on cold winter mornings, he ventured lakeside and listened to the ice crack and race across the lake. This morning, Allie wasn't far behind him, her Bemidji Lumberjacks mug in hand. As she greeted him, they heard the roar of his father's truck and turned to see Francis and Kristopher heading off to join friends at the White Wolf Café.

The wedding was officiated at the Willow Wildlife Nature Center. Woody, his hockey friend, and college roommate stood as his best man, and his father, a musician who owned a Walker, Minnesota, music store where he sold instruments, CDs, and old vinyl records, provided the reception music.

Forrest and Allie didn't need a honeymoon for the sake of romance, and Forrest had plans for a lifetime of honeymooning, so he artfully evaded the subject. The cost of a honeymoon was not worth the lifetime of dreams Forrest had in mind. When she asked what they should do for a honeymoon, he always answered, "Let me surprise you. If you don't like the honeymoon I have in store, then you pick the place, and we'll go."

The day after the wedding, when she thought they were going to town for breakfast to meet his dad's friends, instead of turning west to dip around the lake toward town, he went straight. "You missed the turn," Allie said cautiously.

"I didn't miss the turn. We're on our honeymoon." An hour later, he turned at the road sign that read "Ten Mile Lake," and asked her to close her eyes. "I don't have to blindfold you, do I?"

Giggling, she answered, "You can trust me."

Halfway up Ten Mile Lake, he turned onto a narrow, overgrown gravel road that opened into a clearing. When the car stopped, she opened her eyes.

"Okay, keep an open mind. This could be the best honeymoon, or we're making plans for Paris . . . someday."

When she opened her eyes, her smile turned serious, confused as she stared at a wooden structure overgrown with trees and ten-foot-high unruly, fully bloomed forsythia. A wall of thick golden flowers obscured a western red cedar log home.

As they were walking toward the beach, Forrest said nervously, "We'll have a private cove." Pointing to the infestation of Sting Nettle, "Be careful where you walk—that stuff will irritate the skin." Watching Allie for a reaction, he cautiously pointed to patches of Bull Thistle growing freely. "That too."When they arrived at the beach, they found it overtaken by Creeping Charlie, and a dock partly submerged with several planks missing.

Allie's mouth opened, speechless.

"Don't say anything yet. Let's keep going."

As they toured the cabin, Forrest didn't dare stop describing its potential for fear Allie would say something.Inside the cabin, the two-story-tall windows claiming the entire southern wall provided a picturesque view of the sky and lake. The warped planked ground floor was dusty and water-stained, and the outdated kitchen, with crumbling black tile countertops, looked out to an oversized rock fireplace that dominated the far side of the great room.

Both the up and downstairs bathroom's flooring was hard on the eyes—pea-green linoleum—and rust stained the porcelain tubs and sinks. Large loft, master bedroom windows the length of the room provided a view out to the lake.

In response to Forrest's declarations about future improvements, Allie said little, only huh huhs, and a few ohs, and a lot of head-nodding. They ended up standing on the dilapidated, postage-stamp deck looking out to the lake. Forrest caught his breath, "We'll double the size of the deck, triple it," pointing to the far end of the cabin. "All the way to the end."

Forrest waited, desperate for a response.

After a long pause, Allie spoke. "So, we own this, do we?

Forrest swallowed hard as he watched tears form in her eyes, feeling it wasn't such a good idea after all. "Yeah. This belonged to one of the logging foremen where Dad worked. He's in assisted living in St Paul. I bought it on really good terms. We did. Really good terms. Dad helped us buy it. We'll pay him back." Pausing, observing her for some sign of how she felt. "Is everything okay?" Forrest asked nervously.

Allie inhaled deeply. A smile spread across her face, tears streaming down her face. "Are you kidding? I love it. It's perfect. We'll make this place our own. Our kids will spend their summers here."

# 6

Years passed before they completed the cabin renovations.

The ice on Ten Mile Lake melted on March 31st, a little over a month ago. Forrest climbed out of the icy water after bravely cannonballing into it to cool off on the uncharacteristically hot day. He joined Allie who sat shivering, wrapped in a beach blanket, also having just climbed out of the water. Large droplets of water beaded on her lotioned olive skin, her hair pulled back and tied in a ponytail by a yellow ribbon.

"Who would have thought?" Allie laid back on the dock. "Seems like yesterday we were getting married by the lake and starting a new business right after we bought this honeymoon cabin."

"And now," looking back to view the cabin, Forrest smiled proudly, "We have our dream cabin. Have I said it every year since we built this?"

"Yes, you have. And then you say, 'Allie, did you ever think a New York girl like you would be building a cabin on a northern Minnesota lake someday?'"

"I know. I can't get over it," Forrest said.

"Our whole life has been a dream . . . except for the baby part. It took us a long time to finish this place. I am glad we decided to take our time and do it on our own. It means more, don't you think? You did a great job."

"We did," Forrest argued. "Couldn't have done it without you. I wish I had a picture of you sawing boards and wearing your hard hat, pounding nails."

The property itself more valuable than the existing old run-down cabin, but they decided on a restoration project instead of tearing it down. Finding the property was like finding an antique car covered with hay behind a barn. If not for his father, it would never have happened.

Together they did as much of the work they could handle, except the work of a carpenter—his dad's friend—who constructed a new deck and screened porch, a necessity in the Northwoods, and re-placed the hardwood floors. He also installed windows to add views. They subcontracted for kitchen cabinetry and countertops, road resurfacing, a new dock, and an oversized river rock fireplace. Allie applied her tasteful finishing touch with backwoods log furniture, right down to the antler lamps, Steve Lyman wildlife, Al Dornisch Loon paintings, and wood carved light switches and wall plates.

"Did you ever think the business would grow so big, so fast?" Allie asked.

"I wonder if anybody ever thinks their business is going to grow like this. You go up to the plate and find the bases loaded, and you hit a grand slam. All you can do is round the bases and count your blessings, right? Based on a simple idea—the days of making things had given way to the age of making names. Sounds foo-foo, but you don't know how important a brand is until you lose it, then it's worthless—even your personal brand. It's near impossible to overcome who people think you are. Good or bad."

Niche, Inc., started as an asset management company, emphasizing finance and accounting, then evolved quickly, as the times changed, to assets of all kinds, ones that don't always show up on the balance sheet—company image, marketing, people resources. The way of so many successful companies, first one thing, then it became another. Entrepreneurship, leadership, perseverance, it was simple as that.

Forrest added to the Niche arsenal anything that defined, enhanced, and protected a company's brand. He also added a communication division when he found companies needed help describing their businesses and products consistent with their brand.

Forrest realized companies often knew how to describe their products and services from the inside, or technically, but missed the mark communicating to consumers. Details mattered when projecting brand, from the CEO to the receptionist. The receptionist position was the first impression of a company and could make or kill a brand in the way short time of a call. Every last detail. Niche often rescued companies who claimed they believed in a customer-centric mission but had receptionists who rudely interrupted customers.

Aligning communications around brand became especially important when companies shifted to online sales as they ran brick-and-mortar businesses or transitioned to the global community and needed to communicate to different cultures and languages. These factors merged into a new company mission for Niche to protect and maximize company assets, not the obvious ones on the balance sheet but also the people.

The sun slanted off the water. Deck chimes tinkled in the gentle breeze. Allie shed the beach blanket revealing a yellow two-piece swimsuit and warmed herself in the sun. Forrest wore black Hawaiian swimming trunks and a Minnesota Twins baseball cap pulled down over his eyes. A sweaty bottle of Schmidt beer rested on the dock beside him.

A Golden Labrador named Aristotle had expended all his energy chasing up and down the shoreline after anything that moved, noy lay at the end of the dock, his head hanging over the edge.

Without lifting her head, Allie wondered aloud, "Aren't you glad Woody turned out so well?"

"I was apprehensive about hiring him, knowing it could go off in several directions. I knew he was a special talent but wasn't sure how he'd like working for me. Not as a friend. I was clear about that. We could never be just friends at work. I was committed to being the boss in every way, hopefully, a good one, but I had to be in charge. I made it clear, and he agreed it was the only way. I don't think he has any regrets. He does a great job." After pausing and reflecting on Woody, their friendship, and role in the company, he added, "I love him like a brother, and he knows it."

For several minutes, they listened to the sound of water gently rocking the dock and the whining of a twenty-horse Johnson motor and an aluminum boat slapping at the water as it skipped across the lake.

When he looked over, he saw Allie had fallen asleep. He recalled the night he proposed, a notch in time carved into a favorite remembrance. He could have never planned a night like that. It only happens in the movies. No one would believe it was real.

***

*We were up visiting Mom and Dad during our senior year and took Dad's boat to find a beach and spend the night. She had never been camping. A dark moonless night brought out a million stars and shooting stars like falling rain, the constellations on full display. We didn't want to turn away for fear we'd miss something, like watching our favorite movie. A slight breeze kept the mosquitoes away. How lucky. We had a great day. She had taken to the north woods like it was in her DNA. Everything was perfect.*

*Before I saw it, Allie pointed to the horizon, alarm in her voice, "What is that?"*

*"Is there a city up there? Is the world coming to an end?"*

*I was confused until I saw it, the most brilliant display of shimmering fluorescent lights I ever witnessed—violet, green, yellow, blue, and red. I had seen the northern lights often enough, but she couldn't ever have dreamed of seeing something so beautiful from New York City.*

*I never planned it this way and didn't have a ring. It turned out better. The night had come on so perfectly. I've never been so high on life, before or since. What a beautiful moment to share with the woman I loved and couldn't live without. Not for a minute. So, I proposed. She cried. Then I cried. What a beautiful moment.*

His daydream was interrupted by the sounds of nature's ensemble: soprano birds, woodpeckers providing the beat, frogs singing base, the water kissing the shoreline the melody. In the distance, he heard a forlorn moose. The only thing that could improve the day was a rainbow, but it would have meant rain.

Like the feathery tickle of a fly, Allie brushed the side of his face. Forrest waved his hand and rubbed his face. Without opening his eyes, he said, "I know you're watching me."

"I'll never get tired of watching you." Lying back on her beach blanket, she said, "There is no end, is there? How can there be an end?"

Forrest peaked out of one eye from beneath the bill of his cap. "Blood and guts end, love is forever."

Usually shy about humans, two loons bravely swam close to the dock, an arm's length away, Aristotle nearby, sound asleep.

"Now that's true love," Forrest said. "You know they mate for life."

Startled, Allie cried out, "Look!" Alarmed by her cry, the loons plunged their heads in the water and disappeared. Aristotle jumped to his feet and studied the water.

Leaning upon his elbow, Forrest pulled his hat back and shaded his eyes.

Allie pointed up to the clouds. Excited, she said, "There. That cloud."

Forrest scanned the clouds and looked over to her to see what she was pointing at. Glorious high rising cumulus clouds were moving across the sky like a slow-moving river barge.

"That cloud there. Think of a big mouse with big ears." A minute later, she could see he hadn't figured it out. She waited patiently for him to see it and hummed softly, "When you wish upon a star."

"Mickey. I see it," he exclaimed. "Wow, that's a good Mickey Mouse. That's a happy mouse. Reminds me of Nic Ethics and Professor Smithson. It seems like yesterday, sitting in his class, falling in love with a girl in the front row named Alexandra. I remember him quoting Aristotle and that crazy kid in the back row shouting out, 'One swallow does not make a spring day and one day does not make a man happy. It's a full, well-lived life.' We have a lot to look forward to."

Allie stared up to the drifting clouds as they rose to form white cottony mountains. "They say the day you die, a cloud is created with your name on it."

Rolling on his side, their lips meet in a firm embrace. Forrest slid his hand down her shoulder to the clasp on her bathing suit and stopped.

Breathlessly, she said, "No, not here."

"It's safe here. The lake is a long way off, beyond the cove, and there are no neighbors."

Allie giggled. "Not with Mickey watching. Let's go inside."

They walked up the path toward the cabin wrapped in each other's arms, a solemn walk filled with anticipation, out of the bright sunlight into the shadow of a cluster of paper birch trees to the left and a forest of Tamarack, Eastern White Pine, and Hemlock on the right, and into a cloud of mosquitoes. Aristotle faithfully trailed behind.

When they entered the cabin, they quickly closed the screen door and rushed into each other's arms. Forrest giggled, "Now I know what Hell is like. It's living in a most beautiful place infested with mosquitoes all the time." Allie looked up and smiled. Forrest kissed her lightly. With a sly smile, he said, "Let's light some candles. I'll get the Calamine lotion and start a fire."

As soon as the sun dipped below the horizon, it cooled down. A crackling, birchwood fire sent flickering shadows up the log walls and onto the high, tongue-and-groove pine ceiling. Forrest and Allie lay side by side on a rug atop the hardwood floor beneath the warmth of a king-sized Hudson Bay blanket. Having succumbed to the tumult of chasing after real and phantom feathered fowl all day, Aristotle was lying in his dog bed nearby.

"Do we have to go home? I want to stay here forever." Allie turned her face towards his, and their lips met. "Every time we make love, I hope we make a life."

Forrest contemplated her words. They had recently learned they couldn't have children. Heartbroken, if anyone should have children, it should be Allie.

After a contemplative minute, Allie whispered, "If I can choose a place to die, let it be here. Right here. In this exact spot." A minute later, she asked. "Is there a Hell?"

"Who knows? I know there is hell on Earth. And, I believe there's a Heaven, that our spirits go somewhere, when everyday struggles end and our bodies die, our loving souls rise and live on forever. I don't think the souls of good people ever die, but evil keeps trying to break through and never makes it."

Allie looked deeply into his eyes as if she might glimpse his soul, "I believe with all my heart, we have always been together, and we will continue throughout eternity."

"Oh, Allie, I believe that too. We will always be together."

Forrest and Allie stared into the dying embers. Life seemed out of balance when good people like Forrest and Allie, who badly wanted a child and couldn't conceive, lived in a world filled with unwanted babies. They considered all options, including surrogacy and adoption. They even tried things against the doctor's advice.

At first, the doctor projected optimism, but after three failed in vitro fertilization attempts, his demeanor shifted to more officious explanations. To the Nelthorpes, the doctor's words sounded like a business explanation of what science didn't know and hadn't known when they started. In retrospect, after writing all those big checks, the whole process required luck to play a role in success. Doctors never say that.

Why not them? How often had they asked that question? Far beyond the science of it, beyond species' survival, they always ended in the same place, "Why us?" Why had the universe not selected them for parenting when they were such a good match, loved each other dearly, and were the best candidates for parenthood? In their hearts, they believed in the yin and yang of life's existence and the inescapable cause and effect as baked in as the revolutions of the earth around the sun—reasons are hidden from human view.

"There is always hope," Forrest offered. Only a breath's distance between them, he kissed her gently and held her tight. "Maybe. This place is so magical. Just maybe."

The next afternoon, with a wave of his hand, he requested she stand with Aristotle in front of the cabin. Forrest set his camera on a tripod and positioned it facing the cabin. Allie looked at Forrest and smiled and then to Aristotle standing beside him, a placard hanging around his neck that read, Aristotle. "Happiness forever, huh?" Allie asked as she watched Forrest fiddle with the camera.

"Here we go." Making a mad dash to stand in the picture, they giggled, smiled, and froze. As they looked into the camera, just as the shutter clicked, Forrest said, "A picture for forever, I'd say."

# 7

One acquisition after another elevated Niche to national prominence. Forrest believed marketing to be local, so acquisitions of companies in targeted states earned them Fortune 500 status. Publicity,
not foreign to Forrest, so it wasn't surprising when articles in the
Wall Street Journal and Forbes documented their rise to national
prominence.

Allie had her own budding career. After graduating from law
school and passing the bar, she was offered a professorship at the
University of Minnesota. Recently, she cut back on graduate teaching in favor of teaching aspiring undergraduate law students. She
explained she enjoyed interacting with the wildlife—the less directed
more stimulating.

Rapid growth of the company cast a spotlight in the Nelthorpe
direction. A Minneapolis Tribune article about the philanthropy of
Forrest and Allie described their home as "Magnificent." On twenty-five acres of two-hundred-year-old pines, their home was surrounded on two sides by state and federal forest and three-hundred
feet of sugar sand beach. The quarter of a mile long, cobblestone

approach circled a fountain and a stone archway that connected an attached two-car garage and an unattached three-car garage with guest quarters above.

The interior of the sixteen-thousand square foot home inspired by European architecture featured high beamed log ceilings, liberal use of brass and granite, two fifteen-foot wide hearth fossilized river rock fireplaces, four bedrooms, and eight bathrooms.

The library was Forrest's favorite room featuring the second fossilized rock fireplace, surrounded by dark mahogany, floor-to-ceiling bookshelves on each side.

Their good fortune continued to improve with the hiring of FlorineLasalle as their house manager. Lasalle, her married name which she retained after her husband died in an airplane crash. A notable book collector, she achieved her master's degree in literature from the University of Minnesota and was often called on to evaluate the authenticity of first edition classics.

Her job as a house manager allowed her to withdraw into a world of classic books and first edition collections. Forrest encouraged her to fill the library bookshelves as if they were her own, and she did with luxuriously bound classics and current distinctive works. She said her favorite authors were Jane Austin and Emily Dickenson, but in the stack of books on her nightstand was a copy of Bronte's *Wuthering Heights* and Carl Sandburg's, *Poems that Live Forever*.

When she wasn't reading or caring for the Nelthorpes, she pecked away on her typewriter, writing, hoping to create her own great American classic. The Nelthorpes never pried into her personal life and seldom asked about her writing aspirations.

Forrest usually left for the office at five o'clock in the morning to avoid heavy traffic. Allie left later to avoid the rush hour. He liked to be first in the office for the quiet time before a parade of interruptions. She liked to arrive right on time for her first class.

In the early morning, as dependably as Minnesota lakes freeze over in the winter, Luka was there, leaning on the front fender of the black Lincoln Town Car as Forrest walked across the cobblestone courtyard. The car had 30,000 miles and looked like he just drove it off the showroom floor. Luka Talerico, a ghoulish-looking tall thin Italian man with deep-set, unflappable dark eyes and a long face with puppet jowls. His rounded shoulders reduced his height by several inches. He combed his black, Brylcreemed hair to the side. He stood waiting like a perched bird of prey surveying the field for carrion.

When Luka saw Forrest enter the courtyard and heard the familiar clomping sounds of his black wingtip shoes on the cobblestone, he greeted him and opened the rear passenger door. "Good morning. I hope you enjoyed your time off. Catch any fish?"

"I never took the boat out." Forrest smiled. Luka rarely spoke unless addressed. His longest sentences were about kids and family. Usually, the conversations were short bursts of incomplete sentences, but to Forrest always on point and often profound. Their conversations could be about anything, usually wrapped around extended periods of silence, rarely about the business unless Forrest brought it up. Funny, sometimes, Luka was the right guy to talk through a tough business decision.

As Luka fastened his seat belt, Forrest asked, "How about you?"

"Took the kids to a Twins game. Koosman pitched." Forrest had never seen him in anything but a black suit and a white shirt. He imagined he took his kids to the ball game in the same black suit. "They lost again. Hot dogs and Cracker Jacks saved the day."

"See, they're building a domed stadium," Forrest offered. "Take a couple of years. Domed is good for here."

They enjoyed their time together. For Forrest, it was a transition from an office of scurrying serious faces, all striving to ring the brass bell, using their officious voices to smile "long-lost friend" greetings to a boss who held life and death dominium over their careers. *Was it that way initially—employees feeling like friends? Did the faux friendships grow as the company grew, like moss clinging to the cracks in the sidewalk?* It came with the job, as unwanted as a bad case of eczema. But he recognized the power of it.

For several miles, they drove in silence, in no hurry, as if the Lincoln didn't have a care in the world. Looking back to Forrest through the rearview mirror, "My cousin Benny got out of prison. Remember Benny?"

Forrest nodded and kept watching Luka in the mirror, waiting for more. Luka's eyes were all he could see. Forrest thought his eyes were sad. He knew Luka had a rough upbringing, but he figured it more likely he was born with a sad expression, too. "Prison can mellow a guy out, huh?"

"Five years early. He'll be fine," Luka answered the question not asked.

Forrest thought about saying more. He was his driver, and Luka probably didn't consider himself a trusted friend. Forrest gazed out the window as the traffic whizzed by and listened to the sound of time passing.

More to their story, an unspoken quiet understanding between them, one Forrest preferred but never discussed. He knew Luka felt obligated. More than once, Luka told him he owed him, but didn't know how to repay him, didn't think he ever could. It wasn't about money. Luka knew there wasn't enough money in the U.S. Treasury to repay him for saving his daughter's life.

Luka became Forrest's driver in the early seventies when the company was growing off the charts. He lived in a small Italian neighborhood in Dayton's Bluff, on the east side of the Mississippi, making for a long daily drive to Lake Minnetonka.

A few years earlier, Forrest offered to help relocate him to a house close by, but he appreciatively refused. His wife, Maria, would never leave their neighborhood. All his brothers and sisters and hers too, and cousins, including Benny, all lived within in a five-block area. Talking about his family was one of the few subjects that made him smile.

Luka never missed a day of work. Ever. Even during his daughter's illness, Forrest often wondered how the man could be so stoic. One morning as the Lincoln crawled along in the traffic, in answer to what Forrest thought an innocent question, Luka began crying. An innocent enough question, "How's Annette doing?"

Forrest told him to pull over and joined him in the front seat. Luka leaned over and put his head on his shoulder. Cars zoomed by. He cried as hard as Forrest had ever seen a man cry. The doctor said there wasn't anything more they could do. Luka explained that it was a rare pneumonia. They said they needed to wait, but she was going downhill fast. It was torture to even look at her.

When Forrest heard Luka say the doctors could do nothing more, it triggered the *I can do anything spot in his brain*–the bell's sound for round one. He had learned to tamp such thinking, but Luka's tears challenged him.

He had heard too many "no hope of survival" stories. Sometimes doctors know better, have no faith, are hampered by their training or factor in financial burden; the Talericos could never afford heroic attempts. They would choose homelessness over not doing everything, even when the doctors said her chances of recovery were slim.

Before the day ended, Forrest arranged for a private jet to fly Annette to the University Hospital in Iowa City. A classmate of his, a renowned infectious disease specialist, had discovered a breakthrough in treating the rare pneumonia she had contracted. When she arrived in Iowa City, his doctor friend was shocked at how close she was to death.

The doctor diagnosed Legionella pneumophila, an especially fatal rare bacterial pneumonia. In July of 1976, an outbreak of the pneumonia at a convention of the American Legion at a hotel in Philadelphia killed twenty-nine people and spread to other states. It became known as Legionnaires disease, and Annette Talerico became one of the few survivors, one of the lucky ones.

As they exited the highway onto Hennepin Avenue, past Dunwoody College of Technology, he saw the *Niche Enterprises* sign in the distance. Entering the city and seeing the sign was a "pinch yourself" moment—both a symbol of achievement and a reminder of obligations to over 2,000 employees and clients throughout the country. The iron doors of the underground garage ground opened—it was time to go to work. When the elevator doors opened to the top floor, a bank of windows greeted him, showing off the Minneapolis skyline like a classic oil painting. As he entered his office, he ran into George West, the human resources director.

Smiling at him like a long-lost friend he hadn't seen for years, George stepped in front of him. "Enjoy your time off?"

"Yeah. I need to do it again . . . someday, if the company is still in one piece. Did you find me that marketing guy yet?"

"Better than that."

Forrest cocked his head to the side, awaiting clarification.

"A marketing lady, and she's quite a marketing lady I might add." Rolling his eyes, "Ooh la la."

"Hey, don't forget you're the HR Director. We don't hire ooh la las."

"Of course, we don't, but we can know one when we see one, can't we? Don't worry, she has impeccable credentials, far exceeding what we expected. Two advanced degrees, finance and marketing. A top dog at Goldstein and Fishbohm in New York. So, we can overlook that she looks okay too."

"She's not overqualified for the job? How did we get her away from those guys?" Forrest pressed.

"I covered that. I checked references every which way, up and down and sideways. She's A1 stable. The real deal. She even sought us out. Said she's wanted to work here for a long time. She's from the area—a Minnesota girl. She wants to come home to care for her father. He's in some kind of care facility," he said.

"I know Bob Goldstein, the founder. I could check with him."

Startled, George stepped back. "We already hired her. Her credentials were impeccable," he said defensively. "Should I have checked with you?"

"I'm sure she's okay." Turning the knob on his office door and about to enter, he turned and asked, "What's her name?"

"Kim. Kim Merrymore.

"Who hired her?

"It was Woody's call, wasn't it?"

Forrest shrugged his shoulders and, for a minute stared at George. "Oh yeah, sure . . . she's fine. It was Woody's call."

"I'll bring her by and introduce you. She has been with us for two weeks."

# 8

Minneapolis days were growing shorter. A nip of cold air reminded Minnesotans winter was about to fall out of the sky, and the inevitable blanket of snow would cover everything till spring. Already, most everyone had retreated inside and had put aside their summer toys. In the winter, business picked up its intensity.

Six men and three women dressed in business suits sat stoically around a long, polished cherry wood table, each had a white binder open. On the table, three crystal pitchers of water and glasses glistened. The board room window, stretching the room's length, showed the Minnesota skyline shrouded in winter clouds. Forrest sat at the end of the table.

"Unless there is more to discuss, I want to move on. I know we are in a peculiar situation. We have been off of projections for the past three quarters. I have thought long and hard about calling off any acquisitions and moving forward when it makes better sense. Sometimes, though, in times like this, some of the best acquisitions are accomplished.

"I am going to ask all divisions to cut expenses ten percent. That's all divisions, even the top performers. I know some are doing better than others. I have studied this, and we can all stand for a little haircut, so we'll approach this as a team. Spread the pain, as it were. And no, Chris, we are not becoming socialists. I have always strived for interdependency, so we will remain consistent here."

Forrest surveyed the room, looking for questions and signs of disagreement, like a teacher looking for a confused student. He knew the board members would speak up, but the executives seated in the back might not since the cutback decision affected them on a more personal level.

Forrest found one executive team member hard to figure, not that she had done anything to earn his distrust, but being new, Kim was hard to read and hadn't opened up. She had been there long enough to know Forrest encouraged employees to be direct and well understood he abhorred behind-his-back concerns.

When the meeting ended, Forrest called out, "Kim, if you have a minute, would you come to my office?"

Isabella Garcia, his assistant, one of his first ten employees, ushered Kim into the office without an announcement. Isabella was tall and thin, a first-generation American from a Mexican family who legally immigrated to America. At first, her youth put her behind other candidates he interviewed, but so beyond her years, he had her back a second time and hired her right then. A graduate of St. Catherine University, a woman's liberal arts college in Saint Paul, Minnesota, she was proper in her dress and mannerisms and spoke English like an English professor. Mother of four boys and the wife of a policeman, her street smarts were easy to underestimate

Forrest skipped the usual greeting. When they were first introduced, he said to himself, 'I hope she's not trouble.' She looked to be on her way to a cover shoot for a glamour magazine. Heavily made up, dressed in an expensive business suit, she could easily be playing a movie role as a wall street seductress.

She turned out to be a brilliant top performer, outgoing and friendly, maybe too friendly. She gained a reputation for being a flirt. He discouraged her when he thought she went too far. Always professional, he went out if his way to treat her like any other member of the team, but tension defined their relationship.

Lately, she dressed more provocatively and used sexiness as a tool, which explained why the men in the company related to her better than the women. What was appropriate office attire in an age of changing mores? How should it be defined for the company? He wasn't sure. Though not a prude, he didn't trust himself to be the judge of that, but there had to be some requirement for professional attire. How do you tell one of your executives she's showing too much cleavage? He often wanted to say something about the way she dressed. Today her skirt was too short.

Kim confidently took a seat in front of his desk in one of the deep, tall-backed, mahogany brown leather chairs. "Let's have it."

Forrest could see her reflection in his glass-topped walnut desk. Beneath the glass desktop was a picture of his cabin and Allie, the poem, *If,* his mother had given him, alongside a ten-bulleted list of goals for the year. Behind him was an impressive view of the Minneapolis skyline. Across the room were a full-length sofa and two comfortable leather chairs stationed around a matching burlwood coffee table. A Karastan rug designed in rich hues of cream and crimson dominated the center of the room, and, on the far wall, a coffee bar with a refrigerator and sink, and upper cabinets also built out of walnut burl wood.

"Let's have it?" she repeated. "Did I do something?"

"I don't think you agree with our cutback strategy. I noticed you squirming in the back of the room. Okay, if you disagree, but I need to know what's going on."

"I had to pee," Kim responded and watched for his reaction.

Forrest ignored her remark, their gazes locked in a tug-of-war until Forrest broke the ice. "If you have concerns, I hope you'll speak up."

"I am not going to say anything in front of the board."

"So?" Forrest waited for her to share her concerns.

"I think we need to balance the company. We are delaying the inevitable and not taking advantage of the shift in the business cycle."

"What do you think is out of balance?"

"The future is digital. Everyone knows it. It's the subject of most business journal articles today, but most businesses just wave at it. We are also paying lip service to the coming invasion. We are a reflection of American business instead of leading it. I know how hard it is for companies to let their cash crops go to seed and reinvest in the future. There is a new way of doing business, and soon digital commerce will become a core business strategy for all businesses.

"Even the purchase of cars. Digital is not only about selling books. Amazon is not a bookseller as much as they are a digital company leveraging its capability to sell anything using the internet. Some day they will be selling groceries. Funny how people protest every time a Walmart opens up but ignore companies like Amazon who destroy local businesses like silent flood water. They will gobble up America one brick at a time. Playing catch-up is a losing strategy, don't you think?"

Forrest had a serious, curious expression on his face. "What do you think we should do?"

"Hire a coder, a world-class one. Hell, hire a Russian hacker," she snickered. "Not to code or offer programming services, but we need to understand what the capabilities are and how guys like Amazon are doing it. We need to help companies tear down their brick walls. I can code, so I know what I'm talking about."

Kim eased back in her chair and her already short skirt rose high on her thighs. He averted his eyes and moved out from behind the desk and took a seat next to her. He scooted his chair away and sat down. "I understand you have advanced degrees in marketing and finance. So, when did you have time to learn how to code?"

"I'm not married. I have time." Seductively she added, "I haven't found anyone who measured up."

Forrest ignored her remark and processed her ideas. He searched his memory to recall what he knew about her. "George said you're from Minnesota. You go to school here?"

Kim looked away, hesitantly. "Kind of a Minnesota girl. I was living with my father when I pursued this job. The University of California at Berkley."

Forrest thought her explanation odd but continued, "I'm impressed. Your ideas are good. American discretionary spending is on the rise and will continue to grow. Convenience has become more important while the penny pinching of our parents has waned." Leaning back in his chair, "So, what are your ambitions here?"

Playfully, Kim twirled her long blond hair with her fingers. "I'd like to find a man. God, I have been so focused on this job, I haven't had time for that."

"So, you're here to find a man?"

"You silly man, no, but that'd be nice." Kim stopped twirling her hair strands and turned serious. "I'll tell you what I want. I'd like your job. How's that? Does it bother you?"

Forrest rose and returned to his desk and sat down. "Not in the least. Why should it? I hope all of my employees are upwardly mobile, aspiring for the top."

Confused, Kim searched for a response.

Forrest didn't wait for her. "Do you think I prefer the people who work here to strive for the bottom? No, when the day comes, and I retire, I hope the next CEO is somebody working here right now." Boring in, narrowing his gaze. "Do you want to be CEO?"

Kim smiled and flicked her eyebrows, "I plan to."

Kim rose to leave and when she arrived at the door, she turned back. "You don't remember me, do you?"

Forrest had returned to his desk and stood behind his chair. Narrowing his gaze, he replied. "No. Have we met before?

Kim hesitated and was about to explain when she abruptly turned and raised her hand dismissively. "It's not important," she said as walked away.

# 9

Another acquisition. Another piece of the puzzle.

As Forrest briefed the board on the upcoming negotiation with Sloten, Inc., his gaze kept shifting back to Woody—still the freckled-faced, sandy-haired, mop-top, who seemed perpetually young. Forrest ribbed him often about his youthful appearance.

This acquisition was a jewel of all deals—New York City. Throughout the briefing, Woody's head hung low, and he appeared to be doodling. Mid-sentence, Forrest stopped and looked at him. "Woody, are you okay?"

Woody jolted his head upright like a schoolchild called out by the teacher. "Sorry, Forrest. I'm fine. A little distracted. I'm back. Please go on."

Forrest continued but kept an eye on him. "The negotiation with Sloten, and eventual outcome, either way, will not affect the company negatively. We have the money to do this, and not doing this will not affect our current growth. It's a long-term play for a position. They don't have any products or services that change or add much to our offerings. As I said, this is just a position play. The details of the deal, or no deal, will be above board and shared with you. I have complete faith that what we discuss will always stay in this room.

"I want to emphasize; we don't need to do this, but they do. Niche is a whole lot better off than Sloten. And there is only one way this will happen. Some might report this as a merger, and it may appear we are making some concessions on some product names. I like some of their branding strategies, but, rest assured, this is no merger. Unless we get everything we want, we won't do a deal. Next week Woody and I will go to New York and get this thing done. Charles, you too." Looking back to Woody. "You ready for this?"

"One hundred percent," Woody responded.

After the meeting, Forrest asked Woody to his office. As he entered, Forrest could see something weighing on him. After closing the door, Forrest motioned for him to sit on the sofa and took a seat opposite him. "What's going on?"

Woody stiffened as if there wasn't anything to discuss. Woody was too important, too much of a friend, so Forrest would have to dig a little to learn more. As the two men stared at each other, Forrest could see his eyes were moistening. "I don't think she's going to make it," he gave in.

Forrest raised his hand to his mouth to cover a gasp. Sarah, a sorority sister of Allie's and a good friend, had battled cancer for the past two years and had recently been sick. Still, Woody emphasized her illness wasn't related and avoided talking about it.

The message buzzer on his phone rang and interrupted them. Isabella announced, "Your wife is on line one."

Forrest sprang from his chair and picked up the phone. Looking back, he saw Woody had moved from the sofa and stood with his back to him, looking at the Minneapolis skyline. "Allie, this is not a good time."

"I'm cooking our favorite tonight. When will you be home?"

Hesitating, looking over to Woody. "Favorite?"

"Plank salmon. You're favorite rub. You're favorite Chianti.'

"What's the occasion?"

"Oh . . . it'll wait."

"I'm sorry, honey. I'm delayed. I'll explain."

When he hung up the phone, he went to Woody and put his hand on his shoulder. "Let's get out of here. Meet you at Mulligan's."

A half-hour later, they were sitting at a table, a glass of beer in front of them. Friday night cheap beers and spicy wings attracted a crowd, so they moved as far from the roisterers as possible.

Forrest leaned and talked loudly above the din. "You've got to keep fighting."

"We are fighting for all it's worth, though the doctor told me privately she may not live much longer. He said to get things in order. Do you hear me, Forrest, he said to get things in order! She is failing so fast. Right before my eyes."

"Why haven't you shared this with me before?"

Woody picked up one of the beer coasters and studied it. "You know how things are. Things are crazy, right?"

"Why are you even here?"

"I haven't been around much. I've taken a lot of time off."

Forrest looked confused. "Oh." Forrest took several minutes before responding. The bar was standing room only, and loud conversations and laughter were stifling. "Yeah, crazy time for sure. You're my best friend. I hate when business gets in the way. What can I do?"

"What can I do? I bet I've heard the question a thousand times. Everybody says that. I know everybody wants an answer, but it's a question without an answer. I say that to Sarah all the time. She says she has accepted dying, then a while later, she wishes for more time. One minute she is counting her blessings, and the next, she is asking 'Why me?'" Woody dropped his head into his hands. "I don't know what to do, what to say. I don't want her to give up, but . . . I'm lost. What can I do? What can I do? I'll tell you what you can do. You can tell me what to do."

"No doubt you're already doing it. Sarah's a strong woman. She knows what is going on and has you to talk to," Forrest replied sympathetically.

"Stronger than me in this deal." Nodding his head, "Yeah, I can see it in her eyes. She's probably been shielding me. It's just like her."

Frustrated by all the noise, Forrest moved his chair around the table to sit closer to him. "I understand how you feel. I don't know what I'd do without my Allie. I can't even imagine that." Forrest looked across the room then up to the ceiling, imagining the unimaginable. "It's like way down the hall, in another room, behind a steel door. I can't imagine."

Woody chugged the rest of his beer and raised his glass to get the attention of the barmaid. "Why do some people have all the bad luck? In less than a year, I lost my mother, father, and now Sarah."

Shaking his head, Forrest lamented. "You've had it rough. It's hard to understand. Just random, I guess. I've been fortunate, but I've always known just like that . . . ." Clicking his fingers. "Anytime."

"You have all the luck," Woody reflected.

"Luck." The word hung in the air. Forrest's gaze drifted away from Woody's sad face as he studied the bottom of his glass, watching the air bubbles float to the top seeking freedom. In the silence between swallows, Forrest processed Woody's situation. *How could I ever stand up to losing Allie? What would I do? Was there such a thing as luck, good or bad? Can a person go forever with just good luck? What do we know about luck anyway?* People like to attribute the randomness of events to luck all the time. It's only a word.

One thing, life isn't always simple. It's never one thing. And, what does anyone know about a man's luck until he puts a gun to his head and blows his brains out? Humans like things to fit into neat little packages—complete and explainable. Forrest believed there were consequences—everything was not just good and bad luck. Measure for measure, life reacted like a field of energy, a poke in one place reacts in another. *Professor Smithson always said ethical breeches came with price tags. Even a peccadillo could have a price tag. No, not Woody. Not Sarah. It's never one thing. Not luck. Things like this are hard to understand but not just luck. Smithson used to quote Ralph Waldo Emerson, "Shallow men believe in luck. Strong men believe in cause and effect."*

Both Woody and Forrest reflected on the situation until Forrest broke the silence.

"Are you worried about business?"

"Well, sure, I'm a bit concerned. Aren't you?"

"Doesn't seem all that important at a time like this. Put it out of your mind. Focus on

Sarah and yourself. It's a cycle thing. We go through this from time to time. Will again. Once in a while it's good for the company to lose some weight."

"No, I understand that. Of course. I'm more concerned about the Sloten deal. Not letting you down."

"How long have we known each other?"

Woody looked up with a questioning expression. "A long time, long before you started this thing."

"I love you like a brother. You're not going to New York. Give me your files. You need to take some time off. Sarah is the only thing right now."

"But . . . ."

"No."

Knowing Forrest as he did, Woody shrugged his shoulders in resignation. "Take Kim then. She's incredible. She knows more about this deal then I do. She'll be a great asset."

Forrest looked away, searching for a way to respond. "You know Kim may be a super smart person, but she sure has another side."

"I know. Trust me, Kim does have another side, but when she's in her business mode, there's none better."

"I'll consider it but go be with Sarah. Let me deal with this."

***

Forrest called and told Allie he was on his way home, but an hour behind his promised arrival. Forrest worked long days, Luke as well. The long and short days evened out. More than a driver for Forrest—Luka was an everyday, everything man. Both felt equally privileged in the relationship. They liked each other.

As they started home, the roadways were slush-covered, but soon it snowed hard, and the windshield wipers waved frantically side to side. Way too early for winter. Forrest could still remember the warmth of the summer sun while lying on the end of the dock with the woman he loved.

Forrest sat in the front seat. The workday over, no papers to read, no more meetings. The day ended on such a sour note. All he wanted was get home to Allie. He'd decide whether to take Kim with him to New York over the weekend. He dreaded discussing it with Allie but knew he should.

The Lincoln seemed to have one speed through rain, snow, or sunshine. Luka calmly watched the road disappear inch by inch. Up ahead, they could see red and blue lights flashing from side to side. An accident? A delay? When they arrived at the accident scene, they found only two abandoned cars, not even policemen.

As they entered Wisteria Lane, the headlights showcased sagging pine tree boughs heavily laden with wet snow. The only sounds were the hum of the motor and tires crunching on the virgin snow atop the cobblestone lane. Forrest couldn't remember ever being so happy to be home. They circled the snow-covered fountain and pulled up to the side door beneath the archway that connected the garage/guest quarters and the house. Forrest hopped out of the car, wished Luka a good weekend, and heard him drive off.

Shoulders slumped to shield against the blowing snow. He entered the side door into the mudroom that led to the kitchen. He took his shoes off and laid his coat over his arm. Allie was leaning on the granite center island, studying a cookbook. Laying his coat on the center island, he went to her and kissed her like a returning soldier and held her close.

Allie pushed back and looked up to him. "Wasn't sure . . . I nixed the salmon. I wanted to cook a special dinner. Glad you're home." His eyes showed her the love, but they betrayed he was a thousand miles from the kitchen. "What's up?"

"Sarah's not doing well. She's given up, according to Woody. Says the doctor told him he should prepare."

Allie's mouth dropped open. "How awful. I thought her cancer was in remission."

"Guess it came roaring back. No more heroics, the doctors said."

Speechless, Allie moved close to Forrest and laid her head on his chest and cried.

Through her tears, she asked, "How's Woody holding up?"

"Hell, he's doing better than I would be. Not good. I pulled him off the New York trip. He needs to spend all his time with her. Every minute."

"What are you going to do? That's an important meeting."

Forrest dreaded any questions. "I guess I'll take Kim. Kim Merrymore. Do you know who that is?"

"The floozy?"

Forrest jerked his head back. He couldn't recall ever hearing Allie say anything like that. She was such a positive person. Shaking his head. "You know who she is?"

"I remember the cocktail party for Wesley's retirement. I thought she was going to fall out of that dress she was wearing."

Shaking his head, "Yeah, I don't know what to do about it. Do you have any suggestions?"

"Have George deal with it."

"Nah, I'm not sure that would be appropriate. George is no match for her. She's not as bad at work, although she is the worst kind of problem: a high achiever of questionable morals."

"Any man should fear a woman like her," Allie said dismissively.

"Anyway, Woody says she knows this deal inside and out. I'll decide later. For sure, Charlie is also going."

Without comment, she eased away, "I put a quiche in the oven. I'm sorry. You hungry?"

"I could eat."

"Give me twenty minutes. Go change, and I'll set up in the dining room."

When Forrest entered the dining room, he saw place settings for two, a full bouquet of yellow roses and lit candles. While she was in the kitchen, he poured them each a glass of wine and sat down.

As Allie entered, balancing a hot pad, ceramic baking dish, and salad bowl, Forrest asked, "What's the special occasion?"

"You know we never need a special occasion." As she set the quiche on a trivet, beside a basket of artisan cracked wheat bread, she said again, "I'm sorry it's nothing special. Just something I whipped up."

Smiling and touching her forearm, "I know your nothing special dinners."

Their attention focused on serving up salad and quiche and the tinkling of silverware on ceramic plates for the next five minutes.

Allie watched Forrest move the food around his plate. "That was a big sigh."

Forrest nodded and smiled. "Woody says we have all the luck. He feels he's getting all the bad. Do you think it's bad luck? We certainly have had our share of good luck."

"Luck? We are blessed for sure. You have to take it one day at a time, I guess. So,

speaking of blessings." Allied raised her wine glass in a toast. "Let's toast."

Curiously, Forrest raised his glass to hers. "What's the occasion? It's bad karma to celebrate a deal before it's done."

"Then, let's toast to us." They clinked glasses, and Allie continued, "All of us."

Forrest looked at her curiously and then broke out in a broad smile. Hesitating, he asked, "You mean like all of us?"

"I mean the three of us. We're expecting."

Forrest slid his chair back and rushed to her. Allie rose and met him. He plucked a yellow rose from the bouquet, smelled it, and offered it to her.

"Do you think . . . ?"

"You mean the magical cabin and Mickey smiling down on us."

"That is a special place. As you said, if I could choose the place to grow old with you, it is our cabin on Ten Mile Lake."

# 10

Every trip to New York from the Mini Apple was an experience. Sloten, Inc's office, on the thirty-third floor, overlooked an incredible view of the East River and the Brooklyn Bridge, an easy walk from the Beckman Hotel, which was in One Chase Plaza.

A black acrylic conference table with stainless steel trim and legs and gray textured walls fit perfectly with several modern twisted chrome wall sculptures. There were six people in the room. Martin Van Sloten sat at the end of the table with two of his vice presidents on one side: Vice President of Finance, Rory James, wore a black, chalk-striped suit, an NYU graduate who had been with the company only five years, and head of operations, Marilyn Carter, a grandmotherly woman in her sixties, wearing a blue print dress with a royal blue silk scarf tied in a French-girl-twist knot, who had been with the company since the first day.

Forrest, Kim Merrymore, and Charles Gunn sat opposite them. Dressed for success, Forrest wore a Southwick, charcoal wool suit, a starched, white button-down shirt, a muted, garnet paisley silk tie, and black wingtips. Kim wore a Ralph Lauren, navy blue business suit with a short skirt, an off-white, scoop-neck silk camisole, and her platinum blond hair in a high bun held together by long, dangerous-looking hairpins. She drew glances from men, and as many women, on their walk from the hotel. Charlie went all out to wear what many believed was his only suit, clean and pressed, a nondescript gray tie, and a white shirt.

When Forrest met him in the lobby for the walk over, he did a double take seeing his beard so neatly trimmed. Charlie seemed a man larger than his usual unkempt self, and Forrest's hockey roots came out when he said, "Well, if we don't win the negotiation, we're sure to win the fight."

In his sixties, Martin Van Sloten was eager to sell the company and proud of his negotiating skills. His expanded girth belted uncomfortably tight, and his average height made him appear smaller than Forrest remembered. His receding hairline had reached the point when some men were deciding between a toupee or going bald.

Martin Von Sloten gifted the Niche team a leather portfolio notebook and a Mont Blanc fountain pen to begin the meeting. A platter of almond and chocolate croissants, silver plates, and white monogrammed cloth napkins beckoned, and behind them on the buffet, a silver coffee urn, cups, and a silver cream pitcher and sugar bowl. Forrest poured himself a cup of decaf before he sat down. He always said he didn't need to be caffeinated to be alert. Martin dug into the croissants and, Charlie, never shy about food, matched him croissant for croissant.

As they neared lunchtime, Kim proposed Charles, Whiten, and herself meet over the lunch hour and iron out some of the operational/financial details that had arisen in the morning session. Martin proposed he and Forrest dine together in his office.

As they broke for lunch, Kim whispered to Forrest, "Give me an hour with Whit, and he'll be eating out of my hand." Forrest saw Martin was watching and waiting for him at the door.

When they reconvened after lunch, late in the afternoon, after three more hours of grueling negotiation, Forrest retrieved his brief-case from the floor behind him and collected the papers in front of him. Looking at Charles, then to Martin, he announced, "We've been talking about this deal for several months. And we've been sitting here all day going through the same stuff. I'm wearing down. I know these things can be hard but near impossible when things aren't lining up. When they aren't, sometimes it's time to call it."

Slowly, Forrest stacked his papers inside his briefcase and snapped it shut. Pushing back from the table and looking over to Kim, "We're leaving." Rising from the table, Forrest continued, "We're done here. This isn't going to happen. Let's shake hands and wish each other the best."

Charles remained seated with his arms folded across his chest. As Kim opened her briefcase and collected her papers, Forrest walked to the head of the table with his briefcase and offered his hand. "Thanks for your time." Stunned, Kim stood nervously behind her chair. Looking back to Rory and Marilyn, Forrest smiled, "It was good to meet you guys. I wish you all the best."

Martin took Forrest's handshake and gripped it tightly, not let-ting go. As Forrest loosened his grip and tried to pull away, Martin gripped it tightly and pulled him back. "I hope I haven't offended you in any way. What is it you don't like about this deal? We can do this."

Forrest saw the panic in his gaze. "An hour ago . . . ," Forrest looked at his wristwatch, "I looked at my watch. You said we were close, and since then, you offered up one significant change after another, changes unrelated to the foundation of the deal, that took us way off course."

Forrest and Martin stood face to face, still locked in a firm uncomfortable handshake as if letting go was the end.

"Okay, Forrest. Sit down. Let's get this thing done."

When Forrest took his seat, he laid his briefcase on the table in front of him and didn't open it. "Charles, review where we are, please. Is that okay with you, Martin?"

Charles moved to the end of the table and plugged his laptop into a projector. The image of an excel spreadsheet came to life. "This represents where we were before lunch." The slide showed a double column with the header Niche on one side and Sloten on the other. It was an impressive bulleted listing of the issues going back to their first discussions months earlier.

Items agreed to were check-marked. There were only a few items of disagreement. Slide after slide showed the few remaining highlighted areas. Charles led them through each page, paused at the end of each slide, rubbed his beard, and asked for comments. There was little discussion. On the items highlighted, Forrest clarified what issues were important to Niche, and why some were important to the Sloten employees who would become Niche employees.

From the beginning of negotiations, months ago, Forrest knew the issues involving money were the ones Martin cared about most.

Clear to everyone, Martin twisted things into knots to avoid any hint the discussions sounded like money. Forrest insisted they stay on the issues. When Martin shifted to money issues, Forrest forced the conversation back to the pending list, which made Martin uncomfortable and cut right to the heart of the problems—yes or no. It wasn't long until Charles checked off the last remaining issue.

Martin leaned back in this chair and looked over to his vice presidents, then back to Forrest and Kim. There was an awkward silence before he spoke. "Okay, Forrest. We can do this. I will have my attorney draft up a memorandum with this documentation." Waving his hand at the blank screen behind him and then back to the projector, "Charles, can you give me a copy of the spreadsheet we agreed to? We'll sign off on it then turn the attorneys and accountants loose."

# 11

Still warmed by success, they walked back to The Beckman Hotel, an easy but brisk one from One Chase Plaza. They hadn't worn coats.

By the time they arrived, darkness had set in. Too excited for dinner, and no one wanted to eat late, they agreed to one celebratory drink. Charles said he would join in for one but was on the first flight out of New York and had to get up at 3:00 am. Forrest declared he wanted a good night's sleep and to get home, but he wasn't leaving town without signing something. Success was like melatonin to him. His best night's sleep came after victories on the Niche gridiron.

The lounge was empty. They took a seat near the piano. Kim insisted they order a bottle of champagne to celebrate, and Forrest relented. Kim laughed, then sipped her champagne. "I was looking right at him. I thought he was going to pee his pants. He blinked all right. You even had me for a minute."

Charles sat and listened.

Forrest couldn't resist smiling. "I was serious. It was not my intent to make Martin look bad, but I had had it. Negotiations were over. Charles, did I handle that okay? I hope I didn't show him up."

Charles jumped in. "No, I thought you handled it fine. I could see where it was going, and you weren't bluffing. I knew Martin would retreat."

"Yeah, he was trying to get everything he could. It was his baby." Forrest paused and reflected, "Wonder what it's like to sell off everything you built. No, I'm not going out that way. When it's time, I'll walk away, and I'll know the company is in good hands when I do." Forrest sipped his drink. "That's pretty good stuff."

Kim poured another drink for herself, then Forrest's glass. Charles covered his glass with his hand and rose. Standing behind his chair, towering over them, stroking his trimmed red beard, Charles said, "That is good stuff. If I have one more, I'd have six. See you guys back in Minneapolis."

As Charles was walking away, Kim beamed and raised her hand in the air playfully, inviting a high five from Forrest. "This is a big deal." He slapped her hand, and she caught it and held it briefly before he broke away. They made eye contact before Forrest looked out uncomfortably.

"Huge. Really huge," Forrest reflected. "You know the one piece I wanted was their position in Atlanta. I don't think Martin understood how all the pieces fit together and how important they were to the deal. New Yorkers sometimes think they are in the center of the universe. Atlanta is exploding."

A Black man sat up to the piano a few yards away and began to play.

Kim raised her glass. "To the merger . . . er acquisition . . . and to a great leader. I always knew that about you. I am lucky to be on your team."

"You did a great job today, Kim. They were impressed—nothing like having the facts ready to keep the negotiations on course. And, you worked well with Rory. You guys figured out some pretty complicated stuff over lunch."

"I think he likes me," Kim said suggestively.

Out of the corner of his eye, he saw a man enter the lounge and survey the room. A few minutes later, he was standing at their table. "Are you Forrest Nelthorpe?"

Forrest nodded.

"Mr. Von Sloten asked me to deliver this to you tonight. He said he would see you tomorrow morning at nine. His office."

"Thank you." Turning to Kim, "That was fast work." Tearing the envelope open, he read through it quickly.

"May I tell him you'll be there?"

Filing the papers back in the envelope, he looked back to the man who stood by the table patiently. "Yes, I'll be there."

The piano player's smoky voice crooned a Bing Crosby tune, "Pennies from Heaven." They sat silently and listened. When he finished singing, Kim poured another drink, and before Forrest could say anything, she ordered another bottle. As the waitress served a new bottle of champagne, the piano player looked over to them and called out, "Say, you love birds have any requests?"

Forrest ignored the comment. He noticed the fedora hat resting on the piano. "You do Sinatra?"

Smiling from ear to ear, "Do I do Sinatra?" Reaching for the hat and theatrically pulling it down over his forehead, "I'll let you be the judge of that." He sang in his Nat King Cole husky voice, "Luck be a Lady."

"God, it's hot in here," Kim said as she slipped her suit jacket off, revealing a silk spaghetti strapped low-cut silk camisole, and, leaning over, exposed much of her breasts. Releasing her hair from the bun, she shook her hair from side to side until it fell evenly over her shoulders.

When the piano player finished singing several Sinatra songs, he pulled his hat off and sat it on the piano, slid back, and announced it was time for a break. Forrest rose and put a ten-dollar bill in the tip jar, hesitated, then added a twenty.

Forrest stood by his chair, about to announce it was time to turn in.

Kim leaned forward and almost in a whisper asked, "Let's stick around and dance. It's early."

Forrest bristled and wanted to put a stop to any notions she might have. Ever. He also realized he needed to be careful of any word games she might be playing. "You know this is a business trip."

Laughing playfully, "Of course it is, silly boy. It doesn't mean we can't enjoy ourselves a little."

Shaking his head, Forrest returned to his seat and scowled. "Sorry, I'm a boring guy. All business."

Kim smiled and nodded confidently. "Oh, come on, here we are in New York. We don't know anyone. We're alone."

Angrily, Forrest stiffened. "There is no way in hell. I could give you sixteen reasons. Start with: I'm your boss. And that's not even the number one reason. The other fifteen are all named Allie. Look, we hired you based on your credentials. Top of your class. Your experience. That's it. Not how you look. I want none of that in my company."

Clinching her champagne glass so tightly he thought it might break, Kim jerked her head back and glared at him, then she softened and reached up and twirled her fingers in her hair. "Whatever are you thinking?"

"You know this is business and always will be," Forrest persisted.

Pouting over his remarks, she said, "Of course this is business. What were you thinking?"

Sliding his chair back, he stood. "I need to go to the men's room. And when I get back, it's time to call it a night."

Forrest walked away, weaving unsteadily between the tables. A few more people had arrived and were engaged in quiet conversation.

Disgusted, Kim watched him leave then looked around uncomfortably.

When he came back, she asked him to sit down and finish his drink. "Please. I said some stupid things. Of course, I find you attractive, and how's a girl to know what the possibilities are? Let's finish our drinks and call it a night. This job is important to me. I have big plans."

As a peace offering, Forrest sat and sighed heavily. Between sips and awkward subdued small talk, Kim shared how she loved working for Niche and complemented the creative talent. "I'm excited at my prospects here." She looked forlorn. "I have a lot to learn from you. It's going to be a ride." He couldn't tell if her humility was an act, but it appeared genuine. Eager to end the evening, Forrest gulped his drink down quickly and slid his chair back.

As they headed to their rooms and were about to enter the elevator, Forrest wobbled and leaned against the wall. Grabbing his forehead and shaking his head, he tried to focus his gaze on the different faces of people who passed by. "I'm not much of a drinker. I can't remember the last time I drank champagne. That's potent stuff," he tried to laugh it off.

By the time they reached the top floor, Forrest could barely stand. "I don't know what hit me," he slurred his words.

Kim helped him off the elevator. As they weaved their way down the hall, Forrest nearly fell twice, and Kim propped him up against the wall. "Here, let me help." She pulled his arm over her shoulder and put her arm around his waist. When they arrived at her room, she maneuvered the room key from her purse and opened the door.

As she eased him into her room, he fell back against the wall. His eyes were closed, fighting to gain reality, mumbling he'd be okay. Kim propped him up and walked him toward the bed, "Here, let me help you." Guiding him to the bed, she let him drop.

***

Forrest felt someone shaking him. "You have to get up." Standing beside the bed, in a distant voice, Kim said, "You need to be fresh for the nine o'clock meeting." After several attempts to wake him, he gradually opened his eyes.

As his senses slowly returned, he saw the outline of Kim standing beside him, unabashed, wearing only what she was born with. His mouth dropped open, and he rubbed his forehead, trying to make sense of what he was seeing. He saw he was unclothed and hastily pulled the bed sheet up to cover himself.

"What the hell happened?"

Seductively Kim responded, "Is that any way to say good morning? Ouch."

Looking around. "Where am I?"

"You're in my room. Don't you remember? Where did you think you were?"

"I've got to get out of here."

Smiling, she handed him his underwear. "Here, you'll need these. We need to get some coffee in you and get to the meeting. Do you need help getting to your room?"

***

When Forrest arrived in the restaurant, he saw Kim in a back booth and took a seat. Ashen, head throbbing, holding his head up as best he could, he greeted her. "I'm sorry about last night. That shouldn't have happened. I don't do that." A look of confusion swept over his face, "Whatever that is."

"Oh, Forrest. You mustn't feel guilty. It usually takes two. Men and women do that stuff. Right?"

"I don't. I love my wife. I'm crazy about her."

Kim clenched her lips and narrowed her gaze when she saw Martin Von Sloten enter the restaurant and walk toward them.

"Sure. I understand."

"I'll bet you do," Forrest offered sarcastically. Shaking his head to clear his senses, he continued. "No, I'm not sure you do. I love my wife. Now I'll spend the rest of my life trying to make it up, forgive myself, and live with the consequences."

Martin Von Sloten reached out his hand as Forrest struggled to his feet, trying to hide his misery. "Everything okay?" Looking over to Kim, a mischievous grin on his face, "Looks like you guys didn't get any sleep." Kim dressed casually in a short skirt and blazer with a low-cut silk blouse, her hair hanging loose on her shoulders.

"Travel can do that, I'm fine," Forrest responded in a firm tone.

"Great. Then we'll see you at the office and sign some papers."

As Martin turned and walked away, he gazed at Kim and smiled before he left to join two men at a table across the room.

# 12

The everyday abbreviated conversations with Luka on the ride home went stone silent as Forrest contemplated facing Allie. He hoped she wasn't home.

When he entered the kitchen, Aristotle greeted him with a wagging tail as he smiled over his graying chin. Forrest bent over and touched his nose to his, rubbing his ears. He paused and listened to see if he could hear where Allie might be in the house. As he made his way through the house, he could see the light on the library.

"Allie!" Forrest called out.

"I'm in the library."

When Forrest entered, Allie was sitting on the leather sofa, holding a picture in her hand. Off to the side, a roaring fire made the room stifling hot. She rose, and Forrest kissed her and pulled her into his arms and held her tight, so tightly she let out a deep sigh. When they separated, she looked up to him, searching his face, his eyes, the shape of his mouth, to see what she could learn.

"Congratulations? You're happy with the deal, aren't you?" she asked cautiously.

"The deal went down pretty much as planned. Martin was a bit clingy. You know, selling off his baby and didn't want to let go."

Allie held up a picture of the two of them in front of their cabin on Ten Mile Lake. She wore a yellow two-piece bathing suit, and he was bare-chested in Hawaiian swimming trunks. A puppy wearing a sign around her neck, which read, Aristotle, sat at their feet. "You remember this? I framed it while you were gone."

"Sure. I remember it. How could I forget?" Forrest battled tears welling up in his eyes, dabbing at them with his finger.

"What's going on? Talk to me." Reaching out, she pulled him close. "You're scaring me. Did something happen? I thought the deal went through."

Forrest snickered. "I'll never cry over the business. I love you so much. Life is so good for us. You know that?"

"Is your mom okay? Your dad?"

Tears welled up in his eyes again. "Everybody's okay. I need to tell you something."

The ringing of the phone startled him, and he turned to his desk. "This is Forrest," he said, picking up the phone. When he answered the phone, no one answered. "Hello," he said again.

When he heard the voice of the caller, he stiffened as he walked around the desk and sat down.

"I hope I'm not catching you at a bad time," said Kim.

Forrest looked up to Allie and shook his head. "Well, I just walked in the door."

"Oh, I forgot you lived so far from the office. It's pretty out there, but I live downtown, so it's easy to get home and to the office. Not only am I already home, but I'm sitting on my comfy sofa wearing my favorite white flannel pajamas and snuggling with my feather pillows getting ready for Monday morning."

Allie could tell the call was business and waved her hand to get Forrest's attention. Holding her wine glass in the air, she mouthed, "Wine?"

Forrest nodded.

Kim went on, "The minute I got home, I began to create a summary of the deal—how all the pieces fit together. Knowing Charlie, I bet he already has all the financials summarized. I thought you would want to go over the operational details as well, so you can review it with the team on Monday. How about we meet at the office tomorrow?"

Looking back, he watched Allie disappear through the open door leading to the hallway. "That's impossible. I'm not going to the office," he lied.

"Okay. I'll get it to you first thing Monday morning. Forrest, I want to tell you what a great experience that was. I can't get over how perfect it was. You were magnificent. I'm so proud to be on your team."

Forrest paused and responded uncomfortably, "Okay. Thank you, but I have to say goodnight."

"I hope everything is okay."

Gripping the phone tightly, gritting his teeth, he wanted to slam it down. "Everything is fine. Good night."

Without waiting for her, he hung up. Forrest closed his eyes and eased back. A few minutes later, he looked up to see Allie standing in the doorway with two glasses of wine.

The next morning, Saturday, Forrest drove himself to the office. It hadn't snowed for a couple of days, and the roadway was clear and the traffic light. Working on Saturday wasn't new to him, especially after being out of the office with the Sloten negotiation.

Usually, the office was quiet, just a few people like Forrest catching up or getting ready for the next week. He enjoyed his quiet Saturday mornings at the office. More than anything, he wanted the satisfaction of starting Monday morning ahead of the game. He wore gray slacks and a white cotton, button-down shirt. No tie. No sport coat.

When the security guard saw him enter from the garage elevator door, his heavy wool overcoat draped over his arm; he greeted him warmly. "Congratulations, Mr. Nelthorpe."

"Thank you, Bill." Forrest looked at him curiously. "Word travels fast. How's the misses?"

"She's fine. Miss Merrymore told me you hit it out of the park. A grand slam, she said."

Forrest bristled. "Well, there wasn't much to it." Smiling, "The pitch was right down the middle," he kidded. "But, thanks."

The elevator peacefully ascended one floor after another to the 32$^{nd}$ floor. When the door opened, Forrest was shocked to see Kim standing there.

Dressed suggestively in a see-through blouse and tight designer jeans, beaming with joy, she stood facing him. "I was hoping you'd be here. Can I stop by your office later?"

Forrest shook his head. "That outfit is entirely inappropriate."

"Oh, come on, it's Saturday. Nobody is here. Don't be such a prude."

Forrest could see she enjoyed his uncomfortableness. Clenching his jaw, Forrest sputtered, "It's not appropriate office attire. And . . . you're an executive in this firm . . . you're supposed to lead. I don't see anything we have to talk about."

Kim ignored his remarks and plowed on. "I've looked at all their stuff, client base, past campaigns and lined it up with the stuff we do. I think you will find it interesting. Better than we thought. In addition to what we thought about Atlanta, I think their position is better in Miami. They're on top in Florida."

Forrest eased by her without even a glance in her direction. "I'm sure it can wait until Monday."

Before noon, he straightened his desk and prepared to leave. By habit, like making the bed every morning, he never left the office without organizing it—only those papers that needed to be on the top of his desk first thing Monday morning remained. All other documents were filed away in his desk, a few neatly stacked, color-coded folders on his credenza. The papers on his desk, related or not, were all in the same stack. Other than the few documents that survived in one pile, his desk was clear.

He didn't hear Kim enter, and when he looked up, she had closed his office door. "Is this a private meeting," Forrest asked matter-of-factly as he rose and stood behind his desk, his hands at his side.

Looking back to the closed door, Kim shook her head, "Oh, no." Walking toward him, she held a folder out. "I thought you might want to take my analysis home with you."

Forrest snatched the folder from her, and as firmly as he could, stuffed it in his briefcase. "You don't need to close the door to deliver papers."

When she moved beside the desk, Forrest inched away. "I sure don't want what happened in New York to affect my job here."

"Nothing will affect your job here except for your performance. I'll be sure of that. I'll make sure Woody knows and keeps good records, so you'll get everything coming to you."

Kim tilted her head and glanced at him curiously. "You know what I mean. Things can get complicated in situations like this. I wouldn't want that to happen. For either of us."

"Either of us? It's not clear to me what happened. I'm sure if we stick to business . . . ," Forrest hesitated, studying her smile. *She's so happy with this. What is she smiling about?* "Everything will be fine," he continued. "Let's drop it. I am sure you have a bright future unless things get complicated like you suggest."

He could feel her inching closer and was determined to stay as far from her as he could, occasionally looking at the closed door uncomfortably.

"Dropped?"

Forrest toward her, trying to keep his composure, holding his hands loosely at his side. "Ok, don't bring it up again."

"But . . . ."

"But what?" Forrest sighed loudly.

Kim could sense his anger, but she pressed on and stepped toward him. Forrest took another step back. "I want to be clear. I don't have any regrets. It was great. It happens. I told you that. If it happens again, that's okay too."

Angrily, Forrest lashed out. "Crap. I've made it clear. I'm a married man. Listen to me. I'm married to a wonderful woman."

"Oh, Forrest, that's so corny. Nobody says that. You know some women find that sexy."

Trying to control himself, red-faced with anger, he said louder than he intended, "What woman would find that sexy?" Forrest rushed to the door and opened it. "You need to leave. This conversation is weird. You're not listening to me. I don't know why you can't understand Allie's, not just my wife. Although, that's damn well enough. We're going to grow old together. And, listen to me, she's an angel. A real angel. I know it sounds funny. Still, I believe that."

A sad look swept over Kim's face.

"And I don't have the guts to tell her what happened." Shaking his head, "Hell, I don't even know what happened. Whatever happened or didn't, it will never happen again." Forrest shifted back and forth, "Never." Turning back toward his desk, "We're done here."

"Oh, Forrest," Kim spoke softly, in a calming voice as if a peace cloud had descended on her. "Time changes everything. Everything will be okay."

Kim's eerie smile caused him to flinch. What was it? He noticed her movie star, perfectly aligned snow-white teeth. He didn't remember that about her. *I don't recall much about her background. How does she afford a luxurious downtown million-dollar condo and a glamourous wardrobe? He made a mental note to look at her resume again.* What was he paying her? She wasn't rich from whatever he paid her. She must have inherited money. Maybe she came from a wealthy family.

# 13

In time Forrest covered up the whole episode with Kim with layers of hard work, melding the two companies with particular attention to blending the Niche culture to theirs as quickly as he could. That meant several trips to New York, Atlanta, and Miami.

Fifteen percent of the Sloten employees left during the acquisition period. Forrest thought it was a positive indicator the companies were a good fit. The natural attrition made the deal even better. Some positions didn't fit together in the new company, and based on their skill sets and performance evaluations, he didn't want them anyway. Kim never accompanied him on trips after that but deserved credit for a smooth transition.

Then six months after the acquisition, Sarah died. All funerals are sad, even at the end of a full life, then celebrating years. Overshadowed by the creeping red tide of breast cancer, Sarah's end of life was not one of celebration.

The church tribute turned into a solemn reflection of how death could come to anyone, anytime. Over a thousand people attended. The graveside service for close friends, family, and executives from

Niche followed the funeral. Afterward, well-wishers clustered in various groups and at various times, broke away to offer personal condolences to Woody.

As the crowd thinned, Forrest and Allie drifted to the side and waited for an opportunity to speak with Woody. RJ, who they hadn't seen since graduation, joined them. Of all of his old friends, RJ had changed the most. His hair was short and well-groomed, replacing the long ponytail he wore as an undergraduate. Now a practicing psychiatrist at the University of Iowa, he wore a dark suit and black tie, and his white teeth stood out against his dark Indian complexion.

Forrest had tuned out RJ and Allie's conversation as he could see Kim across the way, watching him. He avoided eye contact, dreading she would come over. When she broke away and walked toward him, he braced himself.

When she arrived, without a greeting, she said, "Funerals are so sad, huh? Woody's a mess."

"Yeah, it's rough," Forrest responded.

Looking over to Allie, Kim stuck out her hand, "So I don't believe I've met the missus."

Allie took her hand reluctantly. Kim's handshake was clammy and stiff. Allie responded coldly, "We've met a couple of times now. We met at Keith's retirement party."

"Yes, I believe you're right." As they were shaking hands, Kim's gaze paused at her protruding abdomen. "Bun in the oven, huh?" Disappointed, looking back to Forrest with a deadpan expression, "Nobody told me."

"You might be the only one in the office who didn't know," Forrest retorted.

"A little Forrest, just what the world needs," Kim said dryly.

Allie quickly responded, a little louder than she intended, "She is a girl."

Ignoring her clarification, Kim reached out and touched Forrest's forearm. "This husband of yours was sure a good catch. I'm fortunate to be able to mentor under him."

Forrest saw RJ standing by quietly listening to the exchange. His penetrating gaze was unnerving, him being a psychiatrist, and given the circumstances.

Allie responded coolly, "Catch? A guess you could say that."

Kim continued, looking over to RJ. "So, who's this handsome man? Do I know you?"

RJ broke out a mischievous grin, "No, we have never met. I'm sure of that."

Forrest made eye contact with Kim, then to RJ. The one-time jokester, now a psychiatrist, smiled.

"Can you read minds, RJ?" Allie asked as she watched Kim turn and walk away.

"Not sure I should say."

Forrest looked away awkwardly.

<h1 style="text-align:center">14</h1>

May showers bring June flowers, and Forrest could see storm clouds gathering outside his window throughout the day.

"What a wonderful surprise." Forrest bounded out from behind his desk when he saw Allie enter his office. "I didn't expect you. I've never seen you look so beautiful. What's the occasion?"

"Oh, Forrest, you say that every time you see me. Is your memory failing?"

"My memory is fine. Every time I see you, I feel the same way." Reaching out for her, he kissed her and pulled her close. Allie was one of the few people who could walk into his office unannounced. Luka was the only other person who felt comfortable entering anytime. Bending down, he placed his hand on her seemingly about-to-burst watermelon belly and kissed it, "Good morning, Chrissy. You being nice to mommy?" Forrest ran his hand through his fresh crew cut. "Getting a little gray already.

Allie leaned in and kissed him. "You'll be a fabulous father."

"So, Christina is the name we settled on. Is there something about the name I need to know . . . Alexandra?"

"I told you not to call me that," Allie joked.

"I thought you were . . . ."

"Just came from there," she interrupted. "Everything is fine. I am dilated three centimeters."

Raising his eyebrows, "Three! What are you doing here? Is it time?"

"Almost. The doctor said soon. I'm going home. I'm not having any contractions." Forrest pulled her into his arms. "It's a miracle. Do you remember after the doctor said we couldn't have a baby, we got a puppy. Aristotle. We said we were done trying—to produce a baby that is. Then we went to the cabin. The magical cabin." Nudging her, "Are you sure you can drive?"

Forrest's assistant, Isabella, poked her head in the door and announced, "Your next meeting is here. I put them in the board room."

They kissed, and Forrest rubbed his hand over her belly, "Bye, Chrissy."

Behind him, she could see storm clouds collecting outside the window, so thick it obscured his view of the city.

As Allie entered the street from the underground garage, it began to rain, gently at first, then harder as the window wipers frantically tried to sweep away what had turned into a downpour. Cautiously, she turned the black BMW on to Hennepin Avenue toward the highway.

Allie inserted a CD in the player, Tony O'Connor, her favorite New Age artist. At one time, she thought it impossible to have a baby and had given up. Now she was about to be a mom, as satisfying as marrying the man she loved and, when thought impossible, to produce a baby—a girl.

Christina, the miracle baby. So much promise. Allie reflected with anticipation and a little fear, what would she be like? What would it be like to be a mom? Nothing in her life could be more important than this.

Exiting the highway, she entered the final road to home, almost safe, off the winding, treacherous road, and out of the rain. The patter of the rain and wipers swishing back and forth accompanied the melodic sounds of New Age strings, an oboe, and a harp. Up ahead, over the hill and down a winding road and over two bridges, and she'd be home.

Today, she would put a fire in the fireplace, mix a cup of hot chocolate—she preferred a glass of wine, but the doctor said no—and would finish the book she was reading, *The Covenant,* by James Michener.

She saw a white SUV in her rearview mirror, riding up close to her with one mile to go. Gripping the wheel tightly, she kept looking back, trying to recall if there was a turn-out or roadway.

She could feel the SUV bearing down on her, as she stole glances in the mirror as often as she dared. The BMW climbed the hill. Down the other side and across the bridge, she would be home. Who is it? No one who lived in the area would drive so recklessly.

As she neared the top of the hill, the white SUV began to pass. Allie shook her head and looked over quickly to see the driver. When the SUV pulled even, she sneaked a peek and was surprised by a flash of white, then a jolt sent her sideways.

Out the front window, the road disappeared. Allie gripped the wheel and jerked it to the left to steer back onto the road. The sound of the beating rain sucked the music into a silent dark black hole and obliterated all thoughts.

The BMW's first roll took her air born and onto its side, then over on its top into a slide on the slippery embankment, where it struck a bolder flipped over onto its side into another fall. It teetered momentarily before deciding on one last roll to the bottom of a ravine onto all four wheels, hammered into the shape of a cigar. Blackness. Silence. Time stopped as nature held its breath until the sound of the beating rain returned.

***

Traveling a safe distance behind the white SUV, Joe Marasco focused all his attention on the slippery road, the route instructions, and the job ahead—fixing a sump pump in a downpour. The blaring music offset the roar of the rain. The side of his van read *Pete's Plumbing*. Pete, his older brother, had had a satisfying look on his face when he sent him on the service call. The call came in as an emergency—a broken sump pump in a rainstorm. He imagined the worst.

He could barely make out the black car and a white vehicle moving into the passing lane. He thought the driver was crazy for passing on this narrow road in these conditions.

Cautiously, he pulled to the side of the road. *That SUV banged right into that car! Right into it. It was an SUV. Where did the black car go?* His first thought was to catch the SUV, at least get a license number. Where did the other car go?

***

Bill Sweet was on his way home from running errands, following a safe distance behind the Pete's Plumbing van. A year earlier, he had retired as a sporting goods manufacturing rep, a million miles a year frequent flyer put out to pasture. A career salesman always on the move—hair on fire—reduced to walking the dog and running errands to help fill the gaps. When he saw the Pete's Plumbing van jerk to the side of the road, he stopped to help. When he arrived at the driver's side window, he could seethe man was on his CB radio. Tapping on the window, he bellowed out over the rain, "You need help?"

Joe bolted from the van, pulled his rain jacket hood up tight around his face, his head cocked to the side. "Did you see that?"

Bill looked puzzled as he shielded his eyes, gazing down the roadway and over the hill through the blinding rain. It was as if nothing happened.

"That SUV forced the car off the road. He just drove off." The plumber yelled above the driving rain.

Bill Sweet stood at the top of the hill, his ball cap pulled tightly down over his head. Soaked, through and through, he could only see beyond the reach of his hand.

Stunned, the plumber repeated himself. "Did you see that? I called for help. They're on the way."

In the driving rain, they made their way down the embankment, slipping twice on the muddy hillside, and sliding the last twenty yards. At first, they couldn't see anyone inside the vehicle because of the caved-in roof. Pressing their faces against the side window they saw a woman. Her eyes were closed. She wasn't moving.

Panicked, they tried to open the door. After several futile attempts, they moved to the other side. The door was also jammed. Yelling to see if she could hear, they tried to rouse her. She looked peaceful as if she was sleeping. They could hear sirens in the distance.

"We've got to get the door open," Joe yelled out. "There is a gap between the door and the back fender." Together they wedged their hands and pulled with all their strength but to no avail.

"Let me get a tire iron." Joe crawled on hands and knees to the top of the hill, up ten feet, slipping back five, clinging to the hillside undergrowth until he reached the top. He pulled a tire iron from the back of his van.

Leaning on the BMW, Bill Sweet pressed his face to the window and stared at the woman, hoping and silently praying she wasn't dead.

Tire iron in hand, Joe stood at the top of the hill, ready to make his way back to the wreckage. The heavy rain made it hard to see and the hillside more and more treacherous. As he considered the best way down the hill, the first EMS service vehicle arrived, lights flashing. The sirens stopped suddenly as if sucked into a vacuum, leaving only the sound of the pounding rain on the vehicles and roadway. Joe rushed to meet them. In the distance, there were more sirens. Yelling out, Joe described a car had been forced off the road and was at the bottom of the ravine. The EMT men strained to see the black BMW. While they were gathering equipment and preparing to go to work, a fire truck and two police cars pulled up.

The police took up positions on the roadway to block traffic from either direction on the narrow, dangerous road. As they set out flares, their red and blue lights continued to flash from side to side. In the distance, they heard more emergency sirens.

When Joe and the EMT team arrived at the ravine, they could see the BMW rolled into the shape of a cigar resting on its wheels and a man standing against the car, his face pressed against the driver's side window.

When he heard the team arrive, Bill turned and screamed out in a high-pitched voice, "There's a woman trapped in there."

The rescue team rushed into action to open the door using an iron claw.

Suddenly the rain stopped. Everyone stood motionless and turned their gaze to a figure standing atop the hill, hands on her hips, wearing heavy, light brown rain gear, lined with illumination strips, goggle glasses, synthetic cut-proof gloves, and a yellow hard hat. Every professional there recognized District Chief Susan Quay. Her presence commanded respect. By reputation, she always showed up at the worst crash sites.

Affectionately known as Suzy Q, but the cute moniker fooled no one. Her commands were brutally direct when required. Cute, stocky, with black hair, blue eyes, and a button nose, but she didn't hesitate to chew anyone out who fell short of expectations.

She didn't succeed at every rescue attempt but never forgot her successes or failures. She was passionate for people, all kinds; she loved them all. "Flawed, every one of them, but God's children," she always said. That endeared her to everyone she worked with: police, fire, and rescue. She was damn good at her job, and confident, and by God, she would save the world if she could.

Like an electric bolt, she charged down the hill, picking her way like a charging ram. She could see the BMW door couldn't be pried open. "Stop! That's not going to work. Get the jaws." The Jaws of

Life could apply 320,000 pounds of pressure and could cut through anything. The front windshield had shattered in place, obscuring the view inside of the vehicle. "Let's get this window out, now."

After cutting around the edge of the windshield next to the frame, they applied suction cups, pulled the windshield back, and tossed it aside. Commander Quay climbed over the front grill and pulled herself over the hood and down into the passenger compartment. Crawling on her stomach she shimmied up close to Allie, checked her pulse, and studied her for signs of life.

"Ma'am, can you hear me?"

Allie opened her eyes like she was coming out of a hard sleep. Commander Quay watched her as she became aware of her surroundings. Allie's eyes opened wide. She could see the roof of the BMW had caved in, the dash and steering column pushed up over her. She couldn't move. She realized she had been in an accident, and the added threat was shock.

"My name is Suzie, what's yours?

"Allie," she answered. Still finding it hard to focus, "Allie Nelthorpe."

"I'm going to get you out of here. We are going to cover you with a blanket, and you're going to hear some noise."

"Chrissy!" Allie screamed out.

Startled, Commander Quay looked at her quizzically. "We're going to get you out as quickly as we can. Stay calm. You must stay calm. I'm going to slip out for a minute, and then I'll be right back."

Panicked, Allie cried out, "Don't leave me."

"I'm not leaving. I will be right here."

"Chrissy!" Allie yelled out louder, shaking her head from side to side.

"Stay calm. Who is Chrissy? Is she your daughter?" Commander Quay gazed around the interior again and saw nothing out of the ordinary in the passenger seat. Straining to look into the back seat, she said, "Was she in the car?" Commander Quay strained to slide forward for a better view of the interior.

"My baby." Tears streamed down her cheeks. Allie's expression turned serious.

"Was she in the car?" asked Commander Quay.

*I've been in an accident. A bad accident.* Allie squirmed, trying to get free her hands outstretched beneath the steering column, feeling for her abdomen.

Commander Quay followed her eyes and hands to her abdomen, pinned below the steering column. In a jolt, she saw the worst thing she could have imagined. She was pregnant.

"Allie!" Loud enough to command her attention, "Allie! I'll be right back. I will not leave you. Stay calm. I'm getting you out of here. We are good at this. We are going to cover you so we can cut this door out, and an EMT will put an IV in your arm."

Commander Quay slid out and stood up on the hood. Long faces looked to her for a command. Her expression looked like a coming death announcement. Instead, she swallowed hard and yelled, like an artillery commander calling out FIRE. "She's alive. But there's an unborn baby on board. We are well into the golden hour, and we need to make this happen. Now!"

Chewing her words and spitting them out. "We are going to get mom and her baby out now. Cut that goddamn door off. Cut the steering column away. Get an IV in her arm. Get a spine board down here. Rig a pully so we can get her up the embankment. Alert the University Hospital. We need a trauma unit standing by that can handle neonates. Now get this damned door off and get her out of there."

# 15

Standing, Forrest gazed out the board room window as his colleagues focused their attention on the speakerphone on the table. A half-hour ago it rained was so hard he couldn't see the building across the street. Now, the sun was so bright he squinted as he looked out.

Voices streamed out of the speakerphone. Forrest wasn't leading the conference call, and thus far hadn't said anything. His thoughts wandered in and out of the meeting. Nowadays, thoughts of fatherhood were never far away from his thinking.

Behind him, he heard the board room door open and turned to see Isabella, his assistant standing there, a look of distress on her face. "You have to come to your office," she shouted, ignoring the meeting taking place.

He moved behind the table and approached her and softly asked, "Can it wait?"

"No. It is about your wife."

Smiling, thinking the time had come, Forrest looked back to his associates and pantomimed holding a phone to his ear, smiling, "I have a call."

Forrest hurried to his office, stepping lightly, expecting good news. Instead, when he entered, a policeman stood inside the door. Forrest's mouth dropped open. He took a deep breath.

"Mr. Nelthorpe, your wife has been in an accident. She's alive. Please come with me, and I'll take you to the hospital. She is at the University Hospital."

"Oh my God," Forrest leaned back against the wall. Behind Forrest in the open hallway, employees gathered and watched. "Is she okay? What happened? What about my baby?"

"I'm sorry. I don't have any information, but her condition is serious. We need to leave right now."

As Forrest walked to the elevator, the policeman at his side, employees looked on. The elevator door opened, and Kim exited. Startled to see him with a policeman, she gasped and stood out of their way.

***

The lights were bright. Everything was white.

Allie wept quietly like a lost, wounded puppy as they evaluated the unborn baby's health, and a applied a fetal monitor. A nurse stood beside her, her hand resting on Allie's shoulder. When the doctor entered, dressed in green scrubs, he circled her. She appeared to be in good health, her skin color good. Married. Judging by her clothes, makeup, and jewelry, she was well off, perhaps a professional woman.

"I'm Dr. Llewellyn. "Your baby is going to be okay. Girl or boy?"

"Girl."

"She has a strong heartbeat. What's your name?"

"Alexandra Nelthorpe," she said, hoarsely, fighting back the tears, trying to find her voice.

A nurse evaluated her vital signs: pulse, heart, blood pressure, temperature, respiratory rate, and drew blood.

Fluorescent lights hummed as the doctor's hard-soled shoes clomped as he circled the bed. "Do you know where you are?"

"I'm in a hospital."

"Do you know which hospital?"

She looked befuddled and wasn't able to answer.

Dr. Llewellyn moved to her side and then her feet and applied pinpricks and watched for her reaction. The ER charge nurse poked her head in the room and nodded. "Your husband is on his way."

Allie shook uncontrollably; a torrent of tears ran down her face. "I want my husband."

"He'll be here soon."

"Your baby, what's her name?"

"Christina."

Reaching out and placing his hand on her shoulder, "What a beautiful name."

Unable to stop crying, she screamed out, "I want my husband, I want . . . ." Loud sobbing replaced her words.

Ten minutes later, Dr. Llewellyn intercepted Forrest in the hallway. "You must be Mr. Nelthorpe. I'm Dr. Llewellyn. I need to brief you before you see her."

"Your baby is okay, and far enough along, we think to be safe. We need to do a C-section immediately. We were waiting for you. I haven't said anything to your wife. There is something else . . ."

Dr. Llewellyn swallowed hard. Situations like this were not new to him, but they never seemed to take the same course. No amount of training prepared him to deliver such news, and it always left a lump in his throat. "Her spinal cord has been traumatized at the lumbar vertebrae, possible thoracic level. She is showing signs of paralysis. As soon as we do the C-section, we need x-rays to pinpoint her injuries' locations and extent. Right now, we need to focus on delivering this baby."

Forrest was speechless. His mind raced. C-section. Spine injury. It sounded like Allie knew little about her condition. *What happens next? What should he say?*

When he entered the room, Allie was staring toward the door watching for him. Reaching out her hand, tears in her eyes, Forrest hurried to her side and laid his head on her chest. With all the strength he could muster, in a clear and calm voice, he said, "Allie, I talked to the doctor. Chrissy is going to be fine. They're going to do a C-section. Then they're going to take care of you. Everything is going to be fine. You are in a good place. They have great doctors and nurses."

The anesthesiologist entered minutes later and asked a series of questions. Urgency filled the air. Weighing the risk, Dr. Llewellyn decided spinal anesthesia was the only option. They rolled her onto her side and inserted a long needle into the subarachnoid space. Two gowned, surgical nurses wheeled her out of the room. Later, she was transported to radiology for an MRI of her spine, then admitted to a hospital bed.

Florine Lasalle, Flo, arrived while she was in surgery. Forrest explained what happened, and they waited anxiously, hoping for the best but dreading the worst.

While in surgery, Forrest met with Ben Culpeper, a Minneapolis detective. A light-skinned, black man, Detective Culpeper was a head shorter than Forrest, dressed in a dark suit that looked a size too big. "There was a witness. A white truck or Suburban forced her off the road." Consulting his notes, Detective Culpeper added, "The witness's name is Joe Marasco. He is an employee of Pete's Plumbing. He was first on the scene and called for help. Good thing he was there to see it. In the rainstorm, she could have been down there for hours. The driver fled the scene. There were no skid marks and little evidence a car had even left the road."

He described where the accident occurred. The spot in the road was familiar to Forrest. "The witness said he saw a white SUV, maybe a Suburban, trying to pass in the driving rain, or

. . . He didn't know the make, model, or year." Hesitating and looking up from his notes, "You don't know anyone who drives a white SUV? Do you?"

"Did someone do this deliberately?"

"We don't know that. The way it was described it could be."

Forrest shook his head. "Why would anyone . . . ? No, I don't know anyone."

"You live on the lake there, I assume?"

"Yeah, she was less than a mile from home."

"Know anybody who lives down there who drives a white SUV?"

Forrest shook his head no again.

"I'm going to hang around awhile. I'd like to interview your wife as soon as she is able. I won't take much time. It would be helpful to talk to her soon."

Detective Culpeper thanked him and wished for the best outcome and left the room. Not two minutes later, he reappeared. "She didn't have any enemies, I suppose?"

"Are you kidding? You don't know her. She has never had an enemy. Not one."

"I assumed so. But you'd be surprised. The world is full of enemies." He turned to leave, then looked back to Forrest. "You don't have any enemies, do you?"

The question made Forrest think. Sure, sometimes a person knows his enemies, sometimes not—people get fired, laid off, someone thinks you mistreated them. Envy can make for powerful but secret enemies.

"You are CEO of Niche Enterprises, I understand?"

"Yes."

"So, you hire and fire people. Fire anybody recently?"

*Do people always know they have enemies? I sure don't think I do.* "No. I haven't fired anyone. We can check with HR and see if they know of any disgruntled employees."

"We need to look at all options. You probably don't. A lot of times, people leave the scene for a host of different reasons. Might have been a drunk driver. We're just starting to investigate."

Later, when Forrest entered the room, he was surprised she to see her holding Christina, a nurse by his side. Allie was groggy. He hadn't noticed before the side of her face was swollen, one eye closed completely, and she had a large bump on her forehead. Worry and fear, the ordeal of the rescue and the C Section all pushed human durability limits.

Forrest hesitated. Seeing Allie so helpless, so innocent, the joy in her face at seeing Chrissy in his arms washed over him. "Looky there. There's your momma. My princess and our special angel."

Laying Chrissy beside her, he announced, "She can only stay for a minute. The doctor will be here soon." Forrest fought off tears, trying not to hint at the conversation he had with Dr. Llewellyn before coming in.

Fighting to keep her bruised and battered eyes open, Allie forced a weary smile. "She's perfect," Allie said admiringly. "Not a scratch. Sorry, Chrissy. I didn't mean to jostle you so."

"See Mommy. She looks like you," Forrest leaned down and whispered to Chrissy. "Are you an angel too?"

There was a joyous short few minutes for Allie, and a torturous forever for Forrest until the doctor arrived. No matter how trained and practiced the doctor was, he couldn't fake delivering unwelcomed news. The doctor moved beside her bed and placed his hand on her arm. Forrest stepped up to the bed opposite him. "Alexandra, I'm glad your daughter is so healthy. It's quite a miracle, given what you went through. I'm afraid the news isn't as good for you. We have the results of your MRI. You have a complete fracture of your thoracic twelfth and lumbar first vertebrae." Dr. Llewellyn paused and watched Allie to see if she understood.

Allie looked up to Forrest and saw his eyes were red. She reached for his hand and gripped it tightly, then looked back to the doctor. "So, that's why I can't feel anything. I can't move my legs." A single tear trickled down her cheek. "I'm paralyzed, aren't I?"

She could hear Forrest fighting back tears but couldn't turn to see him. His hand rested on her shoulder. Her rock, the man with the emotional strength of ten men, was trembling, grasping to hold on. He leaned down close to her. "Oh, Allie, we'll fight this thing. The doctor says there is no way of knowing. It's too early."

"Your husband is correct. You're going to have to learn to walk again. It will take a long time. We don't know. It's too early." Stopping and swallowing hard, "We don't know."

That night Forrest sat in the chair next to her bed and watched her. Each time when she woke, she looked over to see Forrest watching her, smiling. Each time she said the same thing. "You're still here."

"I can't leave."

"I'm scared."

"I know. Nights can be scary. The sun will come up. You'll see."

Allie murmured through her tears. "Remember those days at the cabin when we would lay on the dock and make out shapes in the clouds and listen to the love calls of loons."

"Yeah, and Aristotle would lie on the end of the dock and watch the loons like a schoolchild longing to join the older kids in a game of workup," Forrest added.

In the dark silence, he could hear her weeping. He rose, put his arm around her, and laid his head on the pillow next to hers. "I want to be a mom!" Allie whispered.

"You are. You'll be a great mom. You just wait."

"I want to go to the cabin."

"We will. We'll go there. Soon. And, we'll lie together on the dock and watch the clouds float by. Aristotle will be there beside us. You just wait. Soon."

Allie sighed, and for several minutes only the sound of breathing and dreaming filled the peace.

Forrest broke the silence. "Remember how you always wanted me to go dancing with you and how I said I couldn't dance. Well. I'm going to take lessons, so save the next dance for me."

# 16

After a short stay in the hospital, Allie transferred to the rehabilitation unit under the care of Dr. Alan Whitmore, a bald, ruggedly handsome physical medicine and rehabilitation specialist who had played football at Dartmouth.

Allie's recovery tracked along the extremes of good news and bad news. Paraplegic, the neurologist told her. What an ugly word to describe being paralyzed from the waist down. What aspect of being paralyzed is good news—that she lost the use of her legs only? To Allie, it sounded like dying of thirst and seeing a mirage. Allie told Flo people would refer to her by that ugly word—the paraplegic woman, not mom, wife, professor, but paraplegic.

In time, no longer ruled by pain medication and somewhat clear-headed, she fell under the influence of a new feeling—pessimism. She believed she would never overcome her disability and be the mother and wife she had dreamed.

The first two weeks were important to the proper assessment of her prognosis, at which point Dr. Whitmore finally called for a conference to explain what he had learned and could describe her condition and prognosis.

After morning therapy, a nurse arrived with a wheelchair and took her to see the doctor. Forrest and Flo arrived as Allie wheeled toward the doctor's office. Flo had not brought Chrissy. She always brought her. Allie swallowed hard. *It must be an important meeting*. She felt like she was appearing before the judge—the jury had reached a decision and would deliver a verdict. Would the judge pronounce she was getting out of jail or a sentence of confinement in a wheelchair—a death sentence in her mind. She dreaded the day, but longed for it, the day when the doctor made his ruling.

When they arrived at his office, she pushed up to a round table, Forrest and Flo took a seat next to her, and the doctor arrived a few minutes later. A framed Leroy Neiman lithograph of Muhammad behind his desk felt staged.

When Dr. Whitmore arrived holding x-rays in his hand, he stood next to Allie and squeezed her shoulder, "How's my fighter doing today?" Without waiting for an answer, he extended his hand to Forrest and, with a firm grip, said, "Thanks for coming on short notice. I know how busy you are."

Forrest bristled at his remark. "I am never too busy for this."

The doctor extended his hand to Flo, "I'm glad you could join us. Alexandra has told me what an angel you have been."

He turned on the x-ray viewing box on the wall, inserted her x-rays, and alternated between them, comparing her first x-rays and her last ones. It was difficult to see any difference, even with the doctor pointing to the area. As for her future, he stated many people with her trauma can walk to a degree, some recover, but many can also depend on wheelchairs or other supportive measures.

When he moved back to the table, he stood tall beside her before taking a seat and placed one of his large hands on her shoulder. "Alexandra, you are making good progress, and we're all impressed with how hard you are working."

Allie could see by the doctor's expression serious news was forthcoming. Every day she grilled therapists, nurses, and anybody in range how she was doing, would she walk, any hint about her future, and the answers were always vague. "We need time to tell, or it will take time."

As she listened to him describe her condition, she stared at him, unblinking. She felt like her future was playing as a slow-motion movie, as crucial as any preceding event in her life, one time before the next phase began.

"We want you to return to your home as soon as possible, as independent and productive as possible, prepared to resume your life." Dr. Whitmore said. "After adjusting to their abilities, the vast majority of patients are discharged to begin a fresh start to their lives." Allie heard: *Some people don't go home.* Most everyone adjusts to their disability." Allie heard: *Some people never adjust, never recover.* Allie's eyes became pools, and tears streamed down her face.

Forrest listened with piercing scrutiny.

"The doctor continued. Most people can live in their old environments with their families. Many make full readjustment to a new life by returning to productive activity and employment, despite a severe physical handicap, and whatever we achieve in the rehab process. Allie heard: *I will always be crippled.*

Forrest rose and stood beside her, gripping her shoulders. Flo reached out for her hand as she wiped away her tears. Allie wanted the doctor to say everything would be okay. She wanted him to confidently announce she would walk out of the hospital soon. She knew better. He didn't say it.

Dr. Whitmore retrieved a box of tissue from his desk and laid it in front of her. "Alexandra, this is not bad news. Recovery from an injury like this starts slowly, at best six months, then small improvement for up to two years." The doctor added with a serious expression, "Every patient is different." Allie heard: *People don't recover*.

Allie looked up to Forrest, tears streaming down her face, "So, I might never walk. Is he saying that?"

Before Forrest could answer, Flo jumped in, "No, he didn't say that."

Forrest added, "You will . . . you'll walk again. It takes time." Looking over to Flo, "We are going to be there to make sure it happens." Forrest looked back at the doctor, "I think Allie hears doom and gloom in all your best guesses. "Which is it? Patients recover completely in time or not?"

"Alexandra. What I have given you is the best a responsible doctor can provide. If I were betting man, I'd say you have a better chance than most. Yes, I have seen patients fully recover from injuries like this—no displaced vertebrae, trauma. Lots of trauma."

Allie heard: "*There is a chance, but some people don't walk again.*"

"You met most of the team. They are really good. The best. They all say you're a fighter. That is important. I have asked one of our psychologists to start meeting with you. There is a mental side of this that is as important as the therapy you go through. You will benefit greatly by working with them. This is tough, even for the strongest people."

***

Allie was released from the hospital in a wheelchair to continue her therapy at home in mid-July. Progress was slow. Summer at the cabin out of the question.

The drive home was a silent reflection of her new freedom, a small step in her goal to walk again. On the emotional drive through the canopy of two-hundred-year-old pines along the cobblestone approach to her house, Allie broke out in tears as her home came into view. There were times in the hospital she never thought she would be home again.

Forrest and Allie moved into one of the two ground floor bedrooms, and the other was set up with equipment to facilitate her rehab process. The wide hallways and doorways were a good set-up for her to move around freely. Flo moved into an upstairs bedroom by the nursery. During the day, Chrissy was with Allie, and during the night, she slept in the nursery next to Flo.

Forrest returned to work but not with the same level of intensity. He spent time in his office in the home, but it didn't work after a while, and, slowly, he returned to his old routine as the hard-driving head of a company.

# 17

After months of rehab at home, they agreed to take a week off and go to their cabin on Ten Mile Lake. It felt like being released from jail for good behavior.

She committed herself to walk again but felt lost and defeated, fighting against a superior enemy—filled with despair. Flo encouraged Forrest. Forrest encouraged Flo and together formed an army of two—Flo during the day and Forrest at night. Allie said she'd never give up. He said he'd never give up, too, all the while hoping she didn't detect his fears. He always reminded her Chrissy was a miracle, too, now Forrest's favorite comrade in the battle to keep her spirits up. "Remember how we hoped for a baby, and how until the Ten Mile Lake cabin sprinkled magic dust on us all was lost?"

Forrest, Allie, and Chrissy arrived at the cabin late Friday night. Flo, now a nurse and therapist for Allie, and mother to Chrissy, while tackling expanded responsibilities as Forrest's assistant, arrived an hour later. She also administered the household budget, supervised the property and house, the lake home, and looked after his calendar.

Forrest could not sustain his leadership role in the company without her assistance and be the father and husband he aspired to be.

For a long time, he considered Flo as one of his favorites, not only her competence and all their years together, but her loyalty as well. She was the most interesting person he had ever met. Comfortable in her skin like no one else. He loved that about her.

After Forrest carried Allie up to the loft bedroom, and helped her into bed, and put Chrissy in her crib next to her, he slipped out to the deck and joined the nightly parade of stars. Tonight, a full moon beat a path to where he sat, a glass of bourbon in hand.

When Flo arrived, she joined him to say good night after putting her bag in a downstairs bedroom. When she turned to walk away, Forrest stopped her. "Flo, I don't know what we'd do without you."

Flo blushed at the compliment. "My mother died when I was young," she reflected. "I wasn't able to learn motherhood and to be a good wife from her. But the love of a father can teach you mothering. Since I was a little girl, I kept the house and put dinner on the table. My father never remarried. He worked hard, cooked, and cleaned on the weekends, and until I was ten years old, he tucked me in at night, walked me to the school bus, kissed my owies. Two years later, he died in a plane crash when I was twelve."

Forrest always wondered what the roots of her calm determination were. They had talked little about her childhood, but as he learned more about her life tragedies, he saw her differently, which explained her unwavering appreciation and dedication.

He shared his admiration for her. "You are so much more than my assistant, the way you take care of Allie and Chrissy. Me too. So much more than a job. Family. It's special."

She stared back to Forrest as if pondering his remarks, and not wanting to get sidetracked. She changed the subject. "Anything new on the accident?"

*Accident?* Forrest bristled. "I hate calling it an accident. That was no accident. Has Allie said anything to you about it? Allie had little memory of the event. The doctor's said sometimes people recall a detail or an image."

"No," Flo responded. "I don't think she ever will. You are right; that was no accident."

After she left, he refreshed his drink and returned to the deck. His drinking had evolved into late-night rationalizations, *just a drink or two can't hurt, help me sleep, take the edge off.* Allie didn't approve, but he needed a drink now, and he could stop any time. *I can't let Chrissy see me drinking, and certainly not drunk. The smell of my cologne cannot be remembered to be bourbon. A drink or two won't affect me, my job, and caring for Allie and Chrissy.*

Being a good father was like a steel rod that ran up his spine. The same steel rod to be a good husband, a good leader. But had he been a good husband? The self-doubt raged. Always there, a voice in his head screamed otherwise. He had not been a good husband. He had betrayed the woman he cherished. *Did I do that? Did I?* It was a syrupy dream.

He awoke the next morning on a deck chaise by the first glint of the early morning sun. Startled, bleary-eyed from finishing the bottle of bourbon, he rushed to rejoin Allie. He woke her and helped her dress. Nothing prepared him for assisting her with daily living activities: changing her, bathing her, helping her on and off the pot, and carrying her down the stairs.

Later, resting comfortably on chaise lounge chairs warming in the sun, that only two hours ago had crested the treetops, they watched as Chrissy explored the wooden spindle boundaries of the deck railing. Nothing could be more rejuvenating than waking to the sound of Loons and looking out over the water. Like a glassy ocean, today, they couldn't see the distant shore through the shroud. "Is there any place on earth so peaceful?" Forrest said reflectively.

"I sometimes dream I'm running," Allie said. "Last night I dreamed we were racing up from the beach to the cabin. Then I woke up to this. Sometimes at night, I think this didn't happen."

"I wish this had happened to me and not you," Forrest reflected. "If only it had. You'd certainly make a better nurse. Besides, I was a hockey player. I know how to fight."

Closing her hands into fists and holding them up like a boxer. "I'm fighting. I'm tough." Shrugging her shoulders and relaxing her hands, "But I feel outmatched."

Smiling, Forrest chided, "Not as tough as me. I'll whip this for you."

Still wearing jeans, a sweatshirt, and headscarf from her morning walk, Flo stepped onto the patio and stood behind Allie. It was a windless, cloudless, sixty-five-degree morning. Ever prideful, Flo fed her healthy desires a vegetarian diet and long, morning walks to nourish her soul. She fed her mind with the music of prose or poetry written by authors of the day and yesterday. "Not as tough as me," she corrected him. "Would you like to eat out here?"

Allie answer without hesitation. "Yes. Let's eat out here." Shielding her eyes from the low morning sun, she looked up to her. "Forrest thinks he's tougher than I am."

Throwing her head back, laughing, "Nothing like a little humor to start our day," she scoffed. "He knows you're tougher. He told me."

Soon the air filled with the smell of frying eggs, bacon, and coffee. Forrest lifted Allie into her wheelchair and pushed her to the table's head, then put Chrissy in her high chair. Roused by the smell of food, Aristotle, who had been sleeping at the far end of the deck, joined them. He sat patiently next to Chrissy, who loved to feed him her Cheerios.

After Flo laid out the food, she took a seat at the table. Forrest said, "I feel I just arrived. I'm already planning to leave."

"I wish you didn't have to go," Allie said unhappily.

"I'll take some time off, and we will spend time together here." Looking back to the lake, he continued, "Our little piece of heaven."

"I know you have a business to run. I am sorry I said that."

Biting his lip, he wanted to say: *The hell with business*. He could walk away right now. They had enough money, more than they would ever need. He could retire a young man and devote himself to Allie. Those thoughts followed him everywhere.

"Did you see the message on the counter in the kitchen?" Flo asked.

The business was rolling along—profitable, expanding reserves, and happy customers. He thought he could disappear, and the company would still thrive. He knew that would be true for a while, but every company needed leadership. A leaderless army could win battles but not wars. For the most part, he had a great team, best since he started the company. One team member outperformed them all but was his biggest challenge and never far from his thoughts.

Even now, having breakfast with the two loves of his life, he couldn't escape thinking about the company. Who would take over if he left? The board would probably go outside to find the next leader. That might be okay. But there were people internally who showed promise but needed time. Experience.

There might be five people he thought qualified—two would be on the board's radar. A few people might fight for the job who were not as capable and would never be qualified. Some people weren't cut out for the job and couldn't be trained—skills that couldn't be taught anyway. Then there was Kim, as ambitious as anyone and willing to do anything for the job. *Anything.* He cringed at the thought. It was hard to ignore the combination of high motivation and lack of scruples.

"Forrest . . . Forrest!" Allie's outburst broke the peace. "Where are you anyway?"

Forrest looked up to Allie and blinked, "I'm sorry, Allie."

"Flo asked you a question."

Looking over apologetically, "I'm sorry, Flo, what did you say?"

"Did you see the message from detective Lowell? I set it next to the coffee pot."

"Yeah, I saw it." Pushing his chair back from the table, he went into the kitchen and returned with a drink in his hand a few minutes later.

Allie watched him disapprovingly. "Why are you drinking so early?"

Smiling and holding his drink high, "I'm celebrating this beautiful day."

"You're drinking too much." Flo declared, looking over to Allie. Flo and Allie had discussed his drinking, but it wasn't her place to say any more about it.

"Nah," Forrest took a drink and smiled dismissively. "That place will drive you to drink, that's for sure." Pausing, reflectively staring off.

Allie watched and wondered. Was he worrying about her? Was she too great a burden?

"Allie, when Forrest goes back to work Monday, let's go to Walker and look around. There are some new shops there. We could drive over to Nevis. I know you love the antique shops there."

Allie nodded and looked back to Forrest, unwilling to let go of her concerns for his drinking. "Why are you drinking so much. Is it me or business? I thought business was good."

"Yeah, it's great." Forrest tried to mask his sarcasm. "Business is booming, and it's certainly not that. But there is always people stuff. People will do anything to get ahead. Anything. Climb over anyone. Willing to crush anybody in the way. Think about it. When an Olympic skater falls there are always a few people cheering the calamity, who get the same satisfaction as the ones celebrating the victory."

"If it's not business, it's me then?"

Looking back to Allie and taking another drink, "I'll watch my drinking. Everything's fine at the office. I don't need this business anyway; we have enough money. Like I always said, I could live with you in a tent."

Trying to keep a serious face, Allie responded, "Like I always said, I couldn't."

"You've got to believe. We'll get you walking again."

As they finished their breakfasts, Chrissy squirmed, trying to escape from her high chair.

Flo rose and cleared away the dishes. "You need to call that detective," she said firmly.

"I'll call him." Detective Lowell had replaced the first detective, Culpeper, explaining they were now investigating the crash as murder more than leaving the scene of an accident. By the paint analysis, a Suburban caused the white paint found on her BMW. It appeared to be deliberate by looking at the gash in the BMW and by eyewitness accounts.

"He won't have anything new. He calls me often. I think he feels bad. He doesn't say they've given up, but every time we talk, they give me a song and dance." Forrest's voice rose as his face turned red. "What it boils down to . . . they say nothing I haven't heard. Sure, they feel bad. And take it personally."

Forrest pounded his fist on the table. "By God, not as personally as I do. But there's nothing there." No white Suburban's had shown up in a body shop. We notified all area body shops. They interviewed everybody on the lake—checked for owners of white Suburban's. That yielded nothing. Possibly it wasn't registered to a local address anyway. People from all over come to the area—maybe five million suspects. "Besides, the Pete's Plumber guy isn't so sure anymore about what he saw. But they have the white paint match. They always assure me they haven't given up. Bull. I know better. I can see apology in their eyes and quit in their voices."

With a calming voice, Allie said, "We can't become bitter about this. We don't know if this was deliberate."

"Bitter?" Forrest lashed out, then took a deep breath and continued in a calmer voice, "Yeah, bitter. It makes me so damn mad. Somebody did this. He did it and left you. A coward or a criminal, doesn't matter." Waving his hand high in the air toward the surrounding forest, "Somebody out there. Coward or criminal."

Flo stacked the dishes and silverware onto a tray. "You know how I feel. People always pay. That's how it works. I hope whoever did this goes to blazes." Flo, always quick to say life itself rewarded and punished, added, "For those who slip to the other side, well they die. Whether at the hands of justice or not, they pay. Always consequences." Raising her voice, she continued, "Don't you wonder what happens to people? People say he got away with it, but what do we know? Who tracks a person's life anyway, and there's such a thing as hell on earth, isn't there? If we stepped inside of some people's brains, we'd go instantly crazy."

"That maybe, but I want to know."

As Flo left the table with a tray of dirty dishes, Forrest declared, "This has to be about me. Why would anyone do this to you?" He couldn't imagine anyone wanting to hurt her. Maybe it was an accident. *Or me,* he thought again. Perhaps he was paying the price for that Kim thing? *Professor Smithson used to say we all start our lives as a beautiful fragrant rose, but as we slip down the stem with each little ethical breach, we come into contact with the thorns. Nah. Why would she be made to pay for something I did?*

"Bad stuff happens to good people, is it so simple? Good people don't bring it on themselves," Forrest paused. *Who did this to Allie? Accident or not, someone needs to pay.* "I guess I have to go back to work." Looking over to Allie and seeing the concern on her face. "I'm going to change our life. Please don't worry. You know me, I'll catch the sun. For us."

Monday morning, Forrest returned to the office. Weekend traffic in the summer was heavier due to the vacationers from Iowa and surrounding states. The traffic quickly yielded to congestion as they neared the city. Allie, Chrissy, and business dominated his thinking.

Allie wanted to stay at the lake but knew she had to return for physical therapy the following Monday. She received PT at the cabin during the week, but it was no replacement for what she received at the University. She needed to continue her quest to walk again, but lately, she had lost some of her enthusiasm.

# 18

Forrest's world was divided in two.  On Mondays he returned to a work schedule akin to putting out fires, a schedule so nonstop that when he arrived at their Minnetonka home late each night, he went right to bed. In the mornings, he had a strong cup of coffee, an English muffin with Flo's homemade jam, and friendly catchup small talk with Luka in route to the office.

Friday, the first peaceful time all day, all week for that matter, found Forrest sitting quietly at his desk easily lured to thoughts of returning to their lake home the next day to be with Allie and Chrissy. He turned his back to his desk and gazed out the window—it always took a day to flip the switch to a more neutral position, lower his blood pressure. His mind raced through the past week.

His thoughts were like twisted strands of steel and twine. *Is this on me?* Forrest couldn't shake the notion that somehow his indiscretion had something to do with their circumstances.Shaking his head, *I don't even know if I did anything. And if I did, it happens. A beautiful woman and celebratory liquor. Right? Isn't that baked in as well? Aren't their allowances? Tolerances? The primitive urges of a man?*

*And woman? Don't all the good things balance against the falls? Crap! Stop such foolish thinking. This isn't me. That wasn't me. I am in control and would never. But why punish Allie if any of that is true?*

When Isabella first entered and tried to get his attention, he didn't hear her, so she cleared her throat to gain his attention. Before she could say anything, Forrest said, "I've meant to congratulate you and your husband." He noticed earlier a new picture of her husband on her desk. Over the years, her husband's desk pictures tracked his police force advancements, most recently an official one in his new rank as Police Commander of Juvenile Investigations and Outreach.

"Thanks, I'll pass that on." Looking back over her shoulder and back to Forrest. "Kim is here to see you. She is not on your calendar. Should I schedule her another time?"

Forrest's smile disappeared. "No, I'll see her. Tell her I have an appointment." Looking at the wall clock, "Tell her a noon meeting."

As Isabella exited, Kim breezed in past her. "Forrest, we haven't had a chance to talk. Business is crazy, huh? We're killing it, aren't we? So, how's that wife of yours? What's her name? I can't imagine not being able to walk. And with a new baby to take care of. What's her name again?"

Forrest ignored her questions, turned his back, gazed out the window, and took a deep breath before making eye contact with her.

Kim continued to go on while Forrest tuned out the small talk, waiting for her to get to the point until finally, shifting to a sultry voice, she got his attention. "I hope you've gotten over our little affair. There's always this tension between us. We do need to work together."

Forrest looked up to the clock. "I don't have a lot of time. There was no affair. I'm not going to say it again."

Sitting on the other side of his desk, she crossed her legs, so her skirt rode up on her thigh. She smiled seductively. "Then I'll get right to it. Too bad about Woody's wife." As cold as the winter arctic wind, she added, "What a painful way to go. I guess there are plenty of ways to check out, and she picked an especially painful one. Look, I feel sorry for Woody. For both of them. But the VP job is mine, and you know it. Is this a pity promotion?"

"Good God, you certainly don't know me, do you? Pity promotion? Harrumph. So, you think you're better suited for the job?"

"You bet your sweet ass." Kim threw her head back and let her blond hair flip over her shoulder.

"Woody is qualified."

"Of course, he is." With a smirk, she added, "Just not as qualified."

Forrest interrupted. "This is an important position, and you aren't as qualified. Not nearly."

Kim drew back. "That's BS. You know damn well why you are passing me over. Look, this is the track to the top, and you know it. I swear, looking around this place, it seems to be a liability to be blond with brains . . . and in a relationship with the boss."

Forrest looked away in disgust. "A lot of other people are weighing in on this promotion. Besides, I haven't made a decision, and how do you know what I am thinking?"

Kim grew serious and contemplative. "Sure, others are weighing in, but you're the CEO, it's your call. It's why you get the big bucks."

"You want to get promoted . . . you want the top job, do you? But you don't respect the process. You don't want to earn it."

"Earn it. Of course, I want to earn it. I have. Would you like me to review my track record, new business, client retention, billings? Others weighing in, what is that? You're the CEO. Make a decision."

"There you go. I'm the CEO, but if I ever stop listening to people, then they'll stop listening to me. How do you think it would work out?"

Kim shot to her feet, startling Forrest. Angrily, she leaned over his desk. Her low-cut blouse revealed much of her breasts. "I expect you to fix it."

Forrest remained calm. A devious smile appeared on his face. "How about a promotion to Atlanta? There's a regional VP position there."

Kim eased back and stood at the foot of his desk. "You're not taking me seriously. I hate that. You think you can ship me off to Atlanta and get rid of me. I'm not interested in moving. It would do nothing to advance my career. You know in this company, the path to the top is not through Atlanta."

"I'm serious. We need someone like you in that region. There's a lot of potential there."

"Not interested. Not going. I'm staying close to you. I want to get to the top and need a mentor like you." A wry smile appeared, "You can groom me for the top job."

Forrest pinched his eyebrows and steadied his gaze, looking for more than her words. "Mentor. Do you want my job? You want me to overlook Woody—the most qualified person for the job. Good God, his wife just died . . . and you want me to pass him over, just like that? Because his wife died?"

"Don't give me that crap. This is real life we are talking about."

Kim moved from one side of his desk to the other. "Yes. This is real life. And, yes, his wife died, but he is not the most qualified."

"Wake up. Woody's crumbling right before our eyes. Take this seriously. I want to be judged on my performance. You know where I stand with some pretty big clients and with some board members. It would be a good decision for the company. For both of us." Kim took a deep breath and steadied her gaze. "I will make it to the top. And, I'm not going to make it being a namby-pamby, dumb blond to anyone, and that includes you."

"What the hell are you talking about?"

"Don't worry. I'll keep our secret safe." Kim moved alongside and sat on the corner of his desk, her skirt rising on her thighs, a pensive look on her face, picking through her options. "I still think we make a pretty good team. Look, I know you'll take care of this. Don't let our past get in the way. You know it's the right decision."

Kim slid off the desk, smoothed her skirt, smirked, turned, and reached into her briefcase. Stepping up to his desk, she slid a Kraft envelope across his desk. "Oh, I meant to give this to you. You can keep it."

For a moment, Forrest stared at the envelope and didn't move. He had no idea what was in the envelope, but from Kim, he expected the worst. His first thought was to push it back unopened. He knew to give in to her gave her the edge. He picked up the envelope like it was too hot to touch and began to open it. He looked inside and glanced up at Kim. The look on her face made him cringe.

When he saw the picture, anger swept over him like a gale-force wind—not easily given to anger, the feeling foreign to him. One of his better qualities was to stay calm in the worst situations. Sure, he had flashes of anger playing hockey, but then he could lash out in a popular, somewhat legal way. His dad always told him, "Don't ever let 'em see you are angry. Stay calm and get 'em the next time down the ice."

He felt he could explode into a thousand pieces. The overriding sensibility to lash out was unacceptable in the civilized business. How could a person so talented be so evil? How could those two sides reside in the same person? A total lack of empathy was not a required ingredient for a successful career, he guessed.

Forrest stared at the picture of him, naked, wrapped in a blanket on a bed. Anger turned to sadness. He slumped back, overcome by weariness.

Kim smiled. "I have others. You sure are photogenic, but some pictures might be a bit . . . a bit too embarrassing to show you. Maybe, you'd like to see one with me in the picture." Her smile evaporated into a sad expression. "I always hoped we would be a couple. You remember that night, don't you? The night we celebrated the Sloten deal. That was quite a day, wasn't it? Really put us over the top."

Forrest regained his composure. "This is a nightmare. What kind of woman are you? Do I hear you correctly? You're blackmailing me?"

Kim looked forlorn. "You have me all wrong. I want a chance to prove myself to you. You know how qualified I am. I just want what is coming to me, and I don't want us to get in the way."

Forrest rose. His voice exploded so loud he thought Isabella would hear him. "You need to leave now!"

Unexpectedly his office door opened, and Isabella stepped in. Kim and Forrest looked at her awkwardly. "Your phone conference is ready." Forrest peeked down to his phone to see no holding lights were blinking. "Also, Warren called to see if you were still attending the wedding reception dinner tonight?"

Forrest preferred to be with Allie, but he had committed to attend Warren's daughter's wedding rehearsal dinner. Warren was a good friend and knew how much he wanted him there. He had told him he couldn't attend the wedding the next day. "Tell him I'll be there. I'll stay in town tonight and go to the cabin tomorrow."

When Isabella left, Forrest walked past Kim to the door. "I don't care what you do. Do you hear me? Do whatever you want. See how far it takes you. My priority is . . . her name is Alexandra by the way. Allie to me. And, my baby's name is Christina."

# 19

Usually, a man true to his commitments, but after the conversation with Kim, Forrest left the office and drove straight to the lake cabin. Cell coverage was hit and miss between Minneapolis and Ten Mile, so he made two calls right away on his size-of-a-brick Nokia Talkman. He first called Warren to apologize, then he called Allie to let her know he was on his way, and to let Flo know she could go home tonight if she wanted.

Responsible citizen be damned, Forrest would not make the drive alone without the friendship of at least a nip of Vodka. He stopped at the state-run liquor store and bought a fifth of Smirnoff vodka before leaving the city limits. Something to dull the situation but something else to worry about on the drive home.

By the time he arrived, he had only a few drinks but remembered little about the trip. Towns he passed through were a blur. No matter how hard he tried to bury the conversation with Kim, every thought circled back to it. He could see her devilish, taunting smile reflected in road signs and plastered on the windshield.

He arrived late afternoon. Flo's bag was standing by the front door awaiting his arrival. She was eager to return home and avoid the long, early Saturday morning drive to her writing club meeting, which she faithfully attended.

Allie was lying on a chaise lounge on the back deck. When he stepped onto the deck, he saw she was asleep. He took a seat opposite her and watched. *Why can't life be more like a peaceful daydream? What have I done to my angel?* He couldn't erase the image of Kim standing in his office, confidently posed with her hands on her hips, fearing nothing, basking in her power. The picture. After a few minutes and not wanting to disturb her, he went inside for a drink, to say goodbye to Flo, and to check on Chrissy.

As he heard Flo drive away, the silence of the north woods seized him.

He carried Chrissy to the back deck, where he found Allie still asleep on the chaise. Chrissy was in those first few moments of waking, making new meanings of her surroundings, watching her mom, then to Forrest, mesmerized, as if trying to make sense of his troubled smile.

Allie awoke, with a one-eyed peek at the two great loves of her life. Slowly her senses returned to full recognition of the special man holding her miracle daughter.

Groggy, Allie mumbled, "You're home. What about Warren?"

"Warren understands."

"You must have left the office early."

"Couldn't stay away any longer. How's my little angel?"

"Not very angelic."

Forrest had seen her mental outlook decline. Her progress had slowed so much it was hard to see any improvement. Her physical therapy staff said she was doing great and making steady progress, but not to Forrest or Allie. Maybe they wanted too much too soon. To Allie, anticipating her first step was like wishing for the impossible. It was easier to give up.

Forrest stiffened. *I can't let her give up.* "You know what the doctor said, 'Recovery is not going to be easy. Time and perseverance—a state of mind.'"

Fighting back tears and wanting to change the subject, knowing the truth about her condition, and the apparent depression and not wanting to upset him, she asked, "Tell me how business is going."

"I have a big decision to make, and it's not going to be easy. Woody is going through the motions. He's burying himself in work, but it's obvious he's struggling." Forrest paused and picked through the different ways to answer her question about the business. "I told you I was going to promote Woody to the VP job. Now I am reconsidering. This is not a good time for him. I know him, and more pressure is not best for him, the business, or his career. He'll realize that. He has a great future, and you don't get many chances to be in line, so you have to seize your chances. Now is not his time, and I don't want him to screw it up." Forrest was surprised hearing his announcement. All the way home, thoughts roiled around images of his friend, Woody, and the malevolent Kim. He didn't know he had decided until this moment. "This will work out. I'll see to it."

Forrest finished his drink and set it on the table.

"How many drinks have you had since you arrived?" Allie asked.

"I know, too many. Yeah, and it's not doing any good."

"So, who will you promote? Can't you wait?"

"No. I need someone now. It's crucial." With a sigh, he continued, and braced himself, "Kim." Making the awkward announcement lacked confidence, and he wondered if Allie would recognize his lack of conviction.

"Kim?" Allie exclaimed sharply. "You know how I don't like her. I can't believe you'd promote her. She's a slut."

Forrest drew back. Woman's intuition was a powerful thing. She couldn't know Kim well, but she sure had her pegged. "You're not alone. I'll take some heat for it, but she does a good job—for now. I'll deal with it in the future. When Woody announced that Sarah was in hospice, the sharks started circling in the water. Then after she died, there was blood in the water. It's best for the company. Best for Woody." *Maybe Kim is right; this is not a good time for him.*

In the following silence, they gazed out to the setting sun, only minutes away from blinking goodnight. "Sometimes, I think my main job is to navigate people stuff. This country is in trouble. Dishonesty and blackmail, has become our number one industry and politicians battle for power using them as their primary weapon."

When tears welled up again in her eyes, he thought she was upset about what he told her. *Could she read my mind?* "This isn't like me. Oh, Forrest, I want to be a mom. I want us back. I don't know what to do. I am fighting so hard. I just don't know."

Forrest sat on the deck next to her chair and took her hand. "Would you let me retire, so I can be with you?"

His question brought a smile to her face. "Retire? You're still a young man. Besides, I have to do this myself. You can't do it for me."

What an up-and-down day. He had made another decision on the trip to the cabin. He would resign his position and he wasn't sure how she would accept it. Forrest sat quietly, rubbing the back of her hand. "I'd like to." He recognized this was not the time to go any further. Company troubles were in the cool breeze blowing off the lake. They could talk tomorrow.

"Let's sleep in our bedroom tonight," Allie requested.

The upper-level master suite received special consideration when they built the house and decorated it. After the car wreck, they set up sleeping in one of the first-floor bedrooms. The master suite, on the second floor, ran the length of the room with windows looking out to a magnificent, long view past the cove and over the main body of the lake to the horizon. Allie had furnished it with local hand-crafted log furniture, iron-sculptured, twin bear lamps on their nightstands, elk antlers overhead light, and a bear-print bedspread.

"Let's go to bed." Forrest rose, leaned in, and scooped her into his arms. Allie looked up to him as a bride about to be carried over the threshold on honeymoon night. They kissed, and she nestled her head into the crook of his neck as he cradled her like a small child.

After helping her to bed and covering her, he laid Chrissy in her crib while brushing his teeth and putting on his flannel pajama bottoms and a long sleeve t-shirt. When he returned, he turned off the light. The windows were open, and they could hear a gentle breeze and the water lapping at the shore.

A little before eleven o'clock, sleep was scarce. Allie's faint voice in the still darkness surprised him. "I'm going to do this. Watch me. But you have to quit the resignation talk. Don't give up on me. I'm sorry

I get down sometimes. I don't ever want to be a burden. Never again. I will do this. Wait and see."

"I know you will." Forrest rolled over and kissed her. "I love you."

# 20

Over the past year, Forrest could easily count the number of restful nights—zero. No amount of liquor helped him. The alcohol's numbing effects were addictive, so he drank and hoped and failed to find peace. The drinking had another impact, and in some ways, made matters worse. Usually, the liquor did its job of putting him to sleep. But it didn't last through the night, and during the night, as sure as the sun would rise, images appeared as thoughts bounced around like pinballs.

Tonight's bliss came as a result of falling asleep in the arms of an angel, the woman who told him she'd beat her affliction, vowing to be a mom again, a wife. We'll win this together was his last thought before he drifted off to sleep in search of pleasant memories.

In a dream he recalled an evening, five years after they built the cabin. Forrest built a fire pit, stacking the logs high and soon there was a roaring fire. The moonless, dark sky north woods' night produced a million more stars. Until the fire got going, they huddled together under a blanket draped over their shoulders. The fire gained momentum, and sparks mingled with tens of thousands of twinkling, happy stars.

Allie moved close to Forrest, and their smiling eyes locked and silently issued I-love-you testimonials. He recalled their first kiss outside the Colonial Bowl, a kiss like no other. Her eyes were green with flecks of gold. He would never forget her smile the night of their first kiss—a smile she reserved for him thousands of times since. Her smiles always warmed him like the summer sun.

There it was again, her smile, now fading into a haze of smoke. The smoke enveloped them, and Forrest began to cough. He was startled when Allie cried out, "Fire." Forrest shook his head and rubbed his eyes to clear the smoke and the sting from his eyes.

"Fire!" Allie's scream was ear piercing.

Forrest bolted upright and rubbed his eyes. The room filled with smoke. Outside the bedroom, he could see flames shooting up from the first floor. He rushed toward the top of the stairs. The fire had engulfed the lower level and climbed the walls, curling off the ceiling and shooting flames up the stairs like a fire breathing dragon. Aristotle moved alongside him and whimpered. Outside he could hear sirens and saw two volunteer firefighter trucks had arrived.

Allie leaned up on her elbow—her eyes wide and filled with terror.

"We have to get out of here." Forrest rushed to the crib and swept Chrissy into his arms. Aristotle stood next to the bed as Allie looked out toward the fire. He swaddled Chrissy in her blanket, shifted her to one arm, and turned to Allie. She began to cough uncontrollably. Forrest pulled the blanket around Chrissy's face.

Holding Chrissy in his arm, he slid Allie to the side of the bed, and with his other arm, picked her up and quickly fell backward. Lying on the floor, still clinging to Chrissy, he saw Allie an arms-length away. Chrissy began to cry and cough.

"Shhh, my baby. Everything will be okay." Looking back to Allie, "I got this." Shifting Chrissy to his other arm, he rose to his feet and leaned down to pick up Allie. He rose and shifted them to balance the weight. He thought he could carry both, but as he approached the stairs, he lost his balance and fell again. This time both Allie and Chrissy fell to the floor and him on top of them. Chrissy wailed.

The devil was on a break-out from hell. His long fingers seeking to destroy everything he touched in a frenzy to claim souls. The flames reached out for the second-floor walls. Using the stairway to escape looked impossible.

"Forrest, take Chrissy. Now!" Allie coughed the words out. "Hurry, before it's too late."

Stunned, Forrest started choking. He could see the smoke thickening on the ceiling like a giant thunder cloud.

"I can't leave you."

"Go now! You have to leave! Hurry!"

Forrest knew it was their best chance. He knew he could do it if he hurried. Swooping Chrissy up close to his chest, covering her with a blanket, he said, "Don't cry. We'll be okay." Coughing, he turned to Allie, "I'll be back. I can do this. I will. I promise." At the top of the stairs, he hesitated and picked a path, took a deep breath, and rushed down.

Outside he saw several firefighters. He handed Chrissy to the first one. "Take her. My

wife . . . ." He turned and rushed back into the fire. A fireman's voice yelled after him. When he broke through the wall of flames guarding the open front entrance, he saw the fire had engulfed the entire house and stairway. "Allie, I'm coming," he yelled. "I'm coming."

"Forrest!" Allie yelled out.

The third step gave way as flames reached out for new fuel, his skin and clothing. As he climbed to the next step, he waved his hands frantically to ward off the flames. Another step and he saw Allie leaning forward over the top landing, staring at him, smiling peacefully, her eyes wide, her arms outstretched.

Forrest blinked several times. Aristotle's face nestled next to hers, his paws and legs singed to the bone. He looked back at Allie. Her hair seared to her scalp, her skin turning black. Forrest reached out for her and touched her hand.

Whoosh! The stairway gave way, and the roar of the fire surrounded him.

When the stairway collapsed, he hit his head and lost consciousness. The right side of his body and face took the brunt of the fire, inflicting second and third-degree burns on his face and arm. A firefighter, who had seen him charge into the cabin, and followed close behind, pulled him out.

# 21

Forrest recalled little of the first fifteen days of his hospitalization. The *phuoshh-whooosh* sound of the ventilator helped him breathe and reminded him he was alive, enough to witness white walls and a white bed cover and shadowy serious blurry-faced nurses and doctors. Shock, his friend, dulled his senses, and the IV morphine blessedly pancaked his knowledge of what happened and the gravity of his circumstance.

His parents and hers planned Allie's funeral with Flo's assistance. He wasn't able to attend. Flo and Luka came to visit often, as did members of his executive team. The doctors said he might remember them. He didn't. But the image of Allie, Chrissy, and Aristotle trapped in his head, looped repeatedly. And, his last words, "I'll be back. I can do this. I will. I promise." When Forrest was lucid, Flo nibbled at the edges of his consciousness, but he was more transfixed on the images that appeared in the stark white ceiling.

"Forrest, you gotta fight. The doctor says fighting back is their best tool to get you well."

Forrest heard her, but much the same way he listened to the nurses and the doctors. He had nothing to say.

"I want to bring Chrissy."

"No," Forrest blurted out firmly. He hadn't said a word for days—locked away is a dark place no one could penetrate. His adamant refusal made it clear he understood. The last time he spoke was the last time Flo asked if she could bring Chrissy. She understood he might not want her to see him like this, but she also thought to see her would help revive him.

After removing the ventilator, shock subsided, and the haze that protected him lifted and blew a gaping hole in his existence, uncovering an omniety of intractable pain and the unavoidable, undeniable reality that Allie was gone. Not just gone—died in a horrific fire. Just beyond his outstretched hands. Not once but repeatedly. Horribly.

Now the image of her blackened skin and singed hair, her smile, reaching out for him, dominated whatever life clung to him. The deep seed of the will to live planted at his birth, now was buried in scar tissue and dark memories along with the image of her staring down at him. *Oh, my God. She was smiling at me . . . she was dead. A smiling promise we would be together again. I will be with her again. I will be with her again.*

Pain opened new doors of consciousness.

His time in the hospital was best described by one low point followed by a lower one and then one after that, and another further down—different levels of hell. Step one, the awareness he was alive, then the stark cognizance of lost love, turned his heart to stone: another step-down, the pain, pain as unendurable as the inquisitioner's rack.

The last step down—Chrissy would grow up without a mother and with what kind of surviving father, alive but as a freak. The step he now stood on, his only uplifting emotion—the only way to be with Allie was to die.

What the devil didn't burn on his body, scorched his soul. When he thought the pain couldn't get worse, it did with stunning everyday clarity: gauze dressings, debridement,

twice-a-day baths of burning purple iodine drowned out doctors' and nurses' encouragements. After a thorough iodine soaking, the nurses stripped the bandages from raw bleeding flesh, sometimes calloused nurses aggressively pulled the gauze bandages from his wounds. Other times nurses were brought to tears when he cried out for Allie.

Forrest's mom and dad came to his bedside after the funeral. Francis, the hardscrabble lumberman, now sawmill foreman, was no match when facing Forrest. Holding his Bemidji Saw Mill ball cap in his hand, he softly choked out the words, "It was a nice ceremony."

Saying the ceremony was nice rubbed sandpaper over his wounds. The closed-casket funeral, and the unshakeable image of how Allie perished, had cast a heart-wrenching pale over the standing-room-only sympathizers. Swallowing hard, Francis said, "Her folks were there from New York, they'd like to stop by. I said I'd ask."

Forrest didn't answer but shook his head and turned away. Discussing the ceremony was like rubbing sandpaper on fresh wounds.

Forrest's mother, Ethyl, stood on the other side of the bed. As lumber jack hardened as Francis, she wept softly. "Some of your company associates were there. They sent their sympathies."

Forrest's gaze locked on his white bed cover.

"Pastor Bird came down with us to preside." Francis tried to keep their end of the conversation going. Ethyl added, "He did a nice job. You know she was buried at Lakewood Cemetery."

Francis could tell Forrest wasn't listening. "We'll have a memorial service when you are able."

Forrest broke free of his stare, "No. We don't need to."

The relentless battle of the will to live or give up and die was ruled by believing he could be with Allie if he died. Death always ruled out, preferable to the sting of a thousand bees.

Flo thought she knew what it would take to resurrect him. Late in the afternoon, Forrest had finished his last iodine bath and redressing and was in the safe, lonely quiet of his bed. Forrest repeatedly told Flo he wasn't ready to see Chrissy. He wasn't sure why. Partly, he didn't want Chrissy to see him, the revolting Pazuzu, a terrible memory of Dad. Why did she need any memory of him? Also, she might steal him away from his misery, his most comfortable place.

The burn unit was quiet, reverent. Especially today. He could only hear soft footsteps in the hall, and the slow creaking opening of the door. Flo cautiously entered his hospital room, holding Chrissy's hand. Chrissy wore a pink and white ruffled pinafore, white tights, black patent shoes, and a pink bow clipped to her brown curls. In a soft apologetic voice, Flo asked, "I hope it's okay."

It took a minute for Forrest to gather up the sight of Chrissy, standing like a princess in waiting, looking up to him in awe, wondering where she was and if this was her daddy? Why was he in a bed, in this big white place, with all these strangers?

Forrest moved his lips but couldn't produce a sound. Was it okay? Back and forth, he tried to answer her question. It wasn't. Was it? He recalled when Allie announced the miracle—how they wept in each other's arms. Now, the little miracle stood there, her mouth open, her eyes wide, his little princess, his heart stealer, his flesh and blood, his little Allie. How could he ever desert this little miracle?

He recalled how, not long ago when she sat on his lap, she would twirl her curls in his fingers as he sang her a kid's song. As he sang, Chrissy would playfully put her fingers to his lips, as if to feel the words.

Tears welled in Forrest's eyes, and he began singing softly. Flo strained to hear him singing. Chrissy knew.

A you're adorable

B you're so beautiful

C you're a cutie full of charms

As his voice strengthened, Chrissy smiled and moved closer to Flo and wrapped her arms around her leg.

D you're a darling and

E you're exciting

F you're a feather in my arms

G you look good to me

Forrest's tears freely flowed as Flo walked Chrissy to his bedside. She reached for his hand, "Daddy."

Flo began to cry uncontrollably. Through her sobs, she said, "We need you. You have to win this battle."

Forrest maintained his gaze on Chrissy several minutes longer, then broke away and reached for Flo's hand. Squeezing it tightly, he said, "Thank you, Flo, I'll never forget this."

Forrest spent over sixty days in the hospital. Luka and Flo were regular visitors. Isabella stopped by regularly, usually so proper, she wept openly. Roy King, his attorney, stopped and was always available through Flo if needed. Forrest refused to see anyone else, including Woody.

He conducted any official business with the irresistibly gentle, red-bearded Charles Gunn. His conservative nature could be counted on to not stray outside the lines. He was the obvious choice to run things in Forrest's absence, at least temporarily.

The third time they met, Forrest noticed Charles kept sneaking peeks at his scars, so in mid-sentence, he interrupted, "Charles, get used to it. This is the new me."

"Pretty scarred up, huh?" Charles responded.

Forrest smiled, unprepared for the blatant honesty of the moment.

Kim made a surprise visit, no doubt not wanting to appear unsympathetic. She spent a few brief awkward moments complaining about Woody, but soon she launched into unabashed self-promotion at his expense. Forrest turned her out, and she left in a huff.

Sadness and pain were the companions that marked his progress. Still, his scars were difficult to look at, and the ones in his heart, the invisible ones that would never heal, were like suffering friends, reminders of a greater loss.

# 22

As soon as he could, he met with the police detective and fire inspector assigned to Allie's death and the fire. Forrest asked Luka to attend. "I don't trust 'em, and I haven't even met them yet. Nothing happened with the car crash. They still call it an accident."

When the investigators arrived, Luka offered to pull chairs to his bed, which they refused. Each took a position across from one another at his bedside. Luka stood at the end of the bed. Inspector Raymond Suratt, the fire investigator, introduced himself and Detective Sergeant Dennis Lowell of the Minneapolis Police Department, who he already knew had taken over the case from Detective Culpeper.

Inspector Suratt wore jeans, a sweatshirt, and round, thick, metal-framed glasses. Detective Lowell wore a slick, black baggy suit, a gray tie, and a white shirt. The inspector spoke first in a crisp scholarly manner, "I am sorry for your loss, and we're going to do everything we can to find out who did this."

*Who did this? Somebody did this?*

"How much do you know about the fire?"

"I don't know anything. This is the first . . . ."

Captain Suratt stated the facts coldly. "Okay, let me start by telling you that fires set deliberately to occupied homes or buildings is first-degree arson. The challenge is to find the person and motive to determine the level of added charges. We think it would have been clear to the arsonist someone was home, so first-degree arson charges are in play. The windows and the deck door were open. There seems to have been a blanket draped on the front deck railings, the patio furniture uncovered, the seat cushions out, one of the patio umbrellas was up, and the table set. The hummingbird feeder nearby was full."

*He said this was arson.* Forrest nodded. His mind whirled, stuck on the realization someone had set the fire. Killed his Allie. *Why?*

"So, he knew someone was in the house. Most of the time, it's a man. We're sure it was a man. The accelerant was gasoline—quick to ignite and explosive. It's the most commonly used accelerant. It's easy to ignite and can be purchased anywhere and transported without arousing suspicions. After that, there was plenty of fuel, wood furniture, floor, walls, ceiling, everything quite flammable. A professional might have used a remote ignitor, so likely this was not the work of a professional. We didn't find an igniter. Anyway, arson is started with a match sixty percent of the time."

Detective Lowell interrupted. "We found two five-gallon cans in a witness's truck—or suspect. That's to be determined. That's a lot of accelerant. We found fresh tire tracks in the turnout. You know the turn out when you first turn off the road to your cabin? There were several different tracks, including the tracks of the truck the witness was driving Actually, he's more a suspect."

Inspector Suratt continued, "For a fire to spread that fast, you would need a lot of accelerant. Five gallons of gas weighs over thirty pounds." Leaning into Forrest, "Each. What is that, a quarter of a mile?"

"A bit further than that," Luka volunteered.

Detective Lowell inserted, "Like I said it was a man. That's a heavy carry."

Fire Inspector Suratt continued, "Now it doesn't rule out a woman, but she'd be a pretty motivated one, I'd say. Ten gallons of gas produces 16,000 cubic feet of burn, plus all the combustibles in the cabin, and it went pretty quick. Whoever set the fire brazenly entered the cabin like a pro and spread the gasoline on the more flammable furniture and curtains. Just pouring it on the floor wouldn't have caused this kind of fire. Someone was looking to do maximum damage. Your five-hundred-gallon propane tank relief valve was opened to add fuel and destruction. The breezy night was the final ingredient—fuel, ignition, oxygen."

"This was no arsonist. He was a killer," Detective Lowell added.

*Killer.* There it was again. The cold reality of what happened was summed up in that one word.

Picking at a lunch stain on his tie, Detective Lowell continued, "The one witness, suspect, saw a white something or other, driving slowly in the area at two in the morning and turning around in the middle of the highway. Big white vehicle."

Forrest asked, "SUV?"

"Sure, could be. Our witness drove a silver pick-up. Our witness suspect was arrested for drunk driving at 2:30 am. That complicates matters. He's the guy with the two empty gas cans in his truck. The patrol officer said he smelled like gasoline."

The fire inspector added, "He is in the lawn care business."

Detective Lowell looked at the fire inspector with a blank expression before he continued, "Not much of a witness, but for all we know, he's our guy. And we'll figure out when the fire started."

Suratt moved to the end of the bed and stood next to Luka. "Our volunteer firefighters came from both directions, and they didn't see another car on the road."

"So, what could be the motive?" Detective Lowell asked. "We always start with people in the tight circle of knowns and then widen out. Does anybody come to mind? Did she have any enemies? Do you? Did she ever mention any encounters with anyone she thought odd, or you thought odd?" As an afterthought, he added, "We haven't forgotten the car accident and the white SUV. We still haven't located the vehicle."

"Accident?" Forrest protested.

"Whatever you want to call it."

"I sure as hell don't call it an accident. Allie was the safest driver . . . she knew the road. She didn't just plunge down the hill on her own." Angrily and painfully, he lifted into a sitting position. "We have had this conversation before."

"It's nothing right now. We don't know what it was."

Forrest rolled his head to the side. *Enemies? How could Allie have any enemies? Do I?*

After they left, Luka moved to his side. "Sorry."

"Yeah. They have nothing."

***

Obvious to Charles, Forrest was unable to focus on business. After several meetings, Forrest made it clear the business needed to run without his leadership and explained the vacant VP position should be filled—promote Kim and move Woody to Atlanta.

"You know that is an unpopular decision," Charles resisted.

"I know it's unpopular, but I can't send her to Atlanta, and we need to keep moving. Look. I don't like this, but Kim knows the business. She amazes me sometimes." Waving his hand dismissively, "I know what kind of woman she is. We have to do this. I am more worried about how Woody will take it. When we are ready to make a move, I'll ask Woody to come to see me."

<br><br><br><br>

# 23

<br>

By the time he arrived home from the hospital, his tears were damned up and covered over with anger and remorse. A lost soul crossing the desert in search of a cool drink, he kicked the sand into storm clouds of hating the invisible person who caused the crash and set the fire that destroyed her life, his life, Chrissy's. His destination was reaching the oasis being with Allie.

His mother had taught him never to hate anyone or anything. As a young man, Forrest told his mom he hated Axel, his best friend. She admonished him to never to use that word again, or she would wash his mouth out with soap. When he was nine, she pinned the Rudyard Kipling poem "If" on his bedroom wall and made him memorize it. The poem still lived in his office.

If you can wait and not be tired by waiting,

Or being lied about, don't deal in lies,

Or being hated don't give way to hating,

And yet don't look too good, nor talk too wise

What Ethyl's poetry didn't soften in his heart, Francis' life examples did. He was a tough-barked man, as gnarly as a Ponderosa pine, who never spoke a hateful word to anyone. It was easy to hate his chain saw blade when it went dull after one cut, or when it wouldn't start, but he never had a bad word for it either. The local native American population had their problems, and some of the lumbermen he worked with could spew vile, hateful pronouncements toward them but never Francis. He went out of his way to help them.

Looking back, who was there to hate? Not his hockey opponents who sometimes got the best of him, out skating him, or playing dirty. He never thought the other guy hated him, just trying to win, and at the end of the game, they always met at center ice and shook hands. He did plot to dish out comeuppance to opponents. Was it hate?

The detectives weren't doing anything. Evil always pays for their acts is what Flo said. And professor Smithson said there were always consequences. But in a silent forest, when the tree falls, is there a sound? Without a witness, without evidence, how do you know if life balances out as designed? Does it balance out if Forrest couldn't retaliate or witness revenge?

His bright light, Chrissy, added light to the dark, but even in daylight, he found the land as barren and cold as a frozen Minnesota boundary lake.

Forrest declared he would talk to Woody when reorganization plans were finished. Forrest's heart ached over the conversation. Forrest lightly traced the red crater scars on the side of his face. "I'm sorry for not seeing you when I was in the hospital. I didn't see anyone."

"I understand," Woody responded.

"Woody, we've been friends forever. Right?"

"Like brothers. You know I'd do anything," Woody said. There was an emotional weight to his words.

Forrest flinched. "I have made some difficult decisions. I hope you'll understand. I'm not sure when I'll be back, but the business must go on. It is not a good time to bring new leadership in, but I'm incapable of running things. I am not sure I ever will be. So, we have to make do. I want you to go to Atlanta. The opportunities are unlimited there, and I think your future with the company is best there. I hope you believe me when I say the road to the top may pass through Atlanta."

Woody's face turned red and he tightened his jaw. "So, who is going to fill the VP vacancy."

Without flinching, Forrest answered, "Kim."

Woody lashed out. "Kim, you have got to be kidding. She is a disaster. I thought it was my job. Atlanta? I don't see it. Why are you doing this? Forget we are friends; I wouldn't send my enemy to Atlanta."

Forrest remained silent. He couldn't recall making a more challenging decision, harder than when he first made it, and he had second-guessed the decision a hundred times. Was he doing this because of Kim or for business? He had looked at the decision every way he could and rationalized every alternative.

Woody turned his back to leave without another word, then turned and said, "I don't understand why you are doing this. You know what people will say. And, I say this as a friend." He paused and clenched his jaw. "Or used to be friends. They'll say you are sleeping with her. How else could she get the job? That's the way she works."

Forrest stared at Woody, his friend, his best friend, words drowning in a pool of pity, and mourning, one more ugly side of the whole plague. He lost Allie, and it wasn't just his burned face, but his soul, and now he felt he was tossing his good friend aside.

Woody stared back in disbelief for several beats, regret showing on his face about hus comment about h and Kim. Other might think the worse, but he didn't believe Forrest could stray. He loved Allie too much. No matter, this was important.  He was being shipped to Atlanta.

Finally, Forrest responded, "That's a hell of a thing to say at a time like this." The element of truth, though, soured the moment even more than the announcement. Forrest wanted so badly to say more, but what to say. He made the decision. Maybe it was a bad decision. He made bad decisions before and made them work, but not like this, not with a friendship at stake.

Forrest cringed. Woody was red-faced like right before a hockey fight. When the opponent slashed him, and no penalty called, he would chase the culprit skater the length of the ice and pounce on him. Woody took a deep breath. "Screw you. You're no friend. I don't know what's going on but screw you."

As Woody was leaving, Forrest called out. "Woody, come back here. I know what I am doing. Listen . . . ."

***

A day felt like a month. Forrest couldn't tell what day of the week it was—no Monday morning urges to start his business week, no Friday shoulder slump, no Saturday country club dinners with Allie—no Allie. There were no Twins games they used to attend, no radio by the pool and afternoon naps listening to the Twins baseball's mellow baritone voice, Herb Carneal, call the play-by-play. In the fall, there used to be Golden Gopher football games and tailgating with friends. No more.

There were no friends. No University of Minnesota ice hockey games in the winter months. In late March, Flo announced archrival Wisconsin Badgers had defeated the Gophers in the national championship hockey final game. Forrest lifted his head with a puzzled expression. He never missed a final. The Badgers? How could that be? How could life be like this? Minnesotans loved to win hockey national championships and hated losing to the Badgers—no better rivalry in hockey. Forrest nodded.

When he arrived home from the hospital last summer, friends called on him, but he turned them away. Even Woody, his best friend from high school hockey days, college, were turned away. Flo encouraged him to see him, but he refused angrily. "I told you no one. I don't want to see anyone."

Only three people had ready access to him, Flo, Luka, and Charles—Flo for her mothering of Chrissy and cautious concern for Forrest, Luka, for his non-judgmental silence, a kindred spirit pf pain and anger, and Charles, by necessity his only contact with duty—duty to a company, to stockholders, to employees. Flo, Luka, and Chrissy were co-conspirators to keep him from leaping off the ledge. They rarely asked questions and never made suggestions, but they were steadfast observers and always there.

Even little Chrissy played a part in trying to heal him, doling out large doses of need and love and asking for both father and mother love in return. In the beginning, Forrest tried to sleep in his bed, by habit on his side, but in the night when he'd reach out, he felt the rejection of a cold sheet. Sometimes Flo would take Chrissy to him and announce, "She was crying. She needs her dad." In the morning, he would wake up to flailing arms and legs and cooing sounds. Night interruptions like that always doused the terror, temporarily.

Nights were the most troublesome. Forrest led a Doctor Jekyll and Mr. Hyde existence—by day the loving father and by night, lost in the library, a bottle of Old Forrester on the table beside him, staring into the inconsolable gloom, being tossed around like a Raggedy Andy doll.

The sun always rose out of the east and disappeared into western darkness, tallying another day, a reminder no one escaped, everyone born to die and in between mark their time in the rising and falling. All he wanted was the elusive mirage, one foot in front of another under a cloud of should-haves and could-haves, can'ts and won'ts, and ifs and buts.

The amber potion didn't provide solutions, but it sent demons scurrying to the far corners. In the wee hours of the morning, the once-roaring fire made the library Arizona hot, causing his eyes to droop and dropping him into a deep chasm between alive and dead. The glowing embers of the fireplace, the root of life, smoldered and hissed and cried out for fuel and new life. At times the fire roared and terrified him, but the devil weakened, and the glow always died, the library cooled, and the light of day found him slumped in his old-world, oversized leather chair, his mouth open, breathing heavily.

One night, his slumber was interrupted by a sudden draft. He stiffened and looked around. A whisper broke the silence. "You look so sad."

The vision of Allie appeared standing before the glowing embers. "Allie. It's you. Is it really you?"

He watched the vision move toward him, and he felt the softness of her arms, her cheeks against his, her kiss on his lips. Warmth swept over him.

"I love you so. I don't think I can go on." Tears swelled in his eyes. "I want to be with you. Can I? I would right now. Can you take me with you?"

"Not now, not yet. Chrissy needs you."

"Do you know what happened?"

"I do. You will too, in time. I can't control what happens, but it's always been you and me. You've said that before. We are connected like two pieces locked together and divided by time. We have always been together. I know how much you want to be with me. I want to be with you too."

"I'm lost without you," Forrest pleaded.

"Listen to me. Believe me. I am real. I am not a dream. We will be together. I promise. I

know how hard this is and how time seems to move so slowly. But for me, it will be like tomorrow when we are together. Remember that. Chrissy needs you, and then we will be together."

"Can I get through this?"

"Of course, you can. You are the strongest man I know. You have to. For Chrissy and me."

<h1 style="text-align:center">24</h1>

Winter passed in frigid Minnesota darkness. Forrest never left the house. Occasionally, the doctor came to his home. Time was the only healer of skin and the only ointment for his soul.

Forrest resisted al thoughts about going back to work. Flo never asked. She knew he needed time before he could return. She could see it in his everyday hibernation in the darkened library and his excessive drinking.

Charles Gunn walked a thin line in his meetings with Forrest, as sympathetic as any friend could be, but he faced urgent challenges running Niche, which required him to be as straightforward as he dared be. Charles had reluctantly agreed to serve as the interim CEO while Forrest recovered. He didn't aspire for the position, nor was he trained for it. Being CEO of a large company was not in his DNA. No one likes to fail at anything, and Charles had little confidence and expected no matter what, he could still fail.

Each time he called on him, Charles wondered what he would find, the broken suffering shadow of the man he admired, or the recovering one nearing the time he could take back the reins. Disappointment always walked out the door with Charles after each meeting. As the time stretched on, Charles began to worry Forrest might never return.

The people part of the job was like coaching feline synchronized swimming and wasn't his strong suit. He had a gift with numbers, where they went on a ledger, where they ended on a balance sheet, not people. He could smell test the honesty of a financial report and could reconcile a column of numbers on first sight—some thought it was a trick. He was brave with numbers, not with people.

Charles felt the company's weight on his shoulders and found it challenging to know what to report to the board about Forrest. His respect for Forrest clouded his judgment. He wanted him to make a full recovery, and a speedy return overrode his ability to make a fair company assessment.

When he reported to the board the results of his last meeting with Forrest, he stammered his way through a transparent assessment that more time was necessary. Arthur Garfield Westcott III, chairman of the board, a husky man with a full gray beard and thinning hair combed straight back from a high forehead, questioned Charles' judgment. He announced he would see Forrest and determine when he would return, and, following that, the Board needed to make a plan for moving forward.

Arthur insisted to Flo a meeting with Forrest was of great importance. At first, Flo was reluctant, but she granted an appointment a week later after checking with Forrest. When he arrived, Flo took him to the library. Reverently they clomped across the hallway paver floor. The door creaked like a Boris Karloff movie. Arthur slipped into the dark.

Forrest sat in a leather chair, the crackling birchwood fire the only light in the room. In the flickering light, he motioned for Arthur to join him. As he took his seat He leaned in and offered his hand. Forrest looked away.

Arthur moaned as he eased his large frame into the chair, stroked his beard, and took a deep breath. As he gazed around the room, he sneaked a peek at Forrest, wondering about his mood. Rich, leather-bound books crowded the ceiling-high bookshelves. The fire cast gloomy strobe-like shadows into the room.

Forrest appeared gaunt, his cheeks hollow, his beard unkempt, and, when he turned, the firelight accentuated facial scars running down the side of his face and neck. Always well-groomed before, his usual short crew cut had turned white, was uncombed, and hung wildly over his ears.

Forrest spoke first, "Sorry, I didn't take your hand. That was rude. I don't see many people nowadays and have forgotten my manners." Looking into his lap, "I've turned into a damned unfriendly person, I guess. I'm not trying to be that. I . . . ."

"Forrest, no explanation is needed," Arthur interrupted. He wore a Burl Ives, tweed sport coat. He crossed his arms, rested them on his protruding belly, and rubbed his gray, freshly trimmed beard. Not a man easily intimidated, he now had to broach the subject caught in the back of his throat.

The consummate strong-willed, blunt man searched for what to say next. They were more than business colleagues. They had known each other since Niche formed, and Forrest invited him to be on his board. Not long after joining the board, he became chairman.

In a husky grandfatherly voice, he asked uncomfortably, "Growing a beard, huh?"

Forrest groaned.

"Charles is doing a great job."

"He doesn't like it," Forrest said bluntly.

"Yeah, he's not cut out for it, that's for sure. But he's the kind of guy who won't do anything to hurt the company. You know how conservative he is. Nice to have an interim guy who knows his limitations. But it'll be nice to have you back."

"Not coming back," Forrest blurted out. Hearing his proclamation, Forrest wondered why he said it so forcefully. Sure, he didn't want to go back. He went over that in his mind but hadn't planned to say anything. He hinted at this with Charles and confided in Luka his desire to leave the company in an organized way.

"You mean not now?"

"No, I mean forever."

Even the burning logs seemed to stop crackling. Storytellers of long ago leaned over the shelves, out of their leather book covers to listen. Money didn't matter to Forrest, so he could take or leave the job. Niche had made him a rich man, more wealththan he dreamed possible. What he learned from his customers led him to invest broadly in telecom, packaging and shipping, and even cardboard. He invested heavily in Georgia Pacific.

Pride could be a factor in returning to lead the company—pride of what he had already accomplished and the rewards of greater successes. But pride had been hammered flat. All he ever wanted burned up in the fire.

Arthur didn't expect to hear his declaration. He knew from the first day of the disaster he needed time but felt he would come back and maybe find it good therapy. Looking at the crumpled-up version of Forrest, it was best not to press him. He told the board he would report back and put a plan in place for whatever eventuality they faced. This was the last thing he thought would happen and the least desirable.

Sitting in the dark, facing a man he admired, he processed what was best for the company. If he took him at his word, they should immediately begin a search for his replacement. There would be a lot of disruption. They were damned they replaced him and damned if they didn't. How long could Charles hold on? A year or two? Five?

Arthur decided he couldn't cast him aside. Not yet. Not without a fight. He would stall the board. He'd keep a careful eye on the company, and if anything happened, he would step in. Convincing Charles to hang in there would be challenging.

As Arthur drove away, Forrest felt relieved but also felt the finality of his pronouncement. Everything he built, the woman he loved, Aristotle—all gone. It was his fault. Still, as sure as it snows in Minnesota, he didn't want to go back to Niche.

Forrest remained in the library deep into the night, until the fire turned into hot coals. The only light on in the house was the upstairs night light for Chrissy.

# 25

Small steps of recovery came with the change of seasons as North Star citizens found their way outside to thaw in the early spring sun. Forrest moved outside by the fireplace. Midday, the sun was full and warm. Forrest had removed his hat and gloves.

Flo, his first line of defense, turned away most callers, especially unannounced ones. Luka, the second line of defense, was more protective but left early to take his wife to the doctor. Midday, the sun was full and warm. Forrest had removed his hat and gloves. Flo walked around Forrest to see if he was awake. "There is someone here to see you. He says . . . ."

Both turned to see a man passing Flo and pressing his way toward him. "Forrest, old friend. It is good to see you out here in the sun."

Against the sun's glare, it took a minute to put a name with the man walking toward him Then he figured it out. He would recognize him anytime by his silhouette.

Flo looked back to Forrest for guidance. He waved his hand and motioned for his friend to join him.

Doctor Arjun Dewar, the head of the University of Iowa's psychiatric department, drove over five hours to get there. Forrest hadn't seen RJ since Sarah's funeral, and had refused to see him in the hospital. More than a fraternity brother in college, they had become close friends and spent two summers with him in Bemidji, where he taught him to fish.

When he first met RJ, his sophomore year, he thought him an odd duck. He was a quiet, observant guy who had the funniest one-liners and a unique way of looking at things. At the last reunion with his friends, they had a good laugh over how he ended up being a psychiatrist, how his friends had been his study subjects. He turned out to be the sanest person in the room.

Wearily, Forrest greeted him. "Don't get many visitors. Didn't expect you."

"Flo told me you don't accept visitors," he responded matter-of-factly.

Forrest looked away, considering whether to respond, then back to RJ. "What are you here for?"

"To visit an old friend. I've been trying to see you and decided to barge in—make you refuse me to my face. It's a bit of a drive from Iowa City but good to spend time alone in the car. I've wanted to talk to you for the longest time. I was saddened to learn what happened to Allie. You know I went to the funeral and called on you in the hospital?"

"Are you here to rescue me?"

"Is that why you don't want people to come around? They might rescue you?"

"I don't need to be rescued."

Before RJ sat, he went to the fireplace and added several logs to the fire and stoked it.

"Of course, you don't need to be. I always looked at you as the strongest man I knew."

His remark caught Forrest off guard. "Allie said that to me."

"Well, there you go. Allie would be an authority on that for sure. Hell, what you've gone through would bring George Atlas to his knees."

"George Atlas? How did you come up with that?"

"You know who he is? He was the model for the Alexander Hamilton statue at the U. S Treasury Building."

Forrest laughed. "Allie always said my head was filled with trivia. She used to think all our college trivia games were so funny."

Forrest turned to watch a robin land on the patio and hop from side to side to survey the area.

RJ followed his gaze and said, "Nice to see spring has arrived."

Forrest didn't say anything, but his gaze remained locked on the robin. His psychiatrist friend didn't say anything to disrupt his contemplations. The robin flew away, but Forrest's gaze remained transfixed. He closed his eyes.

The crackle of the fire filled the silence. RJ studied him. Several minutes later, Forrest opened his eyes and looked over to his friend. In the kindest voice RJ could muster, he asked, "Where you been?"

"When I close my eyes, I often see Allie—as clearly as I see you. Not dreams. In color, real, different every time. No holographic black and white nonsense. RJ, do you believe in miracles?"

RJ pinched his eyebrows and pondered the question. "The universe summed up in a simple question. Do I believe? I believe miracles are not always what they seem to be. But do I believe there are miracles? Of course, there are. Miracles today are science of tomorrow. Are you hoping for a miracle?"

"I already had one. Chrissy is a miracle. We tried everything. The doctor said no way. None. Chrissy is a living proof there are miracles."

"What miracle would you like to see now?"

"She came to me and promised we would be together again. Allie did. It happened. It wasn't a dream. When I close my eyes, it's as close to being with her as I can get."

"How is it you will be with her?"

"I never told anyone what I've come to believe. It wouldn't matter. The people close to me think it's sad wishful thinking on my part. You think so, too?"

"Would you think that, if it was me?" RJ asked.

"Probably. So, is that what you think?"

"It's you that sees her. It is more important how you feel. You put a drink in the hand of many scientists when they aren't around their peers, and they might tell you about miracles. I was trained in medical school to stick with science. The more I learned about people, the less I knew. But I get it. Stick to the science. I wouldn't be a doctor if I didn't. But drug studies run a double-blind against a placebo, and the placebo performs pretty well. And the placebo effect becomes an asterisk.

"Science has documented stigmata, voodoo medicine, early death when people give up, people who beat the odds and overcome all sorts of maladies. Are those miracles? A surviving spouse has a sixty-six percent increased chance of dying within the first three months following their spouse's death. So, are you thinking about dying so you can be with Allie?"

"Hey, death isn't our greatest loss. The greatest loss is what dies inside us while we live." Forrest eased back in his chair in philosophical resignation.

RJ didn't respond. He wanted to say more but didn't want to risk affecting the peace hovering over their conversation.

Forrest broke the contemplations. "It feels like a short footbridge away. Death. We all leave this earth eventually. It wouldn't matter. But nah, suicide is such an ugly word. The word itself is repulsive and feels like standing on the edge of a canyon and jumping back in terror at the fleeting thought of falling. No. But I know I'm going to be with Allie again, and if I have to die to be with her, then so be it. It's hard to describe. She came to me. We made a pact. It was real. I will go to her again when it is time. I know it. I don't know when, but I will." Forrest smiled for the first time since RJ arrived and said, "Maybe, if I keep my eyes shut, I'll be with her. I'd like that."

Forrest squinted in the afternoon sun to study his friend, the long hair ponytailed friend who now looked like he was a GQ model. He was no longer his college friend who got straight A's and was in on all the pranks. "You've changed."

"You've changed," RJ rejoined.

Forrest laughed, more at how RJ had changed, than his retort. "I keep expecting you to pull out a pipe and start puffing away."

"We've all changed. We grew up. You ever look at a picture of yourself from our early college days and think, boy I thought I had it all figured out, and now what the hell did we know about anything?"

"Yeah, I thought we had it all figured out. I guess not." Forrest shrugged. "You've become so . . . mindful . . . so analytical. So, are you analyzing everybody all the time?"

"I suppose I am. It's harmless. It's not judgmental . . . more like a geologist noticing rocks. It's who I am now."

In a flash of realization, Forrest observed, "I know what it is . . . you're Sydney on the show *Mash*. Do you remember the psychiatrist on the television series *Mash*?"

Smiling, RJ responded. "Sydney huh? Is that a bad thing? I hope I don't make you uncomfortable." Taking a deep breath and smiling. "Forrest, has your doctor told you, you might be depressed?"

"Depressed?" Forrest had contemplated the question before, and yes, his doctor told him that when he was in the hospital. It would be hard to fool his friend. Especially this one. "Let's just say I'm . . . angry . . . I'm sad."

"Angry?"

"Angry? Angry at whom?"

"With the chase? The chase . . . being Chrissy's father, finding out what happened to Allie. Being with her. What else is there?"

Forrest quickly shifted the conversation, asking several questions about RJ's life. He knew RJ was married with one child, a boy.

RJ never attempted to turn the conversation back to Forrest's state of mind. He knew not to press him. As the sun was setting, RJ announced he needed to get back on the road. As he was leaving, RJ asked, "Can I visit again?"

Forrest asked if he wanted to stay for dinner and spend the night.

The way the invitation was proffered, Arjun knew he was being polite. "I love seeing you, and it's good to hear you are doing better"

"Let Flo know when you might be coming my way, again."

# 26

*I don't remember much of my time in the hospital. I was heavily medicated. The doctor said I couldn't survive without the pain killers. He said the pain of my burns would be enough to kill a man.*

*I do remember a few things. I remember my folks, Flo and Luka, were there. Dad said they had to proceed with Allie's funeral. For days it was all I could think about. I wasn't there. I should have been, if not out of love and duty, then to say goodbye. Dad told me more than once she wasn't there. Funerals were for the living. She was here caring for me, not there.*

*I never expected life to change as it did. We all know we're going to die but don't think about it and don't expect it until death is staring at you with those cold dark eyes. You react with sadness and regret unless you welcome it and look directly into his eyes and say, take me.*

*I remember the moment I decided to live. The smallest things can turn your life around. I had refused to see Chrissy. I told Flo not to bring her around, but she knew better. Unexpected events occur in life when you have steeled yourself against all outside influences. All hope was lost, and then a little girl rescued me.*

*There are things I will never forget. I still recall that day in my office when Allie stopped by after seeing the doctor, about to deliver our miracle baby. That was the same day she was forced off the road and ended up paralyzed—the day I ceased to be Forrest Nelthorpe.*

*The day was like a ride on the Kingda Ka roller coaster. The trip to the cabin to be with Allie was a torturous milepost after milepost of recollections, Kim's words, her devilish smile, those pictures of a night I couldn't recall. Maybe it was the right thing to do—promote her, not Woody. I gave in. I rationalized I could deal with Kim later. I always figured things out, but this was not like anything I experienced before. I thought I'd let things calm down, get Allie back on her feet, walk away from the business. After all, no one understood life's priorities as I did. Things couldn't get worse, could they?*

*I always thought I could have saved Allie. Maybe I should have dragged her out of the fire. When you are young, you are Superman, but there inevitably comes a time in your life when you have to fly but can't. I thought I could carry them both out of the fire. It was hard to shake that thought.*

*Churning memories, weaving the pleasant ones in with the bad ones, always at length connected to the fire. Still, there is no getting over it. I try to forget the fire, but I carry the scars that never let me—Allie's face, Aristotle's. No matter how hard I try, there she is reaching out for me to rescue her. All of my remaining days, weeks, months, and years are stepping-stones to the truth and being united with Allie once again.*

*Lying in the hospital, vengeance kept me alive. No doubt they were going to find the killer, and he'd face justice. But years passed, and the whole thing became a series of technical lectures on law and law enforcement and how hard it was to solve crimes like this—sometimes there were no answers.*

*Now my world has three rooms: one where I sleep, on the ground level bedroom off of the library in the back of the house, the library where I spend my days, and by the fireplace beside the swimming pool when it's warm.*

*The library is the box where dreams and dread are kept. After the tragedy, I spent my days and nights with a bottle of Old Forrester at my side—despair an attractant for gloom. My emotions sleighed all logical thinking. I knew the drinking wasn't helping, but it was essential to my life, the only part that didn't hurt. But I grew to dread it like it was a cocaine addiction.*

*I remember that night when Allie came to me—seared into my memory, seeing her and being together again. It was cold outside and incredibly hot in the library, even with the French doors open. When I first saw her, I suspected she might be an illusion, but she was so lifelike. Not just seeing her, I felt her arms around me, her cheeks pressed to mine. It was no illusion.*

*I remember the first time her image was so clear I thought I had crossed over and was with her. So, years later, after Chrissy brought me into her home, I waited for the time we would be one again. Then it happened again. I thought I was floating up to heaven to join her. I felt suspended in a mystical dreamlike mist, floating away. Allie reached out and took my hand. I remember the rapturous moment was interrupted by a voice coming from the other room. It was Flo's voice. Until her voice came closer, I couldn't make out what was being said.*

*There were other voices in the room. Hands were on me, lifting me, the room was spinning. Allie's smile faded. I lost her again. I couldn't feel her arms around me, but Flo's hand was resting on my chest. I was sliding and then stopped, and there was a banging of doors and faces of strangers and white.*

*Later, I heard the doctor tell Chrissy, "We treated him in time to minimize the effects of the stroke. He should recover. He is a fairly young man."*

*So, I had a stroke. It wasn't my time to join Allie.*

*"His facial paralysis will affect his swallowing and talking. We will know more as the hours pass."*

# 27

Being Chrissy's father came easy. She was his lifeline, a quick learner, and well behaved. When she discovered words and wanted to join conversations, she would string unintelligible sentences without the help of commas or periods, even turn them into paragraphs and short stories. There weren't many things that made Forrest smile, but her babbling was so earnest, so convincing, so rapid-fire at times, it brought him to laughter.

Nighttime reorganized her days and led to early morning questions as only her innocence could conjure. She became the grand inquisitor. One question led to six.

Loss can come in big bites as it did for Forrest, and little bites as it did for Chrissy. When a young child, she would run her fingers over his scars and ask how he got them. The answers he gave didn't mean much to her then.

She starved for stories about her mom as the years passed. What was she was like? How did they meet? Why didn't he go to work like her friend's fathers?

One day, school kids told her that her mom was in a fire. Was she? Dying in a fire disturbed her and lit a match to her curiosity. When she returned from school, she rushed into the library, searching for Flo or her dad. Today they were together—Forrest in his leather chair and Flo on the sofa.

Chrissy wrapped her arms around her father and burst into tears. "Cindy said mommy died in a fire. The other kids said she was in an accident. They all have mommies."

Forrest pulled her onto his lap and held her. "Oh, Chrissy. I wish you had a mommy too. You are a lucky girl, though, to have Flo as a mommy."

Chrissy looked over to Flo, who was dabbing at her tears with a tissue.

Sliding off his lap, she went to Flo and sat on the sofa next to her. Flo pulled her close. Weeping softly, Chrissy turned her head to Flo, "Did you know my mommy? What happened to her?" A year ago, when she asked the question it was about her fear of dying. Flo told her then she was too young to worry about dying. Lately, when she asked, and Flo said her mommy was in heaven, it didn't satisfy her.

Flo looked back to Forrest for the answer. "I wish little girls all had their mommies," she said.

Forrest moved to the sofa and sat beside Chrissy and tried to answer her. "She died when you were a baby. She was in a bad car accident. . ." Forrest looked over to see Flo frowning at him. They had talked before about telling Chrissy what happened with her mom. "She was in a fire too."

Forrest and Flo could see her mind searching for more questions. How did it happen? Where? How could a fire kill you? Can't you run from a fire? A fire!

Questions, questions, questions. Chrissy's mom died when she was young. No amount of Flo's love could explain it. Flo was her mom but not her real mom. Not a wife to her father. There were only a few pictures of her mom in photos she found in the back of one of the library cabinets. Chrissy wasn't in any. And, not in one of her mom and dad standing in front of a cabin, she found hidden away in his desk drawer. There was a dog in the picture too, Flo wasn't in any pictures.

Her dad explained Flo was today's mom, and the woman in the picture was yesterday's. Was Dad married to Flo?

Grandma Wellington was old when she died. Grandpa Wellington was old and would die too. And Gran and Grand Nelthorpe. Dad was getting older, also.

A stuffed dog of Chrissy's reminded Forrest of Aristotle, then Little Miss Make-Up doll, and it wasn't long before she played dress-up with Flo's help, setting up her tea parties, playing hide-and-seek. Chrissy was growing up and her questions more difficult to answer and yesterday's answers did not suffice. More questions about Allie, what she was like, how did they meet? Today dying in a fire questions then heaven ones. Stumbling answers caught in his throat, hinted there was more and the birth of intuition.

Chrissy leaned away from Flo and looked to her father. "Why can't Flo be my mommy now? Why can't you marry her so she could be my real mommy?"

Flo pulled her back and squeezed her tightly. "I love you like a mommy."

As Forrest searched for a response, he recalled Chrissy's first day of school, standing at the front door, dressed in her favorite pink dress, her patent leather purse draped over her arm, she saw tears forming in her dad's eyes. Taking him by the hand, she pulled him down and kissed him on the cheek. "Don't worry, Daddy. I am coming back. I love you."

***

Forrest insisted Luka stay on the payroll, and he came to the house nearly every day but didn't drive him anywhere, not for pleasure, not for business.

Forrest liked Charles and felt a bit sorry for him. He knew he was just doing his job. Charles prepared for his meetings with Forrest as he would for a regular meeting in his office. He had high hopes every visit Forrest would announce he was returning. But he found Forrest distracted and indifferent.

On one occasion, Kim asked Flo if she could visit him. Forrest angrily refused and hid away in the library for two days. Flo never asked again.

Sometimes in the spring, when stubborn remnants of last winter's snow were retreating into the shadows, he donned a winter jacket and stocking cap and pulled a blanket up under his chin and spent his afternoons on the patio in front of a fire reading books from the library. Flo asked, "Are you going to read every book in the library?"

"How long would it take?" he asked. He could see Flo didn't understand his question. "To read all the books in our library?"

"Never, if you are like me. I savor my books. A good book takes time. Besides, I don't always finish a book—sometimes it's the story, other times the writing. But I would read a well-written book even if I didn't like the story. Besides, in case you haven't noticed, I added some new books. So, there is no end to books."

Forrest offered her a rare smile. "You can add all the books you want. Those are your books. It's wonderful how you've taken care of the library. If you want, we could add more shelves to the left of the French patio doors. Call a carpenter. Add shelves over the top of the door, cover the whole wall. Make it the non-fiction wall."

The other guests in the Nelthorpe house—often Forrest called them intruders, were the detective and the fire inspector.

Forrest insisted Luka be in meetings with the investigators. Flo always took Chrissy to the kitchen when they arrived and baked cookies, which added to her suspicions. Her dad would only say he was helping them with an investigation.

Glib officious reports, empty attempts to placate Forrest—to convince him everything that could be done was being done dashed his hopes. After a while, he began to react hostilely to their visits, on occasion, even refusing to greet Detective Lowell when he came to the house. The last time they met, Forrest told him to leave. "You're not doing anything, and you're wasting your time coming here."

Detective Lowell, to his credit, kept coming back. He said he was sorry and doing everything he could. "Not every crime is solvable."

After the meeting with Detective Lowell today, on the warmest day of the year so far, Forrest asked Luka to join him on the patio for a beer. From the patio refrigerator/freezer, he pulled two frozen mugs and two bottles of Rolling Rock. Luka never drank hard alcohol but always accepted a beer. The Golden Wisteria trees were fully leafed. A month ago, they were bent and gnarled lifeless sticks. Across the pool, Boxwoods carved a trail to the guest cottage, Flo's home, and red Champlain Roses, and blue Hydrangeas were in full bloom.

"They're not going to solve this, are they?"

Luka shrugged his shoulders as he searched for an answer. "They might not. They have no idea where to look."

"I'll never accept that."

"Me neither."

"What the hell happened?" Forrest pleaded. "Everything in my life is different. Everything reminds me of Allie, of death, of her life. Years ago, I asked Flo to go through the house and get rid of everything hers. How could she know every plate, every glass, curtains, bedspreads, every piece of furniture held her DNA? She is the air in every room. I should burn the place down. I'm thinking of moving, but Flo likes it here, and there's Chrissy."

Without even a raised eyebrow, Luka responded, "You don't want to do that."

"The grandfather clock in the living room stopped. Why did it stop working? I guess it died too. Every morning when I wake up, I think it's me, but I look in the mirror—it's not me. I run my hand over my face, feel my scars, and say, that's me. Then I look into my dead eyes and say, that's not me. I don't know how to find me. Or escape me. The more I think about how to escape, the more I shrink into the darkness, but like snapping my fingers, when I am around Chrissy, I come alive."

Finishing his beer, Forrest rose and retrieved two more. "She's going to grow up thinking I'm a drunk. You know if it weren't for her, I wouldn't be here."

"I know. But Chrissy's young. You have many more years to be her father."

Forrest sat his glass down and leaned his head back, skyward. He closed his eyes and shook his head and thought about Allie and his life. Her love was radioactive. It could heal, and it could destroy. Love is two-sided. Love is why some people die and why some live and heal. Not having love can empty one's soul, and having it make a person whole. Without opening his eyes, he declared, "I want to be a good father. Allie wants that."

Forrest admired Luka for his silent strength—his loyal friendship. Behind those brooding eyes, he saw wisdom far beyond any person he ever met. His loyalty to Forrest unshakeable—he asked nothing, expected nothing. How does a man do that? Forrest always knew this was more than a job to him. I *could fire him right now, and he would pour me a drink. But if I asked, he would tell me to cut back on my drinking.*"

Out of the silence, Forrest opened his eyes and looked hard at Luka. "This is so hard."

Luka leaned forward in his chair. "I know it is."

"It's hard to live. Everything is hard. I fumble at tying my shoes, and it makes me mad. I threw my shoe and broke the mirror the other day."

"Flo told me."

Raising his foot in the air, he smiled, "That's why I'm in socks."

"I wondered." Luka shrugged.

"All I can think about is being with Allie."

"You will be. Someday."

"Yeah. Someday." Someday seemed so far off. Forrest took a deep breath. "They're waiting for me to return to work. I don't want to. I already told them no, and yet they wait. I'd rather be homeless than go back to that place. You know, sometimes I think being homeless wouldn't be so bad. I could wander around the country moving from park bench to park bench."

Forrest had seen the faces of the homeless—content to be alone, not caring what the averted glances were saying. Forrest could relate. He knew if he left the house, he would feel the stares at his scarred face and the averted glances, the second looks, and the ones he didn't see but felt. "Watch the world go by. I could do that. I don't need a thing. Everything is already lost. But when I imagine sitting on a park bench watching the world go by, there is always Chrissy."

**28**

Years had passed since the fire—too long time for Niche to be without its founding leader. So many times, the board was on the verge of voting to force the issue, but Arthur deflected any action, bought time. Forrest had amassed a team of highly talented, committed executives and Charles, the perfect interim CEO, and up to now, growth was coming from a strong economy, and their client's success kept them busy.

The past year, though, more companies entered Niche's space, as the digital economy picked up steam and offered new ways of worming their way into consumer minds. Companies scrambled to improve their positions.

So far Niche was still ahead of the curve, but Arthur knew they couldn't go on like this forever. Decisions had to be made, and the non-decisions were starting to affect the company—profits and growth were slowing, even client retention slipped for two straight quarters. Internal squabbles complicated things.

The day approached when the board would be forced to address the question of leadership. How could the board wait any longer for Forrest? Could he still lead?

Desperate, Arthur reached out to Flo to arrange a meeting to, at least in his mind, determine whether Forrest was making any progress.

When Arthur called to arrange the meeting, he told Flo, "The board is putting a lot of pressure on me. I think it's time we hire a new CEO. We can't afford to veer out of our lane much further, and risk having to steer this great ocean liner, Niche, back on course. Is there any hope Forrest will come back? Does he ever talk about going back to work?"

"He always says he'll never go back. I know he told you that. But . . . ."

"I always thought he'd come back," Arthur interrupted. "I presented that to the board. Now, I'm not so sure."

Flo continued, "Sometimes, I think he has softened. He is becoming more like the old Forrest, but he hasn't said anything different. He used to talk about running away. I never knew if he was serious. But not anymore. He's so committed to Chrissy."

When Arthur arrived at the Nelthorpe home, it was springtime. Optimism was in the air for even the most hardened Minnesotans. Anxious to see his friend and longtime business associate but nervous about breaking the news to him, he expected he would probably leave with nothing but a handshake, if that.

After going over the business analysis Charles had prepared, he nervously paused and looked up to Forrest before continuing. With a lump in his throat, Arthur declared, "We've reached our limit. We can't afford to go any further." Waiting for a reaction from Forrest and getting none, not even a raised eyebrow, he continued. "Forrest, it's not just the numbers I presented. The natives are restless. We've gone as far as we can without a leader.

"You know how it is. We have a great team, and given the circumstances, we have done better and gone longer than I thought possible. But when the company's head is MIA, predictably human nature kicks up, and there's blood in the water. It feels like we are on the verge of an insurrection. Add to that, it's only natural to be nervous about an outsider coming and taking over, and everyone is concerned about certain people getting the job."

"Kim," Forrest blurted.

Arthur's eyebrows shot up when he heard her name. "You've heard?"

"I don't need to hear. I am not surprised." Leaning forward, Forrest wagged his finger. "She is not qualified. She is the last person you want to lead the company. The only inside guy in the organization is Woody. He's your man."

"Forrest, we agree there. But I have to tell you Kim has made it clear she wants the job, and she seems to be doing anything she can to get it."

Forrest closed his eyes and gritted his teeth. "I know."

"She's been talking to board members privately. So even the board could be divided."

Forrest knew well her capabilities but hadn't thought about her for a long time—another good reason not to go back. He shouldn't have allowed the position to go unfilled for so long. Of course, the vacuum allowed for mischief.

Kim was out of control, and without Forrest there to run things, the company could lose its way. Arthur went on to tell him how Kim was tearing people down in her efforts to prop herself up. She was acting like she was the boss, and it was offending people, especially the ladies in the office. Ever the consummate professional, Linda Gardner had had it with her and was beginning to wear down. "I think Linda's going to leave us. Behind her back, Kim is calling her fat Linda."

Arthur still expected Forrest to come out of his seat and say no to coming back. He didn't. After a long silence, he said he would consider it. Arthur cleared his throat and asked him to repeat what he said. "So, you'll consider coming back?"

Forrest even walked Arthur to the car and shook hands with him. He hadn't walked him to the car before. He said he would let him know tomorrow. As he walked back to the house, Forrest reflected on their conversation. Kim. What a disaster. It wasn't fair to a lot of people. She had to be dealt with.

Losing Linda would be a dagger to his heart—to the company's heart. He always had a special relationship with her. She had been so loyal to the company. To him. *Kim is calling her fat Linda.*

Linda was heavy for sure. She never married. Forrest always wondered if Linda's full-body profile kept men away, or maybe she was full-bodied to keep it that way. Anyway, Forrest thought a lot of men were missing out. *I can't let Kim destroy her. The Company.* But what could he do about her? Could he fire her? It would be messy. Messy for everyone.

29

Forrest and Luka, two men of different backgrounds, might as well have been from a different continent, the industry leader with power and money, and the loyal family man making ends meet. They formed an intractable bond in the silent dark days following the tragedy in hushed tones, mumbles, and long silences. They found no answers. A roaring fire flashed images of Allie's pleading eyes, her charred hand reaching out, and Aristotle faithfully beside her. Sometimes Forrest dozed off in his chair and awoke with Luka still sitting across from him.

In the spring, they moved outdoors and sat across from one another beside the river rock fireplace, the pool fountain behind them like a babbling brook. Looking out was like viewing a landscape painting—the leafy virgin green pressed against a deep blue sky. Forrest always thought it was surprising more people didn't wear sky blue and forest green; they go so well together. "Luka, I am thinking of going back to work."

Luka smiled but didn't say anything.

"No, I've decided I'm going back to work," he announced. "I need to fix some things. I think I am the only one who can. Take me to Allie."

Few words were spoken on the solemn drive to the cemetery. A celebration of trees greeted Forrest. After months of hibernating in minus zero temperatures, trees lining the parkways sprouted new blossoms, and deciduous trees leafed in deep virgin green.

When they turned into Lakewood Cemetery, Forrest was stunned by the postcard views, like taking a right turn into heaven. "Mom said it was a heavenly place, but I didn't know it was so beautiful," Forrest said. "Now, I know what she meant." Stepping out of the car, Forrest looked around to figure out the direction to Allie's grave. Luka pointed west.

A gentle breeze rustled the leaves into a welcoming sigh. Forrest inhaled the fragrance of freshly mown grass as he walked in and around proud, lonely, well-maintained headstones. Flowers grown in six-football-field-sized greenhouses on the 250-acre cemetery grounds were scattered around the cemegarden. Reborn red maple tree, a mere two months ago stood frozen like naked scarecrows, joined hands with white oaks, white ash, and hackberry trees to form a protective canopy that filtered the sunlight. Reverential shafts of misty light guided him to her grave.

Forrest slowed as he saw her headstone and his name engraved next to hers, his year of passing blank. Kneeling in the soft grass and joining his hands as if in prayer, he sighed and shook his head. "Sorry, it took me so long to come here. I know you're not here, but maybe you'll find me." Looking to the heavens. "Can you see me? Can you hear me? I'll be with you someday. I believe that as surely as the next breath I take."

Tears formed in his eyes and began to trickle down his cheek. He dabbed at them with his hand. "This could be my last breath if it meant I could be with you. But I am still breathing, and I go on for now. I am going to be a great father to Chrissy. You'll be proud. I wish I had been a better husband, though. You know that now. Now I need to go back to work. I need to straighten things out—then I am going to be with you. Nothing can stop me. By God, I am going to straighten things out down here."

Luka was leaning against the car when Forrest returned. They exchanged glances, then looked away with red eyes.

***

With a lot of time on his hands, thinking and plotting served his days and haunted his nights. After he decided to go back to work, he began to worry about when and how. He knew a man broken into bits could be strongest even in the broken spots. But how to start?

He immediately began to have daily meetings with Charles, who was delighted with his decision and anxious for his return. He also held off-premise meetings with a few division heads, board members, and a few long-standing local customers.

Finally, he consulted Isabella, his assistant. Given the mixed emotions of going back to work, he didn't want to make anything special out of it and knew she would help. She was always able to interpret goings-on in the company for him. He asked her whenever he wanted to take the temperature of company morale or garner reactions to events. With a confident nod, and with her trusting insider smile, she assured him.

She reminded him Memorial Day weekend was coming up, and people had a holiday on their minds. He could come back Thursday before the holiday weekend. She would get the word out he wanted to ease into a routine, and she'd control the traffic to his office—by appointment only. Everybody would understand. She promised there would be no cakes and banners.

He hadn't seen many of his colleagues since his last day at the office. On that fateful day, he recalled saying goodbye to Isabella and seeing Linda in the hallway and wishing her a nice weekend. He told her he was going to the cabin to be with Allie. Beaming with joy, he added, and Chrissy. He cringed, recalling how he ran into Kim as he was getting on the elevator.

Sitting at his desk in the early morning, daylight was breaking and slanting into a corner of his office. When Isabella entered, she noticed Forrest hadn't turned the lights on in his office. She knew he wanted it that way. She sat across from him.

"It's an odd feeling, sitting here," Forrest lamented, looking out into the office past her. After a long pause, Forrest looked back to his assistant, "Glad you're still here and willing to come back to work for me. Sounds like you left a pretty good job to be here. Thanks."

Forrest rubbed the side of his scarred face and withdrew his hand. "I need to stop doing that. It's a bad habit. Hard to get used to. Nobody ever talks about stuff like this. It's off-limits, like never commenting on a person's obvious handicap. That's BS. I don't want that. I am not handicapped. I know it's a grotesque sight, but I'm not handicapped."

Isabella hesitated. "People will get used to it. My husband wore a beard for years and one day I looked across the breakfast table and said, 'Frank, you've shaved your beard.' He gave me a funny look and said, 'I shaved it last week.' I believe people see people for who they are, not how they look."

"Yeah, you might be right."

Forrest opened his briefcase and began to lay papers and files on his desk in neat stacks, then stopped and looked up. Pointing to a spot behind Isabella, he said. "Allie was standing right there. There are a lot of memories here. Allie had just come back from the doctor." Shaking his head, "That was the day she was run off the road, and this whole nightmare started."

When the first meeting of the full executive staff came, Forrest dealt with the issue head-on. He hadn't been out in public much but enough to be uncomfortable with adults' second glances and staring children. He knew colleagues would find it awkward, not wanting to look and not wanting to pity. The scars would always be there, though, and served as a reminder of what happened and toughened his resolve.

Two weeks back on the job, he called a meeting with the entire executive staff and their support staff. He thanked them for all their good wishes and hard work, then laid out some of the challenges and outlined his plans for the days ahead. He finished the meeting by telling a story.

"The first time I met with Charles after . . . , " Forrest stopped and swallowed hard. *No, I am not going there.* "He was pretty blunt, as only he can be." Looking over to Charles, "First, thank you, Charles, for filling in for me. So right off the bat, he said, 'You're pretty scarred up.' The first time we met, he put it out there, as only he can. I responded: Guess you'll have to get used to it. So, I tell you now, I'm pretty scarred up, so take a good look and get used to it."

He avoided personal contact with Kim for two weeks. When they met, Forrest never said a thing about all the reports of her behavior. He wanted to address her aspirations to get his job, and do anything to get it—tell her no way, discourage her. He didn't.

When they met in his office, she took a seat across from him. She was wearing a business suit and white blouse buttoned to the neck, and the largest diamond stud earrings he had ever seen. She always drove expensive cars, wore the most expensive clothes, and lived in one of the most expensive downtown condos. He knew how much she made. She lived well beyond her means.

After an awkward attempt at small talk, including head-nodding agreement about the weather, she shifted to business. "I think you'll be pleased with what I've done for the company in your absence. I'm sure you've heard how I stepped in."

Forrest remained stoned faced. He knew what a big pain in the ass she was and how she irritated everyone, but he didn't want to pick a fight with her. "Thank you, Kim."

She went on to say, "I've been testing out something for some of our faithful customers who love our total branding top to bottom strategies. I added someone to our communications area, specifically in product support, to test a new service. Or, maybe punch it up.

"We did a project for WIP Irrigation Systems, where we helped them with their irrigation controls instruction manuals. It seems relatively small, but we determined they were spending unnecessary time and money answering customer complaints on how to program their units. What wasn't clear to them was how much it cost to answer customer inquiries.

"Less obvious to them was how the customers were cursing them before they called. That stuff can kill a brand. We found flaws in their manuals, how they used terms their customers had no way of understanding and different words for the same thing—obviously written by some engineer. We found the customer service guides were incongruent with WIP customer's product manual, so there were many callbacks. I think clients will like this addition to our offering." Kim paused to see if she was making the desired impression.

Forrest resisted telling her how much he liked her initiative. He couldn't. The last thing he wanted to do was encourage her. "That should be a good addition," was all he could say.

Kim didn't vary from her business mission until the end when she couldn't resist trying to learn more about his state of mind.

"So, what do you think happened?" she ventured to ask.

Forrest had a puzzled look on his face. "I'm not sure I know what you are talking about?"

"The fire. I'm talking about the fire."

Forrest looked away, irritated she would ask. *If she only knew how much I hate talking about it, even with the detectives.* Forrest clenched his jaw. The words on the tip of his tongue were to tell her it was none of her business. *There was a fire. My wife died. Look at my face, that's what happened.*

Kim didn't wait for an answer, "You had us worried. It breaks my heart what happened to . . . ," Kim fumbled for a name. "Alexandria."

Forrest looked away then back to her, still holding back a response.

Kim continued, "I'm glad your baby is okay." Leaning forward in her most sugary voice,

"We've all shed so many tears, said so many prayers. I started going to church to pray."

Forrest's loathing for her had only grown over time. Often, when alone in the library when he thought about Allie, he thought about Kim. Now she was praying for him, for Allie, for Chrissy. It felt phony. He wished she had never been hired. How different his life would have been. Also, he plotted how to deal with her. He wanted her gone. Gone from the company. Gone from his life. How?

**30**

It didn't take as long as he thought to get back in the swing of things. A few things had changed. Most notably, because of Chrissy, late nights at the office were uncommon. He was quick to take someone to dinner, wine and dine them in the past, and now it didn't seem necessary. He avoided business lunches too. He had a job to do.

Detective Lowell had become a thorn in his side. Intellectually, he thought the detective was doing everything in his power to solve the crime, but he thought him incompetent. Meetings were becoming infrequent until, at last, Forrest refused to meet. Luka continued to meet with the detective regularly, and if anything was new to report, he passed it on.

The maple leaves had turned to gold and red, dried, and fell to the ground—a few desperate ones were clinging to their branches. The previous night's snowfall covered the ground, welcomed by every schoolchild, dreaded by adults.

The city Christmas decorations illuminated the early darkness. Luka encouraged Forrest to meet with Detective Lowell and Captain Surratt, so he scheduled them as his last appointment to accommodate Luka for the drive home and to put off the meeting as long as he could.

Forrest figured he would likely hear the same things, the same promises, the same nothing to report. Detective Lowell wore a wrinkled, stained Christmas tie he no doubt wore every day throughout the season and the same dark suit, bursting at the waist, his coat unbuttonable. Twice the size of the man he first met, Forrest wouldn't recognize him on the street. Forrest thought about making a joke but quickly decided against accusing him of too many doughnuts. Telling a stale joke wouldn't help the relationship and besides, Forrest never made comments like that, even to people he disliked.

Captain Surratt wore loose-fitting jeans and a Minnesota sweatshirt.

Forrest quickly waved off any small talk. Necessity had a way of pushing through to the business side of his brain, a long distance from where he had been dwelling.

Detective Lowell hesitated and looked around before saying anything. Forrest and Luka exchanged glances, wondering what he was going to say.

"We like the drunk for setting the fire," Detective Lowell announced. "His name is Wade Booker. We're close to filing charges. I know it's been a long time. Believe it or not, we have overturned every stone, run all the tests, conducted thousands of interviews. We are close. We can smell guilt on this guy, but it's so damn circumstantial. Tire tracks in the turnout were his, but there were other tire tracks next to his, one that came from what we believe was an SUV like vehicle. There were other old tracks there as well."

Forrest perked up. "An SUV? Like the one that ran her off the road."

"I was referring to the white SUV Mr. Booker insists he saw in the area. That is unreliable, though. It might be a tip but an unreliable one. Not evidence."

Irritated, Forrest resisted, "Or the white SUV that ran Allie off the road."

"The only eye witness to the white vehicle on the night of the fire was the drunk, and as for the road . . . ." The detective hesitated and chose his words carefully. "As for the accident, it was raining, and the eye witness is . . . well, he's a drunk.

"So, the drunk says he saw a white SUV in the area. Swears by it, but he was so drunk the patrolman couldn't get a walk out of him. He makes a better perp then a witness. Beer cans we found on his truck matched an old beer can we found in the turnout. He said he pulls off there sometimes. His prints were on the cans. So, he was there at some point. But that's not enough. He had a book of matches in his pocket, but he's a smoker. I wish he weren't, but he is. Got the yellow fingers to prove it. We still like this guy."

"As I said before, most people use matches to start fires and cigarettes," Captain Suratt added mockingly.

"When he was young, he set his high school on fire," Detective Lowell continued. "With gasoline. The fire didn't amount to anything, though."

In a tired, impatient voice, Captain Surratt said, "Gasoline is the most common accelerant used to start fires. He set the fire on the brick school wall. I doubt if he thought he was going to burn anything down."

Detective Lowell looked disappointed as he continued, "The suspect smelled like gasoline. He says he put gas in his truck earlier. He did pump enough gas to fill his truck at a station a few miles from there, and it was full of gas when we stopped him. He had two empty gas cans in the back of his truck. One was new. Why did he have two? We did detect gas in the back of his truck, but that doesn't say much. He said one of the cans leaked. Still, it's all a bit fishy. I never spilled gas on myself while I was pumping gas. But then he was drunk—must happen to drunks. Surprised they don't blow themselves up."

"A little gas in the back of the truck isn't going to put him away," Suratt argued.

Detective Lowell looked to Suratt with a sour expression and then back to Forrest. "Yep, we need more than that. We still like this guy. All our investigations have taken us down blind alleys, and we keep coming back to him. We'll get him."

"Why do you think he did it?" Forrest asked.

Sliding a picture across the desk, he asked, "So, you've never seen this guy? He does a lot of handyman work in the area. Did he ever do any work for your wife?"

Forrest took a minute, then slid the picture back. "Never seen him before. I'll look through payment records."

"We're working on a motive." Detective Lowell said under his breath.

Inspector Suratt said, "We don't make him out to be a serial arsonist unless he operates a long way from here."

Detective Lowell interrupted. "He's been in the area for years and near as we can tell hasn't left and not the kind of guy who takes vacations."

Captain Suratt continued. "It's been years since we had a serial arsonist around here. Even longer for one that killed anyone. If he is our man, then we need a motive."

On the way home, Forrest sat in the front seat with Luka, and they discussed the visit with Detective Lowell and Inspector Suratt. The snow piled up on the roadways, and the plows were out in full force. "They've got nothing," Forrest spoke first. "They're trying to pin it on some drunk."

Luka watched the cars pass by and kick up snow, blasting the front window. "Yeah. But who knows?"

Wondering out loud, Forrest said, "Yeah, but who knows? Nowadays, you have to have a pretty good case. Everyone is such a damn good liar. For sure, civilization has advanced in the lying department. The thing is, they don't feel there's any connection between the fire and the accident. There has to be a connection. Damn, I hate calling it an accident. That's how they refer to it now—an accident. That was no damn accident."

Luka looked over to Forrest, staring out the passenger window. "It's hard to believe the two things are connected by bad luck and circumstances. That's pretty bad luck."

Twenty miles passed and fifty minutes as they followed a slow-moving snowplow. The wipers strained to push aside the wet snow. "You may want to spend the night if this keeps up, or at least until it passes. The forecast is not encouraging."

For the next painfully slow ten miles, they sat in silence until Forrest interrupted the groaning window wipers. "Luka." Forrest looked over to see his face reflected in the dashboard lights. Did you kill that guy? Salvatore, was that his name?"

"I went to prison for it."

"Luka . . . sorry, I had no right to ask. I never cared to know till now. I've never thought about killing anyone."

The snowplow exited and left them plowing through the snow on their own. "Yes, and I did my time. I was a young man."

"I guess there are a lot of reasons why people kill another human."

"There could be no reason why someone would harm Allie," Luka said. "A person has to be deranged to do that. I mean, there are times when it's okay . . . I killed the guy for a reason . . . I was young, but this was not like that."

"Sometimes, it's ok?"

"I would do it again. There was a lot at stake. The honor of my family. Their safety."

"I can't stop wondering why this happened. Who would hurt Allie? But then I don't even know for sure what happened. It's worse not knowing. Everything is so cloudy. It is like an invisible person wanted her dead . . . or wanted to get at me. For the life of me, I don't understand."

Their conversation paused, and they were left with the sound of tires gripping the snow and throwing it up against the car. The blasting defroster curled hot air off the window into their faces. "The man I killed was a bully. He hurt a lot of people, and he beat my brother within an inch of his life. He would have killed him. I stood up to him. It was easy. I didn't care if I died; I would do it again. In the short time we are alive, what does a man have but his honor? Things like that happen. Life must have its own set of rules."

"Yeah, I'd kill the man who killed Allie."

"I would too. What he did to your wife wasn't human."

# 31

There were no dipping toes in the business for Forrest. That wasn't in his nature. As much as anything, immersing himself in business took his mind off his horrors and was a shift away from the dark syrupy days in the library. But he didn't want to put aside the memory. He'd rather the tragedy be a blanket for holding his memories, never to forget what happened. Whenever he felt distracted from what happened and what needed to happen, it angered him.

The priorities he controlled were clear. Chrissy was first, then putting the company on the right path. The things he couldn't control were not as clear. No amount of money or time, not a hockey fight or a brilliant maneuver, no amount of thinking would bring Allie back. Finding her killer consumed him and, at the same time fueled his commitment to bringing the company back, finding his replacement, and moving on. Be done with Minneapolis, anything familiar, and be with Allie. I know I'll be with her again, became his mantra.

Being a widowed father did not make him a new illegible bachelor. Loneliness in search of companionship was not for Forrest. There-could never be another woman for him. Even Kim had given up on him and turned her attention to her company goals. She was still every bit as attractive, though, and she knew it, and occasionally he thought she was trying to send him signals.

Private, one-on-one meetings between Kim and Forrest rarely occurred. Forrest always included others in their discussions. When on those rare occasions, they were alone on the elevator, parking garage, or hallways, Kim was cautious and relied on her powers of intuition to guide her. "Hope everything is going okay. I'm sure you are a great father to Christina. I'm still praying for you guys. If you ever want to talk."

Forrest stood stone-faced. He had nothing to say. Being alone with her left him feeling anxious, afraid she'd say something that would throw him off, disrupt his resolve not to let her get under his skin. When she paused, he turned to walk away.

"Forrest," she called out to him.

When he turned, tears were welling in her eyes. She stood firm. "Forrest. When I heard the news about the fire, I went to church and got down on my knees to pray for her, for you guys. I hadn't done that in . . . well, forever. It felt good."

Forrest hesitated, unsure of what to say. Befuddled, taking a step back, he raised his hand, "Thank you, Kim."

Only once, in recent times, did Kim venture into sensitive areas. They were standing in the parking garage, no one around. "Haven't heard you're seeing anyone?" Bravely she added, "Maybe you still have a spot for me?"

Forrest shrugged and looked away.

It shocked Forrest that she asked about his plans. "I heard you might be retiring. A bit early, huh?"

Maybe it was something she heard him say, or thought he said, or private thoughts escaping into the collective consciousness? No, he hadn't mentioned it to anyone. He never wanted to come back and regretted the decision every day since. Disappointment washed over him as he searched for an answer.

"Well deserved, I'd say," she added casually.

Scowling, he locked his gaze on hers. "Where would you get that idea?"

"Just a rumor."

A rumor. An easy thing to say. He decided not to pursue it.

"You know how loyal I've been to the company. I passed on plenty of offers. You know how well I've performed here."

Forrest took a deep breath, not having the stomach to argue. "You've done a good job. Yeah. Okay? But what are you saying?"

Kim flinched and returned his scowl. "Good job? I hope you don't think I've just done a good job. We've talked about it before. You know how strongly I have wanted the job when you leave. I expect it, and you remember I took out an insurance policy."

"What job? There is no job. Not my job if that is what you think. And, as for your so-called insurance policy, that's old news. That policy expired. You don't think . . . you don't think I care anymore, do you? You do what you want. You can't hurt me any more than I've already have been." The scars on his face bulged and turned red in testimony. Clinching his fist and tightening his jaw. "You do what you have to."

***

Kim smiled. She didn't believe him. No matter what, he was still human. He'd never stand for the humiliation of being labeled as the guy who sexually abused one of his staff, she reflected. Shame was too high on the list of things humans avoided, shared by most people until there was nothing else, just hopelessness.,

He'd come around. Besides, Kim did have insurance. In the alternative, the company would pay her dearly, and she'd become a media darling. Maybe it was better than being CEO. The media would get lost in sensationalism. They loved stories like this. Never mind the truth if it's a juicy story. It used to be everyone ended up on the losing end of stories like this, not today. She'd be a rich and famous, sympathetic, smart, and beautiful. She loved the moniker and wore it proudly. Maybe she'd start a charity for sexually abused women. She could be a politician.

She knew how dedicated he was to Christina, what a great father, the pride he showed, the love he received from people around him. That, too, was part of the equation. Chrissy was still young—those are difficult years even for the most well-adjusted girl.

Kim had him in the palm of her hand. She got a warm feeling watching him be brave. But she also knew she had to be careful how she played it. The pictures were powerful, but pictures alone weren't going to land her the CEO job. She needed allies.

***

As much as anger was a steel rail that ran straight up his spine, he learned to control it in his hockey days. Maybe he didn't handle it well with Detective Lowell, and he regretted his outbursts. Intellectually, he knew the detective was probably doing his best, but emotionally, Forrest didn't care.

Forrest wondered if he was competent. How could he know? Over and over, he learned what every good leader understood—talented people get the job done. A football coach takes over a hapless losing team, and the next season they start winning. And, some people went through the motions and never succeeded at anything.

Forrest had no way of judging Detective Lowell except by his failures. For all he knew, the detective had a losing record but doubted anybody kept score. There was an element of politics in every business, and who likes who. The school teachers who are political and likeable go far. That is the way it often works and what could he do about it?

Another summer quickly lost, green turned brown, leaves rushed to their death in great piles to be swept up by city workers, then it would be white again. Luka still arranged meetings with Detective Lowell. Once again, a meeting was scheduled in his office at the end of the day to accommodate Luka.

Was time advancing to a solution or abandonment of the investigation? After all this time, had they stopped investigating. Is that what the meeting was about? Detective Lowell said investigations were not like hour-long crime shows. It takes time. Sometimes years. Sometimes after an arrest and attorneys and judges take over, time slows down even more. Trials can take years.

When Detective Lowell entered, Forrest waved for him to take a seat next to Luka. He didn't rise from behind his desk or offer his hand.

"I hope you have something. Luka said you insisted we meet."

Detective Lowell swallowed hard and shifted uncomfortably. "Thank you for the meeting. I know how you feel about these meetings, so I'll be brief." He slid a picture across the desk and continued, "I showed you this picture before, and you said you had never seen this man. As you know, we have a principally circumstantial case, and we've been looking for more evidence. You still don't remember this guy?"

"Remember? No, I don't."

"We continue to keep after Mr. Booker, and his memory keeps improving. Of course, you know how it goes; his attorney says he didn't do anything and wants to cooperate. I don't know, though he's always out of it. He seems to be permanently drunk. Brain's pickled. I've seen it before."

Forrest interrupted, "And this incompetent drunk is the best you have?"

"Anyway," Detective Lowell continued, "he worked for you. For quite a while actually, according to him. Are you sure you don't remember him? Says your wife fired him. She threatened him, and she ran him off. Could be the motive we've been looking for. It was the spring of '81."

Forrest went still and stared off into the room, searching his memory. "It seems like so long ago." Softly he asked, "Are you sure?"

Looking at his notes then to Forrest, he answered, "Yep. I'm sure."

Forrest slid the picture across the desk to Detective Lowell. "Never seen him. And my wife never fired him. She was in the hospital. Paralyzed, remember." Forrest raised his voice to express his irritation. "Remember, she was run off the road by someone—someone you never located. Remember? You still working on that crime too . . . or was that just an accident?" Gripping the desk like he was holding himself in his chair, he continued, "What the hell is going on anyway?" Looking over to Luka, "Jesus, what the hell?" Taking a deep breath and looking back to Lowell, "Must have been Flo, my assistant. She manages the cabin too. You need to talk to her."

A week later, Detective Lowell returned to report his conversation with Flo. He acknowledged what no doubt Forrest already knew by then. He said he was there to confirm what he understood from his conversation with Flo officially. "Wade did work for you for six months, and Flo did run him off the premises after she caught him rummaging through the cabin. Wade confirmed that. She fired him on the spot, and he got all excited. Wade said she threatened him. Said she was going to call the cops, and he better get out."

Wrapping up the conversation and getting ready to leave, Detective Lowell added, the district attorney likes the drunk. He is considering charging him. I'll keep you posted."

Charges were filed the first of August. Detective Lowell called, "Good news," he announced, "We've arrested the drunk. The DA thinks it all fits together. He was a former defense attorney and can look at it from all angles. He said he's going to sew it all together so tight the defense won't be able to find the seams."

Forrest remained silent. He had hoped such an announcement would bring relief, but it felt like kissing a sister. Forrest wondered why the information felt so hollow. What would satisfy him?

Three days later, Robert Westfall III, the prosecutor, requested a meeting in Forrest's office to go over the charges personally. Before sitting down at his desk, he leaned out and grasped Forrest's hand and covered it warmly with his other hand. "Tripp. Please call me, Tripp. Tripp, the son of a Robert who was the son of a grandfather, Robert."

Tripp was a man in his mid-forties, dressed expensively in a gray, chalk stripe three-piece suit and badly in need of a haircut. Luka checked him out beforehand and learned he was married and divorced twice, a hard drinker, bright and destined for a bigger job, maybe a governorship like rumored. Meeting in his office was meant as a show of respect. "It's an honor to meet you," he started. You are well respected in this community, and your philanthropy is legendary. I wish we had a stronger case for you."

Forrest smiled awkwardly. He was ambivalent about the whole thing. Nothing was turning out as he hoped. A weak circumstantial case gave him no relief. The never to be forgotten horror, the everyday aftermath, the hunt for a killer, and bringing Wade to justice left him with more than the reminders burned on his face.

Punishing Wade, the drunk, wouldn't bring Allie back. Would a trial convince him he was guilty? Would it bring the justice he craved? The peace? He realized he might never find peace in the process and would have to live with it, but always like a Minnesota blizzard slapping him in the face. But then, maybe Forrest's expectations were too high and weighed against letting go of his bitterness, his fear Allie could ever become only a memory.

Tripp opened up, "We're going to charge him with first-degree arson and third-degree murder." He watched Forrest closely for a reaction. "You want first-degree murder, don't you? Of course, you do. I would give my left nut to go for first-degree murder, and I'd be there to watch him hang, but we haven't had the death penalty here since the 1900s. I couldn't prove first-degree murder anyway. How could we ever prove he planned this out with the intent of killing her? Or you?"

Forrest exchanged glances with Luka. He knew Luka would be watching him for a reaction. Shaking his head, he looked back to Tripp. After all this time, the same guy as day one? "Isn't there a statute of limitations?"

"There is no statute of limitations in Minnesota for any crime that results in the death of a victim. Let me assure you I don't prosecute until I know I can win."

Pausing, Tripp could see Forrest wasn't happy with his response and seemed to have something else on his mind. He understood how it must be for Forrest and decided a discussion about feelings could gain nothing.

Tripp continued, "So here is the difference. In first degree murder, you have to prove the crime was premeditated. The way third-degree murder reads, intent isn't required. Causing the death of a person by perpetrating an act eminently dangerous to others and evincing a depraved mind without regard for human life is what is necessary. I can prove it. We hardly need a motive. The function of motive here is to give him a reason to be there at the crime scene. Otherwise, we don't need much."

There has to be more to this, Forrest thought.

"So, we also have first-degree arson." Tripp Westfall slid both hands through his hair and pushed them back behind his ears. "It's circumstantial, but we think we can make it. Arson in the first degree doesn't require us to prove he even knew there were people present, only a reasonable possibility someone was present. It is punishable up to twenty years and a fine of up to $20,000." Tripp waved his hand dismissively. "Big deal, huh? This guy doesn't have a pot to piss in, so a fine is irrelevant."

Forrest could barely hear what the district attorney was saying. Arson? Third-degree murder? Why did it feel so odd, so empty? He expected something else, but he didn't know what. This guy was a third-rate burglar, with no motive of revenge, no history of serial arson, nothing to gain—not money, not jewelry, furniture was the most expensive thing in the house. The boat? Why did this happen?

"What can he get for third-degree murder?" Forrest asked as calmly as asking Charles for a clarification of an item on the balance sheet.

"Twenty-five."

"So, he gets five more years for destroying a human life versus a building?" Forrest added sarcastically. "Oh, and a fine too? So, this all sounds circumstantial."

"Hell, sometimes circumstantial is all you get. Look, this guy is guilty. Guilty of something. He's a loser. We need to lock him up. Get this loser off the streets."

Agitated and at a loss for words, Forrest snapped back. "You're kidding me? You think I care about locking him up because he is a loser. Really? I am more interested in knowing we've got the right guy. Loser, huh?" Forrest wanted to ask about the white SUV, but frustrated, the question on the tip of his tongue died there. No doubt nobody connected that crime to this one. Whether he did the crime was a loose end and unimportant to Tripp. Winning a conviction and putting him away was all-important.

# 32

Forrest decided to attend the arraignment Monday morning. Luka suggested they walk to the courthouse since it was such a short walk and easier than driving and parking. On hot days the humidity could be unbearable, but today a string of record ninety-degree days broke into the seventies. In the land of sky-blue waters and frozen tundra, nobody celebrated summers better than Minnesotans. So, when spring arose out of its cold slumber, residents moved outside so the sun could find them.

Luka wore his black suit, white shirt, and black tie, and Forrest gray wool dress pants, black wingtip shoes, and a cream-colored silk shirt open at the collar.

The walk to the courthouse brought back memories of taking young Chrissy to tour the courthouse, a remarkable Minneapolis landmark. It was built between 1887 and 1906 and featured a clock said to be the largest in the world, when installed, six inches larger than the Clock of Westminster. There were fifteen bells in the spire that chimed out the Star-Spangled Banner, in key.

Today their arrival in the courtroom was delayed by a quick stop in the rotunda to show Luka the "Father of Waters" statue. The statue was a copy of the "Father Nile" created by a Greek sculptor in Egypt 2,000 years ago. They arrived in the courtroom as the defendant was seated.

Judge Abigail Hunter entered and gaveled the court into session. Forrest had seen pictures of her in the newspaper. She was a silver-haired, diminutive woman, guessed to be in her sixties. Her grandmotherly appearance belied her reputation as a strict, no-nonsense, sometimes gruff judge. When she brought the court to order, she did so with a crash of the gavel in a wood splitting explosion that startled the low murmur of the courtroom into silence.

The judge read the charges of first-degree arson and third-degree murder against Wendell Booker as he stood at attention, shifting from foot to foot as if he was wearing shoes two sizes too small. Forrest couldn't take his eyes off the defendant.

Forrest reflected on how justice might not satisfy anyone except the attorneys. He figured Mr. Booker would go to prison for a few years and get out for good behavior. Chrissy still wouldn't have a mom, and Allie would still have died horribly in a fire. And, he'd be a free man. Hell, he should get more punishment for killing Aristotle.

Forrest scanned the courtroom, sized up the judge, the prosecutor, the defendant, others who were in the courtroom as observers, and wondered why they were there. He didn't recall hearing the defendant's given name before, Wendell Booker. Detective Lowell referred to him as Wade or the drunk. His mother named him Wendell. Was that a family name or just a name she liked?

He was a 180-proof wiry cowboy-looking man, dressed in a suit two sizes too large, his sleeves dropped to mid palm. The only time Forrest saw him before was in a photo the detectives showed him. Then, he was shirtless, and his eyes were closed, obviously a DUI mug shot. He didn't look much like a criminal today. The evidence was circumstantial. It felt as if they were taking vengeance on a wounded animal.

His attorney was a young man who looked like he had just passed the bar exam. Judge Hunter read the charges and asked the defendant how he pleaded. Wendell Booker answered in a weak quivering voice. "Not guilty." He sounded more like a scared beaten-down-by-life burglar than a cold-blooded killer. If the number of pages on his rap sheet counted, the trial would be quick. He was a nobody who had drifted between welfare, bit jobs, and Stormy's, his regular tavern.

After pleading not guilty, his attorney made a feeble attempt to argue for bail. The defendant could not post whatever bail the judge required, so they quickly settled, and he was remanded to the jailhouse.

As Forrest and Luka were leaving, they ran into Detective Lowell. Forrest wasn't planning to stop and talk, but as he passed the detective said, "Good to get guys like that off the street, huh?"

Forrest turned and growled, "I'd rather know he's guilty." Lightly running his fingers over the scarred side of his face, he froze. Lately, it had become a habit to lightly trace the scars on his face when emotions seized him. "You've got the wrong man, and you know it."

"We'll let the jury decide. That's the way it works, right?" The district attorney thinks he's our man, that he can make a case."

"I could give a rat's ass if some attorney is looking to put a notch in his gold-plated ego. I want to know we have the right man."

Detective Lowell pushed back. "Courts decide guilt or innocence, not victims, not detectives. That is the way it works. Not all crimes come wrapped in pretty paper and bows. Sometimes people get convicted on light evidence, and they did the crime."

"Yeah, and sometimes you get the wrong man."

Nodding smugly, Lowell repeated, "Like I said, that's how it works . . . police work . . . I don't prosecute 'em."

Luka tugged gently on his arm, "Forrest, let's go."

Forrest turned and walked away. Any more conversation with him would not end well.

The walk back was quiet. Halfway back to the office, Forrest turned to Luka. "What do you think? He seems guilty to you?"

"Everybody looks innocent facing the judge."

"I suppose. But everything is circumstantial."

Two blocks passed before Luka spoke again. "Yeah. I wish there were more to it. Hard to explain going from petty burglar to murderer for no reason."

Summer rushed into fall, and the early winter months saw delay after delay in the trial. Then, without much explanation, the judge dismissed the defense attorney, and the trial sidetracked. An accomplished legal observer would have noticed mistakes in the defense were piling up. Tripp didn't resist the judge's concerns, knowing all the mistakes could serve as fodder for appeal.

Time was allowed for a new attorney to be appointed and become familiar with the case. This time a woman attorney who had a successful record of defending higher-profile cases was appointed. The trial ended on June 4th.

Forrest and Luka hadn't reappeared in the courtroom until the day they announced the verdict. Forrest said he couldn't stomach watching the trial. They arrived early and sat in the back and watched as people began to file in, everyday observers, news people, the district attorney, and three members of his team, the defense lawyer, and the jury.

The new defense attorney was a middle-aged woman, salt and pepper hair color, about halfway to complete gray. Sixty percent of the jury were men. Some of the women appeared to be housewives, a couple of men appeared to be professionals. A number of them appeared to be of retirement age. Everyday people tasked to adjudicate the defendant's life, and his, and Allie's, and Chrissy's, sneaked nervous peeks at Forrest, quickly turning away to avoid eye contact.

Judge Hunter entered and immediately went to work. It all happened so fast. She asked the jury for their verdict. Guilty!

Wendell Booker broke down and cried in his attorney's arms and slumped back into his seat. Over his attorney's shoulder, Wendall stared at Forrest as if he was pleading his innocence. The judge announced she would pass sentence the next day, and the court adjourned.

Swede's Tavern was three blocks down a side street in an older industrial part of town, one of the few remaining undeveloped areas. It was raining hard, and they had to park on the street a half a block away. They exited the car, pulled their raincoat collars up around their necks. Forrest flashed open an umbrella, and Luka joined him as they splashed through puddles in route to the entrance.

They entered and removed their coats. Forrest shook his umbrella and propped it by the front door. Three old men sat at the bar. There was an old Wurlitzer in the corner beside a pool table. In a back booth, an elderly couple held hands across the table, sad faced, as if they were saying goodbye or clinging to love. At the far end of the bar, a long-faced man sat alone with his head hung low.

The bartender moved out from behind the bar and met them at one of the side booths. He took their order, two draft beers. The two old men at the bar rose and walked to the pool table. After breaking the pool balls, one of them shuffled to the jukebox, put coins in it, and pushed some buttons. The sound of Johnny Cash singing "Folsom Prison Blues" filled the air.

Forrest spoke first, "That wasn't very satisfying. It made me sick watching Wade break down, the fist-pumping between Tripp and his team. Did you happen to notice the sour look on the judge's face? She wasn't buying it. Wonder if she'll go light on him in sentencing?"

"The worse kind of justice, huh—injustice," Luka said. "But then, what does guilt look like? Every criminal is innocent and hates it when the judge says otherwise."

"I hope there's more to this. I'm never going to believe this guy did anything but ruin his own life. What the hell does a guy do? Just look the other way? One thing I'm not is a

look-the-other-way-guy, but what can I do?"

Another song, "Kiss an Angel Good Morning" by Charlie Pride, began to play on the jukebox.

Several beers later for Forrest, and the same beer for Luka, the conversation circled to hiring a private investigator. Forrest had raised the idea before but dismissed it.

Luka gripped his beer and began to take a drink, hesitated and set it back in the table. "You've wanted to do that for a long time. I guess there is nothing left to do."

"I've looked at investigators before. Some of them are no better than Lowell. I should have."

"I have a guy," Luka's said. "A friend of a friend got in a jam with his company for stealing money. It was a bit tricky since his boss, the crooked one, was the one accusing him. This guy is a bit of legend,"

Two weeks later, they met with the legendary private investigator, Barnaby Willis, in Forrest's office. The murderer didn't look the part, and neither did the private investigator. He was older than Forrest imagined, thought he'd be mid-forties, ex-marine type, police background, not this guy. He was short and overweight, his hair thinning, nearly bald on top, disheveled, wearing a smoky, smelly sport coat and rumpled tie. *The man obviously didn't chase down criminals. He couldn't run across the street,* Forrest reflected. *I'm sure he's never been in a fight, not a Rockford-type PI.*

**33**

Barnaby began talking about the case before any formalities. "Luka briefed me beforehand, so this is a preliminary meeting, an opportunity to size me up. If you decide you want me to work for you, the first thing I want to do is look at what they have on this man. I'd rather start with whether I think they have the right man or not."

Short and sweet. No commitments. Forrest liked that. "That's a good starting place. Fair enough. You do that. Tell me what you think, and we'll go from there."

When they met again a month later, Barnaby had thoroughly reviewed the case against Mr. Booker. "I can see why you are concerned. Tripp is running for higher office and is highly motivated not to let cases sit on his desk or chalk up another conviction and avoid loose ends that can become future campaign issues. Besides, I have it on good authority he is looking for major donors, and he'd love to get your backing. It doesn't make Wade guilty or innocent, but . . . and, he would like everyone to feel he is a man of action. A maximum prison sentence on all counts for that poor guy will play large at election time."

Luka was a man of a few words and rarely spoke up in meetings. Forrest did all the talking. Hearing his comments on politicians induced a raised eyebrow. Barnaby was impressively attentive, aided by thick plastic-framed glasses that exaggerated his eyes' size and gave the appearance he was always boring in on the person talking, looking for meanings behind the words.

Forrest commented that Tripp had already inquired to see if he could support him. "I didn't answer him, but there is no way in hell."

Barnaby continued, "Few crimes are more terrifying than arson. On top of that, bringing an arsonist to justice is difficult. Usually, it's enough to figure out a fire was arson, not in this case, of course, but then finding the person responsible and proving guilt is tough. So hard that, nationally, it is the hardest of crimes to bring to trial and convict. Only ten percent of arsonists are even brought to trial. An arsonist can count on having a ninety percent chance of getting away.

Forrest and Luka exchanged glances. He could tell Luka had something he wanted to say. He probably wanted to say the same thing—I hate politicians.

Barnaby paused. His gaze narrowed as he turned to Luka, then back to Forrest. "Not sure I understand what politicians ever think." A mischievous grin showed itself in the corner of his mouth as if he knew what they were thinking. "In this case, Tripp may have been a little desperate to take action, given how long this went unresolved. Unless we come up with an iron-clad alternative, it will be tough to unravel. He will fight for all its worth to keep his record clean, uphold his conviction. On the other hand, my investigations could find him innocent and never prove who did it. I assume you aren't hiring me to get the guy out of jail?"

Forrest brushed aside the question, and Barnaby didn't wait for an answer.

"A motive is always the investigator's best friend. A good motive gives you a road map for a conviction. As in this case, lack of motive leaves you with a circumstantial case, which is the way it is with most arson cases. Arsonists commit their crimes in the dark of night when no one is around, rarely are there eyewitnesses. They aren't usually trying to time the crime with the arrival of a victim. Okay, they found the gas cans in the back of his truck, one can was new. Why did he need a new five-gallon gas can? He says the other one leaked. I assume they tested it, but I didn't see it in the record. In the trial, they convinced the jury he needed the extra can to set the fire. The defense argued he used gas in his mowing business. Nobody believed that.

"They salvaged a few of his prints at the cabin. That was stunning, pretty incriminating. Of course, we know he was in the cabin before, so his prints should have been there. A drunk man who left finger prints while you were sleeping. . . I mean if he was there to torch the house would he rummage through the house. Or, if he was there to burglarize the place why so much trouble to burn it down?  I guess it's all irrelevant. The defense failed to argue the prints were found on a cabinet, in the back of the house; the only structure left standing with prints. He was a burglar and admitted to being in the house, at one time, but it doesn't make him an arsonist killer.

"Here's what I think. If he was convicted for being a loser, they got it right, but it's a stretch to make him for an arson killer. In all my years, this guy didn't do it. If he was motivated to commit a crime of passion, would he have been drunk out of his mind? No, he would have been stone serious. If robbery was a motive, he sure went through a lot of effort to burn the place down."

Forrest nodded his agreement. "What about the white SUV?

"Yeah. I am coming to that." Barnaby paused long enough to see if Forrest was ready for him to finish his line of reasoning. "So, he drank himself into a stupor before he went sneaking around in the woods and tiptoed, as quietly as possible, drunk, into your cabin while you slept. The same night he was arrested for DUI and couldn't even walk a line. Or maybe he was trying to get his courage up for a contract job but was afraid. There's absolutely no evidence for that. His bank account was overdrawn, and there was no money trail, and he's an unlikely man to hire for a job like this.

"His bar mates said he was drunk every night, so there was nothing special there. Whoever would have hired him would have been nuts to do so. Not only was he a bad choice for the job, but he would turn on whoever paid him faster than you could strike a match. I'd say the one sure crime was the incompetence of the defense. The first defense attorney was incompetent and the last one was a burned-out old hag, earning a living on court assignments and probably tired of the riffraff she represented. Attorneys are humans too . . . oh, I don't want to go that far," he added, smiling playfully.

Isabella entered and served Barnaby another cup of coffee. She had figured out he drank strong black coffee all day long and lots of it.

Forrest learned more about the case's ins and outs in the last half hour than in the years leading up. This guy, Barnaby, was no picture taker. On first impression, he was the kind of no non-sense guy for the job, at home in the seedy parts of town but who could clean up in higher society. He was at ease in any crowd for sure, but he never cleaned up. Barnaby was Barnaby. Forrest liked that.

Luka had checked him out and learned he had served clients in twenty different states, and some well-known murder cases, and some involving financial fraud. As it turned out, he had a master's degree in criminology but wasn't the kind of guy who worked well for other people.

"White SUV. Yeah, I looked at that too. Got nothing really, except . . . ."

Forrest and Luka leaned forward in their chair.

"Well, it's nothing. I don't want to . . . it's just that the eyewitness, the first one on the scene, was driving a white van. The Pete's Plumbing guy—white SUV, white van, rainstorm. Who knows? I'll look at that."

Forrest and Luka looked to him for further explanation.

"Well, it was hard to see, and the other guy following behind never saw anything. Truck? SUV? It turns out the guy in the white service van was the only eyewitness. No one else around. I don't think this will amount to anything. The guy seems pretty straight, and he helped at the scene. I do think it's pretty damned coincidental, those two events."

When Barnaby finished, Forrest hired him.

To wrap up the meeting, Barnaby said some kind words for the police and a few diplomatic ones for Detective Lowell, who he called a bit slow. "His commander likes him. Says he's a team player." Laughing, he added, "They don't call me a team player. That's what makes me such a damn good PI. I've had the police come to me more than once for help. They have rules I don't have. Don't get me wrong; I'm not a lawbreaker. They have some pretty strict policies. Not many guys want to put their jobs on the line to get things done. I get that."

# 34

The recent growth of Niche was the result of several critical decisions. One was an investment in technologies to provide clients an internet search optimization capability. The other decision was to offer a consulting division to help companies compete in the new age digital economy, especially for those companies transitioning from their bricks and mortar businesses to include internet strategies.

The company was back on track and outpacing expectations. Life had sent Forrest to the mat and back onto wobbly feet. He resisted returning, but pride and putting the company in a position to leave on his terms were priorities.

Kim seemed content to bide her time, waiting for Forrest to relinquish his position, becoming chairman of the board would be her preferred scenario. She still had her insurance policy, and it had no expiration date. Ever since he came back, rumors swirled about his leaving and when, but she knew her time would come. Anybody could see how damaged he was, and for now, nothing she could do right now but circle like a scavenger bird.

Nine months passed before there was anything significant from private investigator Barnaby Willis. During that time, he kept Luka informed he had nothing new. In the PI business, Forrest figured, it was zip, nada, nothing, then a breakthrough. He wanted a positive report but hated when people played up to him, told him what he wanted to hear, and treated him like he didn't know better.

March was fickle. One tantalizing minute the sun flirted with city hearts, but today the weather bared its icy white fangs, covering the trees and sidewalks, downing power lines, and causing dangerous conditions on the roadways.

When Barnaby showed up for the meeting, an hour late, Isabella showed him in and poured him a cup of coffee. Holding his rubber goulashes, overcoat, and hat, he extended his free hand to Forrest. Luka extended his hand after he took a seat next to him.

Forrest couldn't shake the image of an innocent man in prison while his wife's killer was free. "I'm never going to believe he did it." He hoped Barnaby felt as strongly as he did. He saw steam rising from Barnaby's coffee. "Isabella makes her coffee hot. McDonald's hot. Be careful." Forrest said.

"That's how I like. Hot." Barnaby blew on his coffee, sipped it, and cleared his throat. "Well, yep, it happens. It's the seamy side of what prosecutors do. Winning a robbery case with several eyewitnesses and a confession might be good for the DA's win-loss record but not as satisfying as proving a circumstantial case like this. But it's his job, and in the big picture, his imperfections keep us safe."

Pausing to let his comments sink in, Barnaby added, "I'm sure you didn't hire me to prove his innocence and get him out of jail. Remember, we might find something to suggest his innocence and end up less satisfied but unable to convict anyone else. Just the way it works on crimes like this. After someone is convicted, it takes a lot to overturn it. So, we find another circumstantial case, and he stays in prison, and the misery goes on."

Long-faced, Forrest shrugged off his comment. "So, no matter, we have to find the person who did this."

"I hope we do." Barnaby reminded him of the challenges, the clandestine nature of the crime, how circumstantial arson often is, ashes for evidence. "Keep in mind if we find someone else, I'll bet you a hundred dollars the prosecution will be as challenging. Double so. Triple."

Barnaby paused to leave the room and waited for Forrest to comment before he continued. "We need a motive."

Forrest squirmed in his seat, sensing Barnaby might not be there to deliver good news, worried he was preparing him for failure. Maybe the end of the road was Wade rotting away in prison, and never knowing—an unsolvable crime, with a patsy serving the time.

Barnaby could see Forrest's discomfort. "We have to uncover a motive," he repeated. "We should consider this a passion fire, or revenge one, not a motiveless drunk in the wrong place at the wrong time. A passion crime is typically impulsive and easier to detect, and motives are easier to find. Emotional crimes typically leave bread crumbs. I'm saying this for two reasons. First, Tripp couldn't find much of a motive and he assumed it wouldn't get any better, and second, without motive it's uphill and we will be fighting the DA. Right now, I don't see any hint of motive. We need to dig deeper. You and Allie led idyllic lives. That is what everyone says. Seemingly no enemies, no jealous lovers, right?" Scrunching his face, Barnaby locked his gaze on Forrest, awaiting an answer, trying to watch for even the slightest subconscious revelation. "I'm sure she wasn't seeing anyone. Right?"

Forrest gritted his teeth. "No, by God. She was paralyzed."

Barnaby drew back. "We are looking at both crimes. It's hard to believe they weren't connected. That would be a lot of coincidence."

Forrest smiled, relieved to hear Barnaby thought the fire and being run off the road were related.

"I need details, relationships. You can go back to high school if you have any names."

To Forrest's surprise, Barnaby went on to reveal he had been looking at people at the University, colleagues, students, employees, friends, any human connections to either of them. "I even talked to students who didn't fare so well in her class, students disappointed with a grade. Hell, nobody had a bad word for her. Even students she flunked. It's hard to believe she didn't have at least one enemy. I've also interviewed many people in your company, even looked at people in the mailroom. It's surprising how the police interviewed only a few of them."

"Well, you're wasting your time there. No killers there. I know those people."

Forrest assumed it was all Barnaby had to offer. In the following silence, Forrest thought they had come to the end of the meeting. Forrest exchanged nervous glances with Luka and was about to ask when Barnaby put his notes down and began again. "Do you know a gentleman named Robert Goldstein?"

Forrest shook his head. "I knew a Goldstein."

"You know the company Goldstein and Fishbohm?"

"Sure. I remember ten years ago they were bought by a Los Angeles company. Assured Inc., I believe. Bob Goldstein, yeah."

"I had a challenging but interesting meeting with Mr. Goldstein. He is in an assisted living facility. He had a stroke. He was quite conversant and bright as could be, but a bit hard to understand. The stroke affected his speech and made it tough to talk. No matter, I figured him out. Your vice president, Kim Merrymore, worked for him before she came to work for you."

Forrest swallowed hard.

Barnaby shifted in his chair, reached into his pocket for a cigarette, and motioned to Forrest for permission to smoke it. Not waiting for acknowledgment, he lit it and blew a thick cloud of smoke off to the side. Smiling, he continued. "It turns out Kim was a bit of a challenging employee for him. She cost him a small fortune."

Forrest leaned forward. "She's a handful all right. If you only knew what a handful she was."

"It is the world's best-kept secret—blackmail." Barnaby went on, "How many politicians, business leaders, people of influence, make decisions based on the fear of exposure. Politicians especially don't want anything to tarnish their image, affect votes. A lot of deals get made for the wrong reasons. I swear, secrets and dishonesty together form the basis of the number one industry worldwide and causes more wars." Taking another drag on his cigarette and pausing to reflect upon how profound his last comment was, he continued. "Seems they had an affair and she had pictures."

The blood drained from Forrest's face, and he began to rub his scars. He didn't think Barnaby noticed, but Luka had a curious look on his face.

"Old Goldstein was a proud and loyal family man," Barnaby continued. "Claims there was just this one little tryst." Raising his eyebrows and smiling mischievously, "At least it's what he claims. Said there was no reason to keep the secret anymore. His wife died, and they had no kids. I think he was relieved to tell someone. He paid her off to leave the company. He never said how much it cost him, but it was a lot of money—a boatload. He said he didn't have a choice.

"He's a bitter man. I wanted more information, like how it happened and how it was she had pictures? He was too embarrassed to go on. I always say if you go to the dance with the devil, you'd better be prepared to leave with him." Barnaby sniggered and looked to Forrest then Luka, who sat stone-faced, to see if they found his comment amusing.

The hair on the back of Forrest's neck prickled. He grimaced as he looked over to Luka to see if he noticed. When he looked back to Barnaby, he had a curious look on his face.

"Kim is always a problem." Forrest hesitated as he searched for what more to say. "I bet she was a problem everywhere she's been. Don't get me wrong, she's extremely competent. A brilliant woman. But how do I describe her . . . she's very driven." Forrest searched for a better way to describe her. "More than driven." Forrest smiled nervously, "She'd do absolutely anything to get ahead. We have to keep her in line."

Barnaby took a deep drag in his cigarette before continuing, then began to cough. Forrest asked Isabella to bring him a glass of water. His coughing spell lasted several minutes before he could go on. Hoarsely, he struggled to talk. "There's a special type person we all mingle with every day. What if I told you five percent of the people in your company, the companies you deal with, neighbors, your city, the state, your gardener, your mechanic. . ." Looking over to Luka, he paused before continuing, "Your driver . . . could all be a type of person who doesn't give a tinker's damn about you or your wife and would love to see you fall on your ass. Some of them would just as soon kill you if they could get away with it. They are socio/psychopathic. That's right, 25,000 or so people right here in Minneapolis. Next time you sit down next to a stranger for a cup of coffee, remember those statistics."

Too stunned to respond, his idea of a psychopath was someone like Charles Manson.

Barnaby went on, "He, or even she, will con and manipulate anyone by relying on refined intuition and charisma. A major difference between a sociopath and psychopath is psychopaths are intelligent people in successful careers."

Forrest was thankful when the meeting ended. Wrapping up the meeting, Barnaby said he would broaden his search and asked Forrest to think hard about anybody he should look at who had even a passing interest in either of them. "We have got to look at this as a crime of passion. We need to find a motive. Go through old scrapbooks. Yearbooks."

# 35

As soon as Barnaby left, Forrest rose, "I need a drink. Let's get out of here." He called Isabella to his office and announced they were leaving, and she should too, that the streets were bad.

As they exited the garage, the weather was worse than what he could see out the window of his 26$^{th}$-floor office. Forrest suggested they get a drink and hole up until all the crazies were off the road and the roads were salted.

When they arrived, the streets were empty, and the Swede's Tavern sign was iced over. The bar was empty except for the same old man and woman, sitting in a back booth, still holding hands across the table, smiling and laughing. The same booth Forrest and Luka sat in before was empty, and they took it. They ordered two draft beers.

The jukebox in the corner was lit up but silent. The only sounds in the bar were the low murmur of conversation across the room, the occasional clinking of glasses, and the heating vent overhead blasting hot air directly on them.

Luka began the conversation. "He makes a lot of sense."

Forrest couldn't wait to get a drink in his hand, but instead of gulping it down and ordering another, he held the glass and watched the foam settle.

"There is something I want to tell you. I haven't told anyone. Have I ever mentioned Kim to you? The lady Barnaby was talking about."

Luka searched his memory. "Sure, but I don't think we've met. She's pretty. Smart. One of your executives, so she's obviously talented like you said. That's about it."

"There is more. Years ago, when we did the Sloten deal in New York, she went with me. It was when Woody's first wife was dying."

Luka nodded. "I remember. It must have been this time of the year because the roads were bad."

"After completing negotiations, we celebrated with Champagne. It went to my head, and the next morning I woke up in her room. I'm not proud of that. I must have passed out. I don't remember. Anything. Mind you, I'm no wimp when it comes to drinking, but I don't recall the time right before I passed out. She took pictures."

It took a few minutes for Luka to fully grasp what he was hearing. Confused, he asked, "Pictures, huh? Why didn't you tell the PI?"

Forrest looked away. "I'm ashamed." Forrest shook his head. "I'd volunteer to go to Hell to protect Chrissy. If any of this became public, and she found out her father had an affair when her mother was pregnant with her . . . that is what they would say. I couldn't stand that. Besides, it's never really been a problem until now. She has performed capably, and I've had no reason to fire her."

"You don't suspect . . . do you?"

"Nah, no way. She's too ambitious . . . lacks morals, but she's not a killer. It takes a special kind of depraved person to . . . She's not the only one doing everything they can to get ahead. Oh, well, her little game won't work with me. But an evil cold-blooded killer, she's not. She said she was praying for me. I believed her . . . No way."

"You heard Barnaby. It's hard to know what's going on in anyone's mind."

"Yeah, I know. We aren't mind readers. Although, if we were, we'd solve more crimes."

Luka smiled and took a drink. "And the mind of a woman? I can't tell what my wife is ever thinking, ever, but, , ," Luka hesitated, unsure whether to say what he was thinking. He was a hundred percent comfortable with Forrest, but they were in a place they had never been before. Forrest trusted him with his most private life secret. But if a warped woman wanted the other woman out of the way—a psychopath would do anything. That's what Barnaby said. No remorse. The road to reality is washed out, and there's no bridge connecting them to the mainland. "You been paying her?"

"No. No, it's not that kind of blackmail. She's been holding it over my head. All these years, just reminding me she had pictures." Forrest drew back thoughtfully. "You know no one could ever prove she was blackmailing me. Like I said, technically, she hasn't. She is successful on her own."

"But she could?" Luka said.

"She never asked for money. She just held it out to get her way when she wanted something. She's never asked for anything she might not have gotten anyway. The thing is, she's talented, so nobody would ever think I did her any favors. Every once in a while, she reminded me of the pictures. I figured she was insecure—didn't trust men. She thinks it's a man's world she is fighting. She still comes on to me, but I figure she is just a flirt. Does it with all the guys."

Forrest stiffened and shook his head. "She may be a lot of things, but she's no killer. Ambitious and ruthless for sure. That woman gets her way, but she's no killer." Gulping down his beer, he rubbed his face's side and raised his glass to get the bartender's attention.

"Pictures? She sounds creepy. Really creepy." Luka waved off a beer for himself.

"I wish we hadn't hired her. I should have stopped it somehow."

"So, are you turning this over to Barnaby? The police?"

"No," Forrest answered forcefully quickly. "No," he followed up in a less emphatic tone. I'm not ready. I need some time. Let's let Barnaby poke around some more."

# 36

Three months passed before they met with Barnaby again. The cliff hanger last meeting left Forrest anxious. When he tried to call him, his message machine said he was out of town.

Forrest made plans for his daughter's wedding and secret plans to leave the company. He made several business decisions to wrap up projects already in development so as not to leave loose ends for the next CEO. He finalized negotiations to purchase the building they occupied. When he concluded the negotiation, they hoisted a new Niche sign atop the building. Niche occupied twenty-three of the twenty-six floors. The other tenants were law firms and accountants and on the first-floor retail space and a bank.

Crocus stalks poked through the snow a few weeks earlier, promising there would be spring again. Spring would soon arrive with longer days and an epidemic of potholes. Soon Minnesotans would again find complaint in mosquitoes and hot, humid days.

Since his last visit, his friend Arjun Dewar, the psychiatrist, called several times to check on him and scheduled to see him in the spring. When he arrived one Saturday morning, the snow had retreated to the darkest shadows of the thick forest, and the crocus were in full bloom along the cobblestone roadway. Flo served them lunch in the dining room, and afterward, they moved outside and sat in the brightest path of the warming sun.

After they were comfortable, they spent the first fifteen minutes talking about the sunny day, Chrissy, and Forrest going back to work.

When they finished catching up, Arjun said, "On the drive up, I thought about how you were always one of my favorites. I never told you, but you influenced me to become a psychiatrist. I wanted to be like you, so confident and self-assured. You never had to go through a series of steps in thinking before you spoke. You seem to understand people so well."

Forrest smiled warmly. "Funny you'd say that. You know I got my masters at the Wharton's School of Business. I had a professor there . . . his name was Charles Dwyer. He summed up the leadership challenge in a series of lectures on human behavior. More than anything else, what I learned in those lectures, and his books, carried over to my career. What's funny is how much I valued the importance of employees in any endeavor. I tried to understand what their values were. Treat everyone fairly. Ironic, in the end, the invisible hand of evil human behavior destroyed my life."

"How's that Forrest? You mean by the guy in prison who set the fire?"

"He didn't do it. I never thought he did. Circumstances, an ambitious prosecutor, and the fact he was such a loser, did him in. I will never understand how someone could ever kill another human so callously, but in my heart, I know he's not the man. You understand, right?"

"That's a projection of your good values. You don't have a little spot in your brain to understand evil. I only understand it textually. There are people in our population who have no empathy, and some are ready to kill under the right circumstances, or just for sport."

"Yeah, I hear you. Barnaby said that."

"Barnaby?" Arjun questioned.

"I hired a private investigator. The guy in prison didn't do it. He is not a killer. Help me understand something. Why would anyone want to do this, other than a deranged person who would do it, as you say, for sport?"

"Looking for motive, huh? I know how important it is. A motive is what ties it all together. Without motive, we can feel lost and never find an ending point. Answers to the question 'why' are essential to moving on. Am I right, the guy they convicted didn't have a clear motive?"

"No, he's a down and out drinker with no apparent motive."

Arjun continued. "Putting context in human behavioral terms in a sea of circumstantial evidence is where we find land. Looking at the evidence and tying it all together is what law enforcement does, but they are not behavioralists.

"First, I look at psychopathy as a more impactful form of sociopathy. All psychopaths are sociopaths, but not all sociopaths are psychopaths. They both fall into the category of anti-personality disorder. Don't confuse psychopathy with psychosis. Psychotics are people who have lost contact with reality. Treatment of psychopathy is rare. It is not an illness, and there is no medication for it, and besides, they can't convince a sociopath there is anything wrong with them.

"Okay, let me shock you. Researchers at Emory University studied the behavior traits of our past presidents and found many of them meet the criteria for psychopathy. Politicians usually score high. Presidents who scored the highest were Teddy Roosevelt, with John F. Kennedy second and then Franklin D. Roosevelt.

"You might think these people are down and outers, loners, trouble makers. On the contrary, they are typically leaders, fun to be around, charming, always have the answers, never at a loss for words. But they are cunning, deceitful, manipulative, and dishonest. They are also apt to coerce others and take pride in their sexual exploits. I can go on. Is that what you want?"

"So, killers?"

"Of course, some are. Not all sociopaths resort to killing, but both the psychopath and sociopath are capable of horrific crimes. They do what they think they need to do. A primary trait of all psychopaths is their lack of remorse. Remorse is not in their make-up. Chances are these traits are passed on in their DNA. Some sociopaths don't possess the intelligence, opportunity, or motivation but it doesn't make them less sociopathic. Like all other humans, some sociopaths are highly evolved, more intelligent, more cautious, more apt to get away with their crimes, and for a long time. They might not be caught. Remember, they take great pride in getting away with their crimes. Fooling everyone might be a high value for them."

Forrest went into one of his elongated silent phases. Arjun looked on, wondering what he was thinking, knowing if he wanted to share it with him, he would.

Forrest finally broke the silence. "A woman?"

Arjun looked at him curiously.

"A woman killer?"

"Of course."

"I hate that woman. If I ever find out she did this, I'll kill her."

"That woman? Do you have someone in mind?"

Forrest had more to say, and after a period of silence, shaking his head, he said. "Never mind. It can't be. This is so confusing. One minute I want to kill someone, and the next, I feel it couldn't be true. Maybe I'll never know. Not in this life. Allie says there will be justice. Maybe it doesn't matter."

"You still talk to Allie?"

"More, when I close my eyes, I am with Allie. It's like entering a different dimension. I can see her, hear her, smell her scent, feel her arms around me. The more often this happens, and the longer this goes, the more convinced we'll be together. She says we'll see justice. You think I'm crazy. You think I imagine all this?"

"Who is to say. I have given a lot of thought to this," Arjun nodded sympathetically. "Haunted by it. I could give you the scientific explanation. I think it's beautiful though—thinking you will be with Allie again. Who is to say otherwise? Science makes us all skeptical. But down through the ages, a lot of scientific truths were later proven wrong.

"The more sophisticated our science, the more we question, but the more we fall into group thinking patterns around the science, the fewer the questions. Already, quantum scientists are raising questions about everything. But as science seeks truth, who says we won't someday recognize God is the great scientist. If God turns out to be a scientist, will it make him less holy?" Arjun wondered aloud.

Forrest was surprised by Arjun's words. *God, the scientist?* What does science know about God and death, anyway? Not much. But they refuse to look beyond the forbidden wall where miracles happen. Death is bad enough—mainly its finality, so we choose between the miracles of our existence or that we become a mound of dirt. As if he was coming out of a syrupy fog, Forrest said, "It seems when death comes on slowly, there is time to decide between the finality of it or the everlasting, but when it's sudden, it's hard to deal with the lack of control, the sudden shift. I know I will be with Allie. I believe in miracles."

"I hope you will."

"So, do you believe in miracles? With your training, I thought you were cleansed of that notion, had it all washed away in medical school."

"Ironically, it was science that taught me to question everything, when I reached the point where answers turned into questions. It happened in a lecture on the brain and a professor's simple comment. The professor said, 'The human brain holds an estimated two hundred exabytes of information, roughly equal to all the digital content in the world.' A gigabyte is like the earth, and an exabyte is the sun by comparison. There are trillions of connections in our brain, as many in a single cubic centimeter as there are stars. It's unfathomable to me. Why? Is it simple evolution? We know so little."

"So, do you believe in miracles?"

"I don't know what a miracle is. It is more unexplained science. Carbon, hydrogen, oxygen move electrons along neurons that gives us the experience of sunsets or fresh cut lilacs. No one can explain that. Miracle today. . .Science can't explain everything, and it was the unexplained that opened my eyes. It was all the answers, and the unexplained explained." Arjun stopped, and a mischievous smile swept over him. "There is a lot to learn about miracles. I also wanted to be handsome like you. That would be a miracle. I doubt God grants vanity miracles."

Forrest shook his head. "And, I wanted to be smart like you."

# 37

For the longest time, Forrest avoided meetings with Kim unless someone else was in the room. On a few occasions, he asked Isabella to join them and take notes. Now, he avoided meetings with Kim altogether. He had delegated so much of the day-to-day business he could pick and choose which meetings he attended.

He frequently met out of the office with Roy King, his attorney, to put his financial affairs in order, prepare instructions for Chrissy, and transfer his assets into a single-administered fund. He made several charitable donations, one to Allie's favorite cause, The Breast Cancer Research Foundation, in recognition of Allie's mother who died of breast cancer, and his favorites, ALS and Wounded Warriors.

It was a surprising warm, sunny April day when Forrest arrived at the office. He hoped another winter had ended. He knew Minnesota weather was unpredictable, and when optimistic Minnesotans started bragging that winter wasn't so bad and began talking about an early spring, eavesdropping weather gods delivered May blizzards to remind everyone to not count on anything.

Isabella came in his office to go over the day's calendar. She reported Linda Gardner had already stopped by to see him. "Ask if she'll have lunch," Forrest requested.

When Linda arrived at his office at noontime, Forrest blurted, "What are we meeting about?" Forrest regretted saying it, thinking it rude and not inviting. Since he returned to work, he was a different guy and often abrasive. He always felt a fondness for Linda. She had grown up in the company. "It's good to see you," he backtracked.

"Mind if we walk down to Amends' Deli?" she asked. "They have added a kale salad to their menu."

After going through the line and ordering their lunches, they took a seat in the front window. Forrest beamed. "You sure look great." When she started with the company, she wore tent dresses and now she wore a size ten, a much smaller version of herself. But behind the same smile, heavy or thin, was a confident woman.

"Thanks. I figured it was about time I took better care of myself."

"We don't get to talk much anymore, so thanks for suggesting lunch. When the company first opened, we spent a lot of time together. I remember watching the world series in my office the last time the Twins won."

Forrest laughed, "That was fun. The good old days for sure. Good old days for the Twins too."

Linda turned serious. "You know I'm all business. I never mix in politics . . . or rumors."

"What rumors, Linda?"

"I keep hearing you're not going to be here long. I know rumors have been around since you came back. It's none of my business. I only wish you the best. But there is a lot of talk about Kim being your replacement. None of my business either. I know she's a brilliant woman. I get that. But a little short on scruples." Linda drew her mouth uptight. "I hope it's okay to say that. But you're a tough act to follow."

"Thank you, Linda. That's nice of you to say. You can tell me anything. I'm not leaving yet. And there is no talk about Kim moving up. None." He began to rub the side of his red, scared face self-consciously. He hated that bad habit.  If he were a poker player, it would be his tell.

Rumors about Kim replacing him angered him. Obvious to everyone, she wanted the job and would do anything to get it. Anything. And, she was up to something, but what? She isn't qualified. She is reckless and insensitive. What kind of a person is so oblivious to what people think? She was not only not in line for the job, but he also had plans for her.

"As I said, it's none of my business, but I guess she's gotten pretty close to a couple of board members."

Forrest dropped his hand from rubbing his face and stared at Linda. "Do you know who?"

"Chris Harrison and James Abbott," she replied. "Who knows who else. That woman has her ways. She has no scruples."

Forrest hadn't heard that before. Two of his board members were talking to Kim. That was out of line. He feigned indifference but made a mental note to have Barnaby investigate. *I can see how Chris and Jim might be vulnerable,* he thought. "I can't imagine they wouldn't have the company's best interest," Forrest offered. "I don't know either of them well. They're fairly new to the board but well placed and influential." *I can see how they might like her. Barnaby said she blackmailed Bob Goldstein, and it cost him a fortune to get rid of her. Well, there is no way she'll ever get the job. Before I depart, I need to deal with her, not leave her for someone else to deal with.*

"Forrest." Linda's raised voice drew the attention of the people around them. Placing her hand on his arm, she said again, "Forrest!"

Forrest shook his head. "Sorry, Linda."

"Well, as I was saying. It doesn't matter. I have a standing employment offer from Brightpath in Boise. I always wanted to live in Idaho anyway."

"I wish you all the best, but you might like my replacement. I haven't announced I'm going anywhere yet."

The silent walk back to the office was a contemplative stroll for Linda and a mind-twisting one for Forrest. Easily the nicest day of the year, they encountered smiling business people eager to offer greetings. When they arrived, Forrest turned to her, reached out, and hugged her. "That was nice. I'm so glad we got to work together all these years. I don't know anyone I've enjoyed working with more."

When they separated, Linda's eyes were moist, and a solitary tear broke free and raced down her cheek.

Forrest smiled, "I'm not leaving yet. Let's call it practicing our goodbyes."

When he arrived back to his desk, he found it hard to concentrate. Lately his thoughts were consumed by what Barnaby had uncovered and anxious to learn more. It seemed implausible Kim could be the evil killer, but Barnaby's and Arjun's lecture on psychopathy haunted him. A top performer in the company, had Forrest been so naive about her?

Thinking about it was bewildering. Everything he understood about people came into question. Like everybody else, people stopped learning when they thought they had life figured out, content with what they believed, stuck in there every day, their jobs, their politics, their religion, their daily routines, and comfortable in their ignorance.

In his absence, Charles developed sophisticated metrics to monitor the business, and all the indicators suggested business was flat but nothing to worry about. That was how it worked. Breathe in, breathe out, expand and contract, intense one minute and relaxed the next. Since Forrest came back, the company had gone through a period of tremendous growth, and the current mini slowdown was welcomed by everyone—time to enjoy their successes.

Finally, Forrest announced his retirement, and plans were underway to secure the company's future, and soon Chrissy's wedding and his life would proceed as he had wished, as he had pledged to Allie.

On Friday afternoon, Luka showed up early to drive him home. He was one of the few people who could meet with Forrest without an appointment. Isabelle nodded, and he entered. Forrest was on the phone. He motioned for him to take a seat.

When he was off the phone, Luka began, "I talked to Barnaby. He may have found the SUV. He discovered a white SUV titled to a man by the name of Merle Simpson. The tags were purchased dutifully year after year until a year after the accident—Allie's crash, and not registered again since. It hasn't been sold. It isn't clear if the police saw this or how they explain it. Get this. Mr. Simpson has been institutionalized for over twenty years. A mental hospital."

"Twenty years." Forrest's mind whirled, trying to see the connection. "So, who is Merle Simpson? He can't be a suspect if he's been in a mental intuition."

"He's no suspect."

Forrest could see by Luka's expression there was more. "He was a foster parent of Kim's."

Forrest's mouth dropped open, momentarily at a loss for words. Another Kim connection. She had a white SUV. Collecting himself, he said, "We still don't have the car, right?"

"Nope. That's the next piece of the puzzle. But its progress."

"I can't believe this. Right in front of my nose. I work with Kim every day. One of our executives. A killer? Really?"

"That's what Barnaby said. People like her are great manipulators, and they are in a world where they don't care, and everyone around them does."

"You think she was the one who set the fire as well?"

"I asked the same question. Barnaby said not to jump too far based on this piece of information. Says, in his business, there are way too many possible explanations. We might find the SUV totaled in an accident. It could be in the junk heap, already crushed. Just another circumstantial piece of the puzzle, and it may not fit."

Forrest and Luka both shook their heads. For several minutes they stared off in silence—Luka going over the puzzle pieces and Forrest contemplating how his attitude toward Kim had changed from despising her and tolerating the situation, hoping time would resolve her threats, to now hating her.

The feeling of hate was new to him, but he hated her with every ounce of his energy. Innocent or not. For the first time, he wanted to strike back, even kill her. But killing someone was easier to intellectu-alize then carry out, easier to say he would kill her until the image of action flashed before him, a face, a real person, even a despised one. It made him shiver to think about.

"Barnaby still doesn't know, does he?" Forrest asked.

"I'm not sure how he'd find out? At some point, he needs to know."

"You know I hate her. She is the only person I ever hated. All along, I thought something would happen to clear it all up, something, not this circumstantial BS. But everything keeps pointing toward her. What are we going to do?"

"We need to find the SUV," Luka answered.

"Is that enough?"

"Probably not. Maybe it's gone or can't be found. Then we're back to square one. How could a motive be proven anyway—that she had some pictures she didn't use, that you will say she was holding over your head?"

"Sounds more like a motive for me to kill her, not her to kill Allie," Forrest speculated. "What could be her motive—to drive me out so she could get my job? To eliminate my wife, to what . . . ? I hate that woman."

"Barnaby said people like her are good at hiding right out in the open. How do we know who they are when, on the surface, they are like anyone else?" Luka said.

"I never thought about it, and now I can't shake it. The whole idea of psychopaths roaming around in and out of our lives . . . I can't stop thinking about that."

Luka went silent. He reacted to the good news about the same way as bad. "Yeah, it's hard to shake."

"Sure, she's promiscuous and lacks scruples, but could she kill Allie and my baby? Could she do all that? I still see her as a successful person, friendly, involved in charities, caring, doing all the things normal people do. She says she's praying for us—can she be a killer? Back and forth I go."

Luka wasn't one to dwell. His thinking process was simple and practical. He had the temperament of a combat officer using an economy of unambiguous words. A get-the-job-done kind of guy. "A lot of time has passed. A lot. The only answer is to find the guy who did this."

## 38

Forrest dreaded even the sight of Kim in hallways, elevators, and especially his office. He despised her so much he worried how he might react being in the same room with her.

He knew she had been angling for his job for a long time but never took it too seriously. The board would never consider her, would they? He announced his departure, and the day approached, and she was doing everything she could to replace him. As best he could, Barnaby monitored her relations with Chris and James, the two board members she talked to. He wondered if there were others. *There is no way in hell she'll get the job.*

Forrest confided in Arthur, the board chairman, at least on what he needed to know, and they were in lockstep on what had to be done. He knew he could trust him. They agreed on his successor. They were ready for whatever trouble she tried to create, and Arthur had plans for Chris and James.

His last day in the office arrived and like all last days for departing employees, he removed anything personal, and what was left belonged there. The next CEO could use whatever files he left or toss them out and start over. It didn't matter to him. Isabella followed his instructions, and there were no celebrations.

The day went as he planned. Several people stopped by throughout the day and wished him well, at least the ones he wanted—private, quiet, one-on-one conversations. His leaving well understood, no one said a thing about his retiring at age fifty-eight. Most people expected him to leave years ago. It was hard for anyone to imagine how he held up all these years. They congratulated him on the upcoming wedding of his daughter, and a few asked about his plans.

Finally, he stood alone in his bare office. Luka would be there soon to take him home for the last time. Life wasn't what he predicted, but when does life turn out as expected? He had skated his way out of Minnesota to attend the University of Iowa, graduated with honors, met the woman he loved, married, and made a commitment to be with her for eternity. A pledge he planned to keep.

He turned his back to the door, entranced, and stared at the Minneapolis skyline. He started the company from scratch, and it made him wealthy and respected. He had money to do anything he wanted, but after events brought him crashing to earth, he bided his time being a good father.

A shuffle at the office door broke his trance. When he turned, Kim stood brazenly in the doorway as Isabella pushed past her. "I'm sorry I must have been in the lady's room," Isabella said apologetically.

"Never mind, Isabella. It's no problem," he said calmly.

Shouldering her way past Isabella, Kim looked back at her and said, "Is this your last day too? Well, good luck." Turning away and walking toward Forrest, she added, "She does a good job of blocking for you."

Forrest had already protected Isabella by finding her a new opportunity outside the company. He shrugged, "It's her job."

Forrest braced himself. He disliked her and had grown to hate her but learned to live with her threats. Everything had changed. Worse than hatred was not being able to expose her, not being able to strike back. Cold calculations left little room for consolation.

He knew there would be consequences if he ever fired her. It would be like lighting a stick of dynamite. Based on what he believed happened but couldn't prove, maybe never prove, it took all his resolve to be in the same building, or especially the same room and this close to her. He felt like a prisoner of war.

Emotionally, he thought her the devil and should be destroyed, but logic kept him in check so far. As irritating as her threats, and as upsetting, he didn't take her too seriously since she was a top performer and hadn't demanded anything special, until now. He bided his time. Hatred with a plan had a surprisingly calming effect. He took a step back as she neared his desk.

Kim was no longer a young woman but dressed like one, wearing a tight skirt, slit up the thigh, and a sheer low-cut blouse. Her youth in the past, but she still turned heads, and at first glance was sexy and available.

Barnaby had prepared a comprehensive report detailing all of her finances and the properties she owned, her investments, her charities, her past relationships, her doctor's and dentist's names. Any company, any community would be proud to have her. She had had breast implants ten years ago. When Barnaby told him, Forrest responded, everybody already knew it. According to the report, she had behavior problems as a young girl, moving from one foster home to another, two abortions before she was eighteen years old. She got one of her teachers fired for inappropriate sexual advances but was a brilliant student academically, never did drugs, and was somewhat of a health nut. She was rich beyond all her successes.

"I understand that fat bitch Linda came to you about me," Kim lashed out.

Forrest responded calmly. "That's so inappropriate."

"I can say whatever I want to you."

Forrest ignored her. "How do you know we met? What makes you think we talked about you."

"She must have. She's one of the people I have to look out for."

"You don't think she is the next CEO, do you?"

Kim ignored his question. "I know you are making plans when Chrissy's out of your life and you've announced you are leaving. It's about time. With or without you, this is my job."

"Out of my life, that's a funny way to look at it. I hope she is never out of my life," Forrest said softly. While she blathered on, Forrest went over the checklist his psychiatrist friend provided—cunning, manipulative, lack of remorse, or guilt.

"I never understood why you didn't leave . . ."

Forrest interrupted and finished her sentence. "Before now? After I lost my wife? After this . . . ," rubbing the side of his face.

"It was a perfect time. You should have."

"You can't wait for me to leave, can you? You think this job is yours, don't you?"

"Look around. Who do you see anyone more qualified? I know who the board has interviewed. That guy from Los Angeles, you know there is no way he gets the job. I know all about his past. I made sure the board knew JPL fired him."

Feigning astonishment, Forrest said, "What? Are you investigating the candidates?"

"It not hard. And the lady from Cincinnati. She's a lightweight. The board knows I'm the most qualified. My interview with them went great. The board knows when you were out of action, I ran this place."

In his waspish state, he had to remain calm. *Keep breathing. Stay calm. God, how I hate her. She could never run this place. How can anyone be so oblivious, so blind to themselves? Is that part of being a psychopath?*

"I made sure they interviewed you, but it's not my job to pick my successor," *I told Arthur to go through the motions, he said to himself,* repressing the smile creeping into the corner of his mouth.

"I heard the board members were pretty impressed with me. We even discussed contract terms. You can't tell me the board did that with other candidates?"

*Arthur did that? Impressive.* "Okay. You're so sure the job is yours; why are we talking about this?"

"How come I haven't heard anything? The board meeting is Monday. How come nobody has gotten back to me? Arthur won't return my calls."

Forrest shrugged, holding back a truthful answer.

"You'd better not get in my way," Kim scowled. "You know I don't need you anymore, but you are my insurance policy. Good news, huh, I never had to cash in my policy until now, but I will. I'll turn you inside out. You like to call it blackmail. Okay, call it blackmail if you want."

"I am not involved. I chose to stay out of it." Forrest stared, sour-faced, in disbelief. In truth, she couldn't hurt him any longer. He was surprised how easy it was to stay calm, staring into the eyes of such an evil woman.

"Yeah, you stayed out of it. You better make sure I get this job. I told you what would happen. I'll accept nothing less. I get the job, or I'll get a settlement of millions. Sometimes I think I'd like the latter better. I might buy a villa in Italy. We don't want a messy finish, do we?" Kim smiled broadly like she had a big secret to reveal. "You know at one point the job wasn't important to me. Being with you was more important. But look at you. You're damaged goods. It turns out you aren't the man I thought you were."

The scars on his face reddened, but he was determined not to let her get to him. He began rubbing the side of his face. He turned away and took a deep breath. Without turning back to her, with surprising calmness, he said, "Sure, I'll make sure you get everything coming to you."

"Don't give me that stuff about my not being able to hurt you more."

Conversations with her always sucked the air out of the room. It was taking all of his energy to remain calm, not appear threatened, not divulge anything. He knew what he had to do. Being so in love with herself blinded her to the possibility he might have a strategy. He remained calm, refusing to wallow in the muck with her. God knows he wanted to lash out. He believed that goodness prevailed in the grand scheme of life.

Alarmed, Kim rushed to the side of his desk, close to him. Forrest took a step back. "Are you recording this?" Excited, looking around nervously, "Is that your plan? Here, record this. Yes, you sexually harassed me. Yes, I have pictures. Yes. Yes. I saved the pictures for my protection and out of loyalty to this company." Kim took a step forward and angrily put her finger in his chest. "You better not try to block me." Abruptly, she turned and stormed toward the door. Without turning around with a wave of her hand, she said. "Have a nice retirement."

Forrest called after her. "No, Kim, I wasn't recording anything and yes, I screwed up. But I don't care anymore. You can't hurt me. I know you think you can destroy me, but no, you can't hurt me any more than you have."

Kim turned and faced him. "So, I can't hurt you? If you don't care about yourself or your company, your legacy, you damned well care about your daughter. I'm sure she thinks you're something. Have you told her how faithfully you loved your wife? That she was an angel? Did you tell her you were screwing around behind her back? I suppose you have all the money you need so you can go into hiding, build yourself a new cabin in the woods like the one that burned down. You can sit on the porch and remember how good life was before you were crushed, before what's her name . . . living your little dream. That could have been us, you know."

Calm swept over her. "I asked you before if you remembered me. You still don't, do you?" Kim waited for Forrest and watched him search his memory. "You were the keynote speaker in Sun Valley, at the American Investment Banker Association annual conference. I was awe struck by all of your accomplishments and your philanthropy. Your speech was so captivating. I've never seen anyone get a standing ovation for a keynote speech. And a bunch of stogy bankers too. God, you were magnificent. I came up after the meeting, and wanted to talk to you. I was wearing. . .I had men hitting on me throughout the conference. You hardly gave me a second glance. You turned away and started talking to some old hag." Kim paused. I looked so good. . .I decided right then I was going to work for Niche."

## 39

Luka showed up to drive him home for the last time an hour later. As he walked past Isabella, she nodded. He found Forrest at his desk, slouched in his chair with his eyes closed, a sad expression on his face. Forrest opened his eyes slowly and nodded. It was time to leave.

Cautiously, Luka said, "You in the mood for an update?

Luka checked in with Barnaby regularly and had talked to him right before he arrived to pick Forrest up. The drive home was commonly a good place for discussions between them. Forrest told him he couldn't stand talking to Barnaby anymore and Luka in some ways was his life line. He never discussed his personal life with Flo, certainly with no one in the company, not his personal attorney, Roy King, and never with his grown-up daughter Christina. Funny how easy it was to hold dark secrets from someone he loved so much.

Forrest could see Luka was anxious to talk. "Sure, go ahead."

"Kim bought a new car the week of the accident. No trade-in. A Mercedes-Benz 380SL."

"I remember that car," Forrest said. "Convertible. She didn't have it long. She gets a new car all the time. So?"

"Barnaby is still looking for the white SUV that seems to have disappeared." When Forrest didn't react, he continued, "When are you going to tell Barnaby what happened?"

"I don't know. Everything points to Kim, doesn't it? But telling Barnaby convolutes things. What does it do for a motive? You know the minute she feels the pressure, she's going to expose me. Maybe I should let her, but it's hard. I need to deal with this in another way. I keep thinking of Chrissy and her wedding tomorrow, then Monday is the board meeting, and I'm off. You know, Kim still thinks she is going to get my job. You should have heard her an hour ago."

The traffic on Interstate 394 was heavy, so they exited onto U.S. Highway 100, which turned onto U.S. Highway 7. Forrest knew the route would take him past the place where Allie was forced off the road.

When they arrived, he asked Luka to stop the car. Peering over the edge to where she crashed, he asked, "Are you convinced that evil woman did this, too?"

"More and more, it seems like it."

"All we got is maybe a car we haven't even seen and may not exist. And some pictures, yet blackmail doesn't seem to play any part of this. Hell, nowadays, a jury might applaud her for protecting herself with pictures. Might help her."

Luka shook his head and frowned. "There's a lot of evil in that woman."

"Yeah, for sure." Looking back to Luka, he asked, "Did I tell you I saw Kim coming off the elevator when I was leaving to go to the hospital after I received the news."

"No, I didn't know."

"I can't get over Arjun's psycho lecture. Since then, I only see her face in his description of psychopathy, and how they go together. But all along, everybody said the odds strongly favored it was a man. It was always a man for the accident and the fire. That's what the detective said, and Captain Surratt, even Barnaby referred to the villain as a man, not a woman."

"There are some pretty motivated women. I remember my second cousin, Siena. She was a born killer if ever there was one. She killed her husband with a hammer while he was asleep."

Looking back over the drop-off to the ravine below, Forrest went over what he understood. "All we know is there was a white SUV she didn't technically own and haven't seen. Drunk says he saw a white SUV. The Pete's Plumbing guy saw a white SUV. We have a drunk and a guy in a rainstorm. Hell, the drunk was almost unconscious, but was convicted of killing her but couldn't even walk the line. A drunk loser who couldn't have done it. Barnaby said all Wade's bar friends said no way. Worse, I know in my heart she did it, but I don't think she'd be convicted. I hate that woman. But hatred gets me nothing."

Forrest never felt so much hate for anyone or anything. It propelled him forward. "I never thought I could kill anyone. *Could I do it? In a rage, maybe, but not cold-blooded and calculating. How can I go to the police? There isn't enough, and she'd get off but take me down. But doing nothing, how does a person live with that?*"

Luka gripped Forrest by his shoulders and looked into his eyes to command attention. "The world is filled with evil people, and we don't know they're evil. They are capable of destroying lives as easily as an evening stroll. We think it just happens in Hollywood movies, or the television shows beaming into our living rooms, even on the news. It's not real when we see it so often in our safe places. Forty-five hundred psychopaths right here in Minneapolis. Imagine that. That's what you told me. People we know. Rub shoulders with. No remorse. No empathy. None. And they can be the most charming people in the room. They can be our political leaders. So much evil."

Usually a man of few words, Forrest had never heard Luka go on like that.

Luka took a deep breath. "Nowadays, the system doesn't always work." Sighing angrily, he said, "Look what they did to Wade. She'll have the best attorneys and will weep for the jury. She'll say her father abused her . . . and you." Then, almost in a whisper, "You've always known about my past friends. I could take care of this."

Forrest was stunned and fought back the tears. "You would do that for me?"

"I would. It wouldn't be just for you."

Forrest couldn't remember Luka stringing sentences together like that before. After several moments of silence, Luka re-started the car, and they drove on. Pulling away, Forrest watched out the window as the ravine disappeared from view. He hoped for a revelation, renewed strength for the next few days, or a vision of Allie.

"Allie and I met in a college ethics class," Forrest broke the silence. "Our professor said there were consequences for all of our behaviors. He felt all ethical breeches had a price; the larger the breach, the greater the penalty. I wonder."

Forrest felt tired as they neared home. The wedding was tomorrow; then there was the board meeting and the announcement of his successor. He had to deal with Kim. He mulled over his choices.

Driving through the pine tunnel along with the quarter-mile-long cobblestone approach, his house came into view.

Monday, he was leaving—he hoped forever. He couldn't stick around for whatever happened. He knew it could be challenging for Chrissy, and he hadn't decided what to say to her. He had made a pact with Allie. Plans were set. There was no turning back. He already gifted the house to Chrissy and Tom. When they arrived and circled the fountain, sadness swept over him and a tear came to his eye. Staring up to the house, it was like saying goodbye to an old friend.

Another Friday night but not just another day to cross off the calendar of not too many more. Exhausted from years of hanging on and the stress of running a company, he had no heart to continue. He planned to eat and go to bed early.

When he entered the kitchen, he greeted Flo, "I'll eat in the dining room." Instantly he recognized his insolence, turned, and tenderly placed his hand on her shoulder. "If that's okay with you? If you prepared something?"

Florine smiled. "That'd be a first, don't you think?"

"Of course. Thank you."

After changing into more comfortable clothes, he made his way to the dining room. Flo had set the newspaper on the polished long walnut dining room table, beside a single place setting. There in front of him, a fully bloomed yellow rose in a walnut vase. He secretly wished Flo would stop. It reminded him too much of Allie. But at the same time, he appreciated her thoughtfulness. The newspaper headline screamed the world gone mad, another terrorist attack, this time closer to home in downtown Minneapolis.

Forrest was deep in thought when she served him a half Ahi Tuna sandwich on lightly toasted sourdough with a special caper sauce and a cup of clam chowder. She always seemed to know his mood, and tonight she served a light dinner. The French doors were open to the patio—not a hint of a breeze.

"Flo, I swear you must be a mind reader. You always seem to be one step ahead of me." Picking up the newspaper. "Do you remember the Y2K scare?

"Sure, I do. You told me there was nothing to worry about. And there wasn't. You said it was more an opportunity for hysterics and entrepreneurs, and there was always money to be made from a crisis."

"Yeah, then January 2, 2000, the whole memory of it began to disappear into the wind, just a footnote in history. Not even a story for Chrissy to tell her kids someday."

"Wonder what the survivalist did when they climbed out of their hole and found the earth still intact?"

"Started looking for another crisis, I'll bet." Holding out the morning edition of the Star Tribune, Forrest asked, "You see this article? A good summary of what happened. What the disruptions were. Seems like not much, except in the United Kingdom, over 150 pregnant women were given incorrect Down Syndrome risk assessments due to an age miscalculation. There were two abortions. Probably more stories like that."

Flo searched for something to say. She could tell Forrest had something to say.

Shaking his head, Forrest turned solemn and looked away. *How does it happen? Life is going along, and then just like what they said about computers, suddenly everything is screwed up, and everybody is doomed. It's like life is waiting for an accident. Then it's a matter of luck, whether it's fatal or whether life gets back on track?*

"Flo, I won't be back for a long time. You can live here as long as you wish. Monday, I have arranged for you to meet with Roy." Roy King was his attorney. "I have made some arrangements for you. I think you'll find everything to be most satisfactory."

Florine's smile disappeared as she dropped her head. "I know something is going on, but don't feel it is my place to ask questions."

Forrest reached for her hand. "Flo, you have a right to ask anything. You have been a part of my life for . . . for a long time. You know how I feel about you. You have been at my side through the worst times. But I know the questions, and I don't have any answers for you. It is just my time."

Flo pulled away, turned her head, and dabbed at her eyes. "Will there be anything else?" she asked.

Initially, Forrest hired her as a house manager, then his assistant and mother to Chrissy, then promoted to lifesaver. She was now in her sixties. They had grown old together, their hairs whitened, and skin wrinkled. He never asked her age, caring more about good health and her velvet touch.

Reaching out for her and drawing her back, he said. "There is one more thing. I've never told you. I love you."

Flo drew back. A tear broke loose and rolled down her cheek. "I know. You've been so good to me. These have been the happiest days of my life. Being here and being a mom to Chrissy makes me the luckiest woman alive. You rescued me."

Forrest squeezed her hand. "You rescued me. You're a special person." With a chuckle, he continued, "I'd say I was pretty lucky to have a wife like you."

"Funny kind of wife. I live in the back cottage, and this is the first time you held my hand."

"One-woman man, I guess."

"I love you too."

Forrest nibbled at his sandwich and didn't touch the soup before he pushed it away. The time had finally come. His time. In control again soon, Monday, a day he had patiently longed for—the end and the beginning.

A half-hour later, Flo returned and noticed he hadn't touched his dinner. Forrest was deep in thought as he looked out across the patio toward the setting sun darting in and out of the branches of a large stand of pine trees. "Is there anything wrong?"

Forrest looked up and by habit turned the badly scarred side of his away from her. A man of two faces. Behind the scars was the life story of the man Forrest Nelthorpe.

"No. No, everything is perfect. I wish I was hungry. It looks so good. I had a late lunch meeting and ate more than I intended," he lied. "Sorry. You can put this away, and maybe I'll eat it later."

"Forrest, do you want to go over the wedding arrangements?"

Are there any changes?

"No."

"Then, I am sure everything is ok."

**40**

Forrest went to bed early as planned, but a little after 10:00 pm, he put on his robe and went to the library to pour his first drink. Even on the hottest days, Minnesota nights cooled off. When he wandered into the library, he saw Flo had already stacked wood in the fireplace. He smiled as he struck a match to the wadded newspaper and watched as the flame ignited the kindling and licked at the sides of the logs. He held his hands out to warm them against the roaring fire. He would miss Flo. She was always taking care of him in surprising ways.

Warming himself in front of the fire, he scanned the perfectly organized bookshelves with hundreds of books, authors living their everlasting life in perpetual silence. A mere glimpse of any one of the books screamed, read me.  Flo's books. Every one of them standing tall and proud on the library shelves, shoulder to shoulder, authors from Hans Christian Anderson to Virginia Wolf, dusted and perfectly aligned—bards and word painters who strung words together in high order propositions that told stories of pain and sorrow, inspiring ones and entertaining ones, everyday men and women heroes and villains.

The birchwood fire crackled and popped and sent warm flickering shadows around the room as he slumped in his desk chair. In the dim light of the moose-antler desk lamp, he stared at the framed picture he held. Periodically he paused and listened to the warmth of the fire. The dancing lights cast by the fireplace accentuated the rippling scars on his face and made them appear to be plastic, one ear grotesquely disfigured, an eyebrow missing and covered over with scar tissue. He kept the picture stored in his desk drawer, and only occasionally did he pull it out. It always transported him back in time to a place of dreams and nightmares.

When he was in college, long before the cabin fire, people talked about him behind his back. He was going to be rich. Funny how often people can look back at their youth and predict friends who would succeed and the ones who might end up in jail. Maybe he would be president, some said. But for Forrest, the one thing for sure, he'd get the girl. The one in the picture. He did. It was destiny.

Not only the head of his company, its founder, but he had been the industry leader. Nelthorpe wasn't a household name but digging deep in his bio, he triggered billions of dollars of wealth worldwide. In his company, and among his circle of friends, he was true north, a man with the right answers, the first to see the bright side, quick with a joke, and the first to laugh—the company parking garage attendant must have thought they were best friends. He didn't have an enemy in the world, except one. For the longest time, he wondered how that happened and blamed himself.

The fire had diminished to glowing embers. When Chrissy was a teenager, she used to scold him for drinking in the library late at night, so he usually set the bottle of Old Forester on the floor in the desk kneehole at his feet, careful to keep it out of sight. Not tonight, the bottle sat half-empty in the middle of his desk.

During daylight hours, the library was a warm, friendly place, but at night the heavy air bore witness to anguished contemplations, under the watchful eyes of dead authors whose works were reverently bound inexpensive leather. Why was the sun always so hopeful and the nights so filled with gloom?

The man outside the library played the reluctant executive's role and still stood as tall and sturdy as the Minnesota pines lining the narrow roadway to his house. At night, though, Forrest, the lonely tormented man, tried to drown the silent ruminations of what-ifs and what nows with his favorite bourbon in his only safe place.

So much time had passed, months and years of going through the motions of living extra years—years of survival, years of why me? Now as the time approached, decisions made, he was more committed than ever. He wanted to be with his wife, Alexandra. He smiled. She didn't like to be called Alexandra.

The heavy commitment he made long ago brought him to the precipice. Could his spirit be whisked away, so he could once again hold Allie in his arms? He could feel her. She filled the air he breathed. He was awash in her. He could smell her perfume, feel her hand resting on his shoulder, see the in and out of her spirit breathe with the certainty every breath he inhaled contained atoms of her.

Forrest didn't hear footsteps clomping on the polished hallway pavers, handpicked from the streets of old Minneapolis, echoing off the high ceiling like horse hoofs. Like in an old Boris Karloff movie, the heavy wood door creaked open, flooding the library with the bright hallway light. Standing in the doorway, Christina's glowing image radiated into the room. He laid the framed picture on the desk face down.

Christina had been the perfect baby, the model adolescent, and now the grown woman, a painful spitting image of her mother, which at times made him smile or brought tears to his eyes. She was a five-foot-five, blue-eyed brunette with a magna cum laude intellect that towered over her colleagues. She graduated from the University of Minnesota and was a second-year law student.

As she approached, she saw a bottle of Old Forester bourbon sitting on his desk. She leaned in and kissed him. "Dad, you know how I hate you drinking down here alone so late."

"Just a nightcap."

"It's after one o'clock." Chrissy picked up the bottle and tilted it on its side to the light. "This is not a nightcap." After she set the bottle down, she picked up the picture and studied it. "I remember seeing this picture when I was a little girl. Was this before I was born? You guys were so young."

"Yes, a long time ago. Your mom's favorite picture, and mine." Forrest reached for the picture and paused. He laid the photo back on the desk face down, hoping to avoid further discussions.

Frowning, she asked, "Why aren't there more pictures of mom?"

"She was a young woman. There weren't many pictures."

"Was that our cabin?"

"Yes. We used to have a cabin on Ten Mile Lake."

Christina reacted in a gush of rapid-fire questions. "You never told me about it. What happened to it? Why don't we have it anymore?" Christina paused and sighed. "There is so much I don't know. Was I ever there?

"It wasn't important."

"So, was I ever there?"

"When you were a baby." Forrest turned away, slid the picture off the desk. The moose antler lamp cast angular shadows across the desk and onto the right side of his face. The bones in his face were sharper than she remembered. She recalled when she was young, and he would pick her up with one arm and toss her over his shoulder like a sack of feathers. But even then, she wondered what he thought when he looked away or when the glint in his eyes turned serious. She sometimes thought he was disappointed with her, but she never said anything. She never saw the sadness as a chink in his armor, though. She wouldn't allow it. He was the ledge she stood on.

When she asked her grandmother if he was sad, she always answered, "When you are older, your questions will get answers." Then as an afterthought, she added, "But the answers won't always be what you want, and you'll have more questions. Yes, he does have some sadness. When you're older, you'll understand." She was older now, and she still didn't understand.

"What was Mom like?" Chrissy wondered aloud.

In the dim light, she didn't notice her dad's eyes were moist, fighting back the tears. "Look in the mirror. You could have been twins. You know she had green eyes, with a glint of gold. Like you. I still have never seen anyone with eyes that color." Forrest's voice was soft, almost a whisper. Gathering himself, he cleared his throat. "All your life I've seen her in everything you do, the way you wear your hair, the way you put it up in pigtails, the way you walk, talk, the way you look off to the side and cock your head when you don't understand, the way you love with your eyes, your knack of peering into a person's soul. That was your mom. I've lived remembering and seeing your mom in you ever since you were a small child and every day since."

"How old was she when she . . . ?"

"Too young."

"When I was young, I thought she died of cancer, but some kids in school said it was a car accident, some said a fire. When I asked Flo, she always said talk to you. When we talked, everything was vague, or you didn't want to talk. Why did it take so long to tell me she died in a fire."

"Dying in a fire is such a horrible thing. . ." Forrest looked over to a large antique grandfather clock. It was almost 2:00 am. "And, all your questions. That too. That was your mom. It's late. You have a big day tomorrow."

Holding out her ring finger, "I'm getting married tomorrow. Can you believe it?"

Forrest rose, held his arms out, and pulled her to him. "Oh Chrissy, I'm so happy for you. You couldn't have done better. I like Thomas." Holding her at arm's length, "I set up a trust for you as a wedding present, and you know we have already discussed you now own this house."

Forrest anticipated a reaction and placed his finger to his lips. "No more discussion. It's a financial move, and I don't need a place like this. In the next couple of weeks, Roy will contact you and go over the details."

Alarmed, Christina pulled back and looked up to him. "Dad, I don't understand what's going on."

Forrest shook his head and waved his hand dismissively. "Who could understand retirement. It's time to retire and change my life. Time for a change in the company, too."

"So, tell me more about mom," Chrissy asked.

Forrest turned and tried to maneuver by Chrissy toward the door. "Not tonight." Looking to her he eased by, "So how's our Mr. Bradley holding up?"

Chrissy moved to block his path, cocking her head to the side, her gaze pleading for answers. "So, there you go again. You're avoiding me."

"Not tonight. It's too late." Forrest stopped and turned off the desk lamp. The hallway light lit a path out of the library. "We'll talk in the morning."

Easing by her, he walked toward the door. Chrissy stood her ground. "It drives me crazy when you won't talk to me. I'm getting married, and you're leaving your company and running off to Australia, or God knows where, for God knows what reason, and for how long. You won't talk about it either. You're so mysterious." Angrily, as he exited, she added. "This is so maddening."

Forrest turned and looked back. "Chrissy, I'm sorry. Yes, some things are hard for me to talk about. I hope you will understand someday. But not tonight. It's too late to start." He turned and disappeared into the bright hall lights, leaving her standing in the dark library.

# 41

St. John's Cathedral was built in 1907 in downtown Minneapolis with donations of old mining and timber money. A full football field long and nearly as tall, its granite walls rose nearly one-hundred feet, where they adjoined a classical Baroque gold-leafed domed roof reaching up fifty feet. At its peak, a bronze cross pointed toward the heavens another fifty feet.

When Forrest arrived with Florine and Luka, the church pews were full, awaiting their arrival. Luka had taken a circuitous route that turned out to be blocked by two cars along the side of the road and a life flight helicopter evacuated one of the crash victims. By the time they arrived at the scene, people were standing around two crunched cars no all that damaged except an airbag had discharged in one of them.

In the pews, curious faces turned, wondering, and waiting for the ceremony to begin. When Forrest saw Chrissy standing with her bridesmaids in an alcove, they exchanged smiles and shrugs. The priest saw him and smiles all around sent him scurrying to the front of the church, and with a nod, a hundred organ pipes trumpet arms filled the nave with the sound of Wagner's "Bridal Chorus" from his Lohengrin opera. Warm smiles and full hearts looked on anxiously for the bride to walk down the aisle.

Standing before the altar was the groom, Thomas Bradley, stoned faced and stoic—all slender six foot five inches of him, his dark, thick wavy hair parted and combed to the side. His gaze focused on Christina and Forrest. Beside him stood his best man and three others all dressed in black tuxedos.

Thomas was destined for success. If they had been further along in their careers, they would have called the marriage a merger—she the brilliant law student specializing in financial law and he the investment banker, five years older than Christina and already setting a new pace for the seasoned veterans of his investment banking firm. Chrissy's undergraduate degree was in finance, and she minored in literature.

When Forrest and Christina arrived at the foot of the two steps leading to the sanctuary, they paused. She wore a snow-white jeweled strapless princess gown with a cathedral train. Her maid-of-honor stretched her train back, fluffed the edges, and stood by.

Forrest, his white hair brushed stiffly back in a crew cut, wore a single-breasted black tuxedo with black silk lapels and a black waistcoat. Forrest and Christina faced each other. Holding her hands in his, he beamed, raised his eyebrows, and leaned in, "The road leads here." Turning away, she followed his gaze to a smiling Thomas Bradley. "I certainly approve. He's a good man."

Thomas smiled lovingly at his about-to-be wife. He and Forrest had hit it off from the first moment she brought him home. He never told Christina he had Luka check him out, wanting to be sure

Thomas was a good match for her. Fathers worry about who their daughters marry, especially when they are about to receive a generous financial gift at such a young age.

Standing on the sanctuary steps, the bright daylight streaming through six, twenty-foot-high, arched stained-glass windows accentuated the glistening scars on his face. Throughout the nave and sanctuary, hundreds of depictions of angels appeared. Gazing back to Forrest, Chrissy's radiant smile turned serious.

Reaching up, she laid her hand on the side of his face. The shiny red scars covering the side of his face glowed in the bright sunlit nave. She couldn't stop herself. In a hushed tone, "I know something is going on. Does it have anything to do with mom?"

The music ended, and the nave went tomb silent. Surrounded by angels depicted in glass, marble, steel, bronze, plaster, and wood and the marble statues of the apostles witnessed their quiet exchange.

Forrest looked away, then smiled at her. "You are relentless." Taking her hand in his to comfort her. "Chrissy, this is your day. We'll find time to talk."

"Dad, let me in, please. I want to know what's going on."

Peeking back to a church full of witnesses, then back to Chrissy, he pressed his lips together to stifle a smile, "That's a bit longer conversation, don't you think?"

Squeezing his hand, she leaned in and kissed him. As she turned back to Thomas, she said, "Let's find time soon."

Behind them, a few coughs and anxious shuffling of friends and family broke the silence. Forrest held on to her hand, gazed deeply into her eyes, and smiled. "We'll find the time. I'll tell you one thing; she'd be proud of you."

She turned and proceeded up the two stairs to the sanctuary where her about-to-be husband awaited. Thomas Bradley's pinched face fought back emotions when she turned to him and they made eye contact.

The ceremony lasted fifty minutes. A Holy Communion service followed the exchange of vows, an option Forrest requested. On bent knees in this most magnificent house of God, Forrest prayed for forgiveness and made his peace.

# 42

The wedding reception was held at Forrest's home on Lake Minnetonka. Exercising home privilege, Forrest changed into comfortable slacks and a short-sleeve silk shirt, then followed the music and murmur of conversations to the back patio. Men dressed in suits, women in formal dresses, bridesmaids and groomsmen milled around the sculpted swimming pool. Black coated waitstaff weaved their way through the guests balancing Champagne and hors d'oeuvres on their sterling silver trays. The bride and groom had not yet entered.

Forrest spied a group of his business associates milling around a river-stone fireplace sitting area at the far end of the pool. Making his way along the mortar cut stone patio, he stopped and shook a few hands, offered a few polite shoulder hugs, and nodded to others.

Fit for a man his age, by appearance anyway, he was capable of taking on the workload of men much younger, not of a man about to retire. When he arrived, he greeted his associates with firm handshakes and congratulations. Woody embraced him warmly.

Linda Gardner breezed by; her swishing long full skirt caught the attention of Forrest and his colleagues. She paused momentarily to congratulate Forrest. "It's been such a pleasure to work for you. You're a good man Charlie Brown." She always said she never married because she couldn't find a man like Forrest.

Forrest's current status with the company and plans were uppermost in the minds of his circle of colleagues. John Bolten, his fine blond hair was neatly parted to the side, congratulated him next. A long-time board member, his polished fair skin seemed never to need a shave.. "Another acquisition. You should be proud. The votes are all there." Niche had acquired another company in Phoenix.

"Woody gets the credit for that one. He did all the work."

Charles Gunn, the imposing, red-bearded, gentle giant, added, "It's a perfect fit."

"Thanks," Forrest responded warmly. "It's good for both companies. Good for employees and how novel, good for customers." Looking up to him, he gripped his arm. "I'll never forget you stepping in for me. You did a great job."

Charles looked away sheepishly. "I'm glad nothing serious came up and," pausing to add emphasis, "I didn't screw things up too badly. I've enjoyed working with you all these years. You know both boards want you to stay on and meld the two companies."

"I've made myself clear." With a side glance to Woody, he added, "And, my successor will be announced Monday, when the board meets."

Woody had been with the company for over twenty years and was a big part of its success. As he worked through his life tragedy, Forrest promoted him to Atlanta against his wishes, and for a long time their relationship devolved to business only. His freckled face and red hair still gave him a youthful appearance. He smiled and placed his hand on Forrest's shoulder. "You know they'll sweeten the pot."

"What I get out of this deal is a matter of public record. It's more than I deserve. So, they want to offer me more? For what? I've done enough. Besides, there's nothing left in the tank."

John jumped in. "But, Forrest, you know . . . ."

Interrupting him with a firm wave of his hand, he said, "No. It's a final no. Not a politician's no. Don't bring it up again."

Forrest turned and saw Chrissy dancing with her new husband. John and Charles walked away, and Woody stayed behind. "So, you're walking away from it all," Woody said. "You're still a young man."

"Woody, don't BS me. I'm definitely at retirement age. Okay, a bit earlier than some, but damned glad to be doing what I've wanted for a long time."

Raising his eyebrows, Woody nodded. "A well-kept secret, I might add." Sighing, "You know I was pretty mad at you when . . . you know . . . but, maybe it was best. No, it was best. I was a wreck."

"That was a rough time. I understand how you felt," Forrest said.

"Rough time, but no excuse to be upset with you."

Forrest and Woody watched as more guests joined Chrissy and her new husband. "It's time for me to move on and for you to move up." Forrest smiled.

"I see Kim didn't show up."

"She wasn't invited."

Woody jerked his head away from the dancers. For a minute, their eyes locked. "Is she going to be a problem?"

Across the room, Woody's new wife waved and began to make her way toward them. "I sure like Toni," Forrest said.

"I'm lucky to have found her." They both watched her cut in and out of the guests, stopping once to say hello. "I'm surprised you never found anyone," Woody said.

Guests gathered around Christina and Thomas, cheering loudly as the song ended; he dipped her low and kissed her.

"There's no other. No more Allies. Just the one." Pausing, Forrest looked skyward. "No one. I've missed her every day since . . . every day."

Woody's wife, Toni, an Italian blond many years younger, with sandalwood bushy eyebrows and a toothy smile, joined them. She reached out and hugged Forrest.

When he broke free, out of the corner of his eye, Forrest saw Arthur weaving his way toward them. When he joined them, before even looking at Forrest, he reached his hand out to Woody. "Bet you are glad to be back in the mini apple." Gripping his hand warmly, he added, "I'll be seeing you Monday. Big day."

Tugging at Woody's shirt sleeve, Toni pulled him toward the dancers. "They're playing our song."

Looking back as he pulled away, he grinned and replied. "Big day for sure. I'll leave you two to talk business."

Forrest and Arthur watched Woody and Toni dance their way toward the music and the other dancers. "He's a good one," Arthur said.

"It's good to see him happy again. I understand Toni's a top-notch IT person."

As they watched Woody and Toni dance, they saw Isabella standing at the edge of the dance floor with her husband, the police commander. Arthur nudged Forrest to get his attention. "They don't get any better than that."

"Both of 'em. None better. Toni could have advanced in the company, but she always liked what she was doing. I understand she's going to work for your company. Thanks. Hope it works out, for both of you."

"I know it will." Arthur reached out for Forrest's hand and gripped it warmly. "So, you're really leaving the company." Pulling at his straggly gray beard thoughtfully, he added, "Time flies huh? Sure glad you came back. You did a hell of a job."

"Thanks for all your years on the board." Forrest swallowed hard. "Now that Chrissy is married, it's time to move on. I've been waiting for the moment."

"You've been as good a father as a CEO. I have never seen anyone so dedicated to a daughter. Are you sure you don't want to be at the board meeting? A lot of board members would like to wish you well."

"Nah. I've said my goodbyes."

"Can't imagine you'd miss the big show."

"It's enough to know it will happen."

"It's all set. Everyone on the board is with us. I have set up a meeting with the two board members. I think they are nervous. The votes are cast, and I've briefed each member personally." Raising his eyebrows. "A couple of board members had some . . . shall we say conflicts of interest? By board time, that'll be fixed."

The music stopped, and the DJ announced, "So the next song is for the father and bride. Let's see if we can locate a father for this beautiful bride."

Standing in the middle of the dance area Chrissy surveyed the room. Spying her father, she waved for him to join her. Forrest smiled, looked back to Arthur, and walked toward her. The Lee Ann Womack song, "I Hope You Dance," began to play as they met. Nestled in the crook between his head and shoulder, they swayed back and forth.

"Honeymoon in Paris. That husband of yours is quite the romantic. You're leaving next weekend?" Forrest said.

"He surprised me. It was a last-minute thing. He's waiting for his passport." Across from the swimming pool, a cobblestone footpath led to Flo's private quarters. Along the footpath was a line of Golden Wisteria trees. They were in full bloom, the branches filled with dangling racemes of yellow chrome flowers. "I don't ever remember those trees blooming. Not like this. Everybody is commenting on them."

"We imported them from China. Your mother's idea. It is said Golden Wisteria trees only bloom where there is love. They haven't bloomed for a long time." Forrest swallowed his words and continued swaying to the music. Other dancers joined them as the music played, and the message of the song sweetened the moment.

She pushed back and gazed deeply into his eyes, tears streaming down her cheeks. In a rush, she pleaded. "There is never a good time. Here we are, and once again, it's not the time to talk. Why won't you talk to me? Why Australia? I don't even know how long you'll be gone. Tell me what's going on. I don't want to lose you. It's like you're going to the outback to live. Alone. You're always alone."

Forrest couldn't resist smiling at the barrage of questions. It was so Chrissy. So, Allie.

Pulling her close. "Australia. I needed a place as far from here as I could find where there are no distractions. I want to be alone now. You are all grown up." Pushing her back gently. "Look at you. I am so proud. Your whole life in front of you. Oh, Chrissy, what can I say. What can I tell you? I have to leave. It's my time. Well deserved, don't you think?"

"I'm so worried about you. This is all about Mom, isn't it? I don't understand, but I feel it."

"She was special, your mom. Brains and beauty, she could tell a joke as well as anyone and beat me like a drum in golf. But put her in an evening gown, and she turned every man's head, and envious ladies too." For several moments they listened to the music and smiled at the other dancers. "Here's something you don't know about your mom. She had two toes that crossed. Like crossing your fingers."

"Like mine do?"

"Yeah, just like that. Another reminder. Whenever we were by the pool or on the beach, whenever I would catch your cousins looking at them, I'd tell them that's how you spot an earth angel. You know I think it's true."

Chrissy smiled but didn't respond. As they continued dancing, her still moist eyes sought an elusive truth, not about her mom but the story about the scars on his face. "Tell me what happened. I always felt there was more. I deserve to know."

Sighing deeply, he said, "At your wedding? Is this the time to talk? Here on the dance floor?"

So many times, Forrest prepared to discuss everything with her. The thought of talking about his past life and his plans were horrifying, and he was never sure what to say. What happened, and what he was going to do. Should he tell her everything, or just what he wanted, like before—to protect her, to protect him.

He didn't want to have secrets from her, but every time he got close to telling her, he couldn't do it. *She knew I was in a fire; the side of my face told the story. Her mom was in the fire. A man was in prison. No doubt, she sensed I didn't think the man in prison was guilty. There was so much she didn't understand. I need to tell her everything. She deserves to know.* Just going over what to say in his mind made him instantly tired, in want of a drink. It was so easy to put it off. He would talk to her someday.

"Honey, tragedy appears when we least expect it. But it happens. It can happen to anyone. Leaves scars, not only these." He raised his hand to his scarred face. "All scars can take time to heal. Sometimes, scars like this don't heal. In the interim, we make choices to go on with life, or stop living."

"I always wondered what choices you faced, what choices you made? What happened? I've never seen you with another woman. Didn't you ever want to be with anyone else?"

Looking skyward, smiling. "There are no other women like your mom. She was the only one."

"I always wanted you to marry Flo."

They danced as Forrest fought back tears gazing into Chrissy's green eyes, like her mothers, the rarest of eye colors, two unique women. He pulled at the practiced lines he so badly wanted to share, but in the end, he carefully selected his words from the unspoken truth hovering around them.

Suddenly, the moment was shattered. Over her shoulder, he saw Luka leaning against the brass railing leading up the cobblestone steps to the library. Luka nodded. His black wavy hair was untouched by the gray that was infecting other men his age.

Christina turned to see what her father was looking at. "He's so mysterious. Don't get me wrong, I love him. But he's so mysterious."

"He is. Prison does that to a man. He's a man of secrets, but I trust him with my life.

"A house of secrets," Christina said sarcastically.

When the song ended, they separated, and the DJ reintroduced Thomas Bradley, who offered several toasts to his new bride, his parents, bridesmaids, and groomsmen. He told a story about his best man, which sparked some heckling. He finished by asking Chrissy if she wanted to say a few words.

Christina joined Thomas in front of a semicircle of well-wishers. Pointing to the heavens, she tearfully related how much she wished her mom was there and how Florine was the closest thing to a mom any girl could ask for. "Flo . . . where are you?" Searching the faces, finally, she spied her standing in the back with her head down, trying to avoid recognition. "I know you weren't my biological mom, but you were my mom in every other sense. I love you with all my heart."

Looking back to the semicircle of well-wishers, "Dad says I look like my mom." Pointing back to the heavens, "I know she's here watching over me. She is up there smiling at what a good catch Thomas is." She leaned over and put her arms around him. "And, my father raised me and gave me every ounce of his love. Dad, thank you. I love you. Dad . . . ?"

Gazing out over the tops of heads, she searched for her father. At last, she saw Forrest in the distance, opening the library door for Luka.

Unaware Chrissy was pouring her heart out, he looked back to the guests and over the top of their heads to a panoramic view of the lake.

# 43

The wedding magnificent, the reception a joyous occasion—there were congratulations around, and everybody was complimentary of his mansion and the fully bloomed Golden Wisteria trees.

When Forrest and Luka arrived in the library, away from the din of the music, the dancing, and the laughter, Luka pulled out an iPad and searched for something. "Kim owns a farm," he said.

It was an odd sight, seeing him holding such a sophisticated piece of technology. Forrest nodded to the iPad and said, "I never thought I'd see that."

Luka responded, serious, unclear about the gist of his comment. "It's my daughter's. She showed me how to use it." He fumbled to find what he was looking for. "I went there. It's in Monticello, an hour north of here, halfway to St. Cloud. It isn't being farmed. It's registered under the name Merle Simpson. Remember, Barnaby said he was her foster dad. The one in the mental hospital. I talked to Barnaby about this, and it turns out he was her birth father. Well, he is still in a mental institute. Hard to believe he is still alive."

"She probably drove him crazy."

"It's quite a spread. Out in the middle of nowhere, surrounded by trees and fallow fields. The nearest neighbor is a mile away as the crow flies but over two by washboard back roads. A John Deer tractor beside the barn had weeds growing up to the steering wheel. The empty eight stall barn is so clean you could live there. I didn't go inside the main house, but it is for a gentleman farmer if this is a farmhouse. There was an empty swimming pool in the back. Look what I found in the barn." He held the iPad out so Forrest could see it.

The picture of the inside of the barn showed an open beamed ceiling with plaster walls and polished hardwood floor, a full open kitchen, a bedroom, and bathroom, all decorated in a cowboy theme—straw stacked halfway to the ceiling on one side.

Forrest shrugged as he studied the picture. At first, Forrest couldn't make out what he was trying to show him.

Luka took the iPad back and slid a different picture into place.

Shocked, he looked up to Luka. "This the SUV?"

Luka nodded.

"This is it, right?"

Luka had unstacked several bales of hay and pulled the tarp back, revealing the front end of a white Suburban."

Forrest's mouth dropped open. Outside he could hear the guests singing along to the Kenny Chesney song, "How Forever Feels."

"There's more. At the far end of the barn was a locked cabinet, which I was able to jimmy. I have a picture of what I found there." The next photo showed a medicine bottle sitting on the countertop. "You know what's in the bottle? Chloral hydrate. In the day, they called it a Mickey Finn. It's been around forever. Today they call it a roofie. I'll bet she slipped it in your drink and helped you to her room."

Forrest was stunned into silence. "It must have been before that last drink. I left to use the restroom."

"There's no way you cheated on Allie. She drugged you then snapped a few pictures and waited until morning. No doubt she did the same thing to that CEO guy; what's his name? The eerie part of this is she had a scrapbook of you—pictures, newspaper clippings, company announcements, memorabilia from college, even your wedding announcement, the birth of Chrissy."

Dumbfounded, Forrest moved to the leather chair and sat down in a huff. "It's still so hard to believe. It's so hard to see Kim doing all this. Is this enough?"

"You bet. There were even gas cans. It was safer to hide all this then dispose of it. She figured selling the Suburban was risky."

"We should share all this with Barnaby."

Luka sat opposite him in the leather chair. "I did. He was with me."

Forrest rubbed the side of his face and looked away in silence. "I'm not so sure. Gas cans—it's a farm. We can't be a hundred percent sure this is the SUV yet. And the SUV is not connected to the fire." Shaking his head, "And they already convicted someone. Barnaby said its tough to get anyone to listen."

The music stopped outside. Forrest starred at Luka, hoping for some clarity.

"I'll bet they can match the tire prints to the turnout, too," Luka said. "She's what your friend described. And Barnaby too."

"Yeah. Maybe. It'll be complicated and uncomfortable. Kim will get a top attorney. Wade was easy to convict . . . she'll make it messy."

"Barnaby said that too. He's waiting to hear."

"Not yet. We've talked about how complicated this is. We know how the law works."

Luka shook his head. "I hate to think about how this could turn out, how unfair that would be."

"What the hell can we do? Doing nothing is not an option. God-damn, the attorneys. They'll find a way to get her off, and things will be said. And Chrissy . . . ."

Luka forced a weak smile and offered hesitantly, "You know I've told you I have friends." Then with a wave of his hand and shake of his head, he awkwardly tried to downplay his remark.

When Forrest first heard Luka say it, he couldn't fully grasp what he was hearing. There it was again. He had thought about it since then. "You would do that?"

Luka couldn't tell if Forrest was asking a question or making a comment. "You know I would."

Forrest's flinched and looked away. Looking back to him, he squinted, "I know you would." His expression became serious as he admonished him. "This is my problem. I'll deal with it."

"This is my problem, too."

**44**

Usually, the board met the first Wednesday of every month, but Forrest insisted they meet early Monday morning. Sunday afternoon, he called Arthur to confirm he wouldn't attend and discussed what had to happen. Arthur was still disappointed but understood.

Monday morning, Luka picked Forrest up early. He helped load his single suitcase into the car, and Forrest instructed him to take him to Arthur's office. After reviewed the plan they met with Chris Harrison and James Abbott, two board members, one at a time for fifteen minutes. At a minimum, they had a conflict of interest. Barnaby had produced a slew of evidence but nothing to justify anything more than dismissal from the board. The other option required them to recuse themselves from voting on the next CEO, but Arthur insisted they leave the board in deference to the new CEO.

When they met, Arthur offered to call it a resignation but warned them there would be severe ramifications if the circumstances weren't kept confidential. They were professional men, with their status to protect, so there would be no community discussions. Forrest remained mostly silent, and Arthur did most of the talking, but he added at the end of each meeting, "I know you are both happily married, and you may not appreciate my words but count yourself lucky." Neither of them resisted, and both nodded their agreement.

Arthur planned to call the special board meeting to order at 7:30 am, a little behind schedule. Since Forrest elected not to attend the board meeting, they said their goodbyes in the parking lot, which delayed Arthur's arrival. He hastily proceeded to Kim's office. She was there waiting, hoping for positive news on the upcoming meeting. When he entered her office, he shut the door. Alarmed, she bolted from her chair and moved beside her desk. "What is this?"

"Kim, perhaps you know the board has selected Woody to be our next CEO."

Kim stiffened. "No, I didn't know. Who was supposed to tell me?"

Arthur ignored her question. "The board felt he was the most qualified."

"Most qualified. This is a sham, and you know it. I met with the board and each member individually. You know this position is mine. You all know what I've done for the company. Where is Forrest? I want to talk to him?"

"Forrest is not here. He elected not to attend today."

Kim's face turned beet red. Holding her breath and reaching up, she began to twirl long blond strands of hair. "That coward. We'll see about that. I'll address the board."

Arthur held his ground. "I'm sorry, that will not be possible."

"We'll see about that. You know this was a setup. That's why Forrest isn't here. He's too chicken to face me. He set the whole thing up. Oh, I'll address the board. You'll see. You can't keep me from doing that. They'll be glad I did. It will save them a lawsuit worth millions. The board will love to hear what Forrest has been up to."

"You do what you need to do. But right now, you need to leave."

"Leave? I work here. I don't have to leave."

Arthur took a step back toward the door. Forrest had told him she had a vicious side.

With one hand on the door handle, he told her, "Yes, you have to leave. You don't work here anymore. You need to leave immediately." He opened the door and called out, "Bill, please escort Kim from the premises. We will deliver all of your personal effects to your condominium, or . . . wherever you wish. Your farm? Let us know."

"Farm?" Stunned, Kim said softly, loud enough to be heard but not expecting an answer.

Turning back to the security guard, "Bill, escort her out of the building and off the premises. I want this to happen quickly." Looking down at his watch, "I'm late to the board meeting."

As Kim was escorted off the premises, she turned to Arthur, "I'll be back. Soon. This is the worst decision you ever made. If you talk to Forrest, tell him he's a dead man."

When Arthur arrived at the board room, the members were seated and drinking coffee, chatting amongst themselves, awaiting his arrival. Executives of the company and invited staff sat in chairs at the end of the room.

Arthur called the meeting to order, noted the minutes, attendance, and then informed the board Chris Harrison and James Abbott had resigned from their positions for personal reasons. "I know you will join me in wishing them the best. I will appoint a committee to begin searching for their replacements." Minutes of the previous meeting were approved without discussion. The next order of business approved a motion waiving the board notice requirement. There were a few housekeeping announcements, including the obvious one and approval of the last meeting minutes.

Arthur reported Forrest was unable to attend. He proceeded to read a letter from him. The meeting room went church quiet. Forrest thanked the board members and acknowledged their role in making Niche so successful. He regretted not being at the meeting, his last, but he had met with each of them personally in the past few weeks, and they knew how much he appreciated their service and friendship. "It meant the world to me. I will always think of each of you whenever I think about Niche."

After reading the letter, Arthur added his reflections about Forrest, his unique leadership qualities, his vision in founding the company, his high esteem nationally, and his well-known contributions to the community. "He became a friend to many of us, and I will miss him, and I know you will as well. Forrest, old buddy, he did a great job, and I wish him the best. I tried again to talk him into staying on a bit longer. He's too young to hang it up. Sadly, we have to honor his wishes." Looking skyward and stretching his hands out. "He wouldn't tell me what he was up to." With a chuckle, he added, "I think he thought I would pursue him where ever he was.

"Before I ask our next CEO to assume his new position and say a few words, I have one other bit of business. As of today, Kim Merrymore is no longer employed here. You all know she was one of the candidates interviewed, and she was qualified. However, with Woody's selection, her disappointment, and my desire to put everything in order for the next CEO, it was best she leave. I would be happy to answer any questions after the meeting."

Arthur surveyed the room and observed tacit agreement of each member. He continued, "Now is the time to turn the page. I want to thank each of you for your cooperation in the special approval process. I have no doubts about the quality of your choice. I am also pleased the board has selected one of our own. Just as one era ends, I expect with our choice of the next CEO, we will be entering a new one, one filled with as much promise and even more success. Woody, please join me." When he arrived and shook hands, the company communication director snapped a few pictures.

***

The trip to the airport took a little over an hour. Forrest usually sat in the front seat, but he sat in the back this morning, staring out the window. No words were exchanged for the first half-hour. Luka's dark, brooding eyes kept glancing back in the rearview mirror, as if he had something to say. Forrest looked away, not wanting to invite conversation.

Halfway to the airport, Forrest was ready to talk. He explained what happened at the board meeting and Kim's firing. "Arthur called me right before the board meeting. She was upset and stormed out of the office. You said Barnaby has the police waiting for her at the farm."

Luka had a concerned look on his face. "They won't find the pictures there. Trust me, the police will get all the evidence, and Wade will be cleared."

Both men had used the silence to contemplate what had happened leading to this moment, the horrors, the recovery, his early retirement, this planned trip, what Luka just said—the police were going to be there. Each man processed the most recent events, their conversations, turned them over in their minds, seeking the best way to think about it, the right things to say, not wanting any misunderstandings at this critical time.

Their gazes connected; neither one blinked, neither wanted to look away. Forrest wasn't sure what to say or whether to say anything. He took a deep breath and looked away. "I had given up for sure," Forrest's voice cracked. "But time always plays a role in how things turn out, huh?"

"You have to believe this time it'll all work out. True justice," Luka affirmed.

Shaking his head, confidently, "I do. Like my college professor said, actions have consequences, measure for measure."

The car grew quiet as they neared the airport exit. "How do people become monsters like that?" Forrest asked. The traffic whizzed by as the car eased over to the exit lane.

When they arrived at the airport, they stopped beneath the skywalk between the parking garage and the terminal. They exited the car at the same time and met at the trunk. Luka retrieved his suitcase and set it on the curb. The sun darted in and out of racing cumulous clouds. Wind gusts shook the car. "Traveling light for such a long trip. Looks more like a guy who isn't coming back," he chortled.

Looking skyward, he responded solemnly, "That'd be okay. I need a change of scenery. Give my best to Maria."

Luka reached out and pulled Forrest close. "What you've done for my family and me, I'll never forget. You know I'll look out for Chrissy too, but she's in a good place." Speaking softly, "It's over. I . . . ."

Forrest slid back and raised his hand to interrupt him. "I have faith in what happens . . . true justice, right? Luka, you've done more for me than I ever did for you, more than any man could ask." Shaking his head, Forrest added, "You never asked for anything."

Luka responded. "No matter, I'll never forget you. I'm a free man, thanks to you. You learn a lot about yourself when it's real life and not just talk."

"Goodbye, my friend."

# 45

Standing in the Quantas ticket line, anxious travelers all around him shifted from foot to foot, looking at their tickets, their watches, the ticket agents, bags, and the people around them. Forrest stood patiently, stiffly, in a daze.

When it was his turn, a smiling middle-aged, dark-haired female ticket agent greeted him. "Good morning. Where are you going to-day?"

"Heaven I hope," Forrest joked half-heartedly, shaken by his last conversation, imagining the end, hoping to appear normal. "But if not today, Sydney, it is, and heaven can wait."

The ticket agent's name tag read, Naomi. Without looking up, she asked for his name as she typed it into her computer. Quickly, she glanced at his passport, handed it back to him, and asked if he had bags to check. Forrest indicated he only had a carry-on suitcase and preferred a window seat. "If you don't assign the seat next to me, that would be great."

"I think I can do that." A few more keystrokes and the printer spit out his ticket.

Handing him his ticket, she said, "Have a nice flight."

Soon after Forrest arrived at his gate and took a seat, an army soldier dropped his duffle bag and took a seat nearby. At the end of the row, a short, slight man held on to a young boy's collar while he scolded another. Behind him a woman, as much girth as height, ate out of a bag of potato chips. They were an unlikely couple, he thought.

In the adjacent row, an old man and woman were holding hands. His gaze stopped there for a minute. She leaned in and kissed him for no apparent reason. They looked over to Forrest and exchanged smiles. As his gaze wandered around the room, he noticed a young mother with a small girl, maybe ten years old. Both were wearing their hair in a ponytail, tied with a yellow ribbon.

Forrest eased his head back and closed his eyes.

*What happened? One-minute I was pinching myself for reality— married to the woman of my dreams, my company a huge success, our private piece of heaven on Ten Mile Lake where we produced a life after doctors said we couldn't. We had a beautiful home on Lake Minnetonka. How futile it was to try to figure out why things happen. Maybe life just happens, and we make the best of it. Or perhaps life is held together by invisible bands, pull too far, or in the wrong direction, and the bands stretch and break and add predictability of all-seeing consequences.*

*Now it ends and begins. I am alone, off on my journey*

A woman's voice announced on the overhead speakers, "Quantas Airlines flight 1087 to Sydney, Australia, is now ready for boarding. We invite all first-class passengers to board at this time."

In camos and tan desert boots, the army soldier had stretched his legs out over his duffle bag. His hands were folded in his lap, a peaceful smile on his face. The two boys were now sitting between their parents playing games on their Gameboys.

Glassy eyed, Forrest stared in the direction of the mother and her daughter, but at nothing. In a daydream, he pictured Allie in Professor Smithson's class, smiling up to him—a moment embedded in his memory, one that would follow him to his grave.

The repeat announcement for first-class passengers brought him to his senses. The young girl smiled at him as her mother retied her ponytail with the yellow ribbon. He returned her smile then looked up to her mother, who was smiling at him as well.

The first-class cabin was half full. The ticket agent had honored his request for a window seat and to leave the seat next to him vacant. Once situated, a flight attendant leaned in, and looking at a piece of paper, said, "Mr. Nelthorpe, would you like a glass of wine?"

"Yes, I'd like that." Smiling, "Anything dark red."

"May I get you a pillow or a blanket?"

"Thank you. That would be nice."

She quickly returned with a glass of wine, a pillow, and a blanket, as passengers squeezed by. The young mother and daughter he had seen in the boarding area sat across the aisle from him. Brushing the hair of her doll, watching Forrest, the little girl asked, "Are you famous?"

Smiling, Forrest answered. "No, I'm not famous. Are you?"

"My daddy is famous."

"How nice. I'll bet that makes you famous then?"

"Oh, no. He's a pilot."

"Is he flying this plane?"

"Oh no, he's at home. We are going to visit my relatives."

Her mother looked up from her magazine to Forrest. "Now, honey, let's not bother this nice man."

"It's no bother. Really." Forrest couldn't take his eyes off of the yellow ribbon in her ponytail. "She reminds me of my daughter, but she's all grown up. She likes to wear her hair in a ponytail, too."

Flipping her head around, the little girl's mother showed off her ponytail, also tied with a yellow ribbon. "Allie wanted me to wear her hair like hers."

Forrest steadied his gaze on the little girl. His expression turned serious. "Is your name Allie?"

"Why yes, my name is Allie. What is your name? Mine is Alexia. My grandmother's name is Alexia. Mom and dad call me Allie."

A television screen popped out from the bulkhead, and heads turned in unison to watch and listen to a blond-haired woman provide flight instructions. Forrest turned away, finished his wine, set the empty glass on the seat next to him, laid his head back, and closed his eyes. He smiled like a new sunrise had washed away the nightmares, and all his life burdens lifted—only blue skies ahead.

Seconds later, he glanced over to the little girl who was staring up to the screen open-mouthed. *Allie? Her name was Allie. Like my Allie.* Leaning his head back and closing his eyes, soon, the sound of the flight attendant's voice drifted away.

They pushed back from the gate. The engine idled as it inched its way toward the takeoff position, stopped, then the roar of a million silent explosions catapulted them down the runway and pushed Forrest back against his seat. The rolling runway caused the wings to flap like a bird taking flight.

Reverent, serious faces filled the cabin hoping the plane was up to the challenge and once again would break its bond with the earth. The concrete runway released them with a groan. The gray quickly changed to rich patches of crinkly green, buildings became boxes, and cars crawled along the concrete compass like bugs.

*The little girl's name was Allie, just like my Allie. And she was wearing a ponytail tied up with a yellow ribbon. Just like Allie. How did a New York girl end up in Iowa and fall for a hockey-puck-Minnesota guy? I knew the minute I saw her in ethics class she was the one for me. I never had a doubt. Looking back, I was fearless in pursuing her. It was as if the secret combination of life tumbled into place and opened a door, and we found each other again, this time so quickly and in plain sight.*

*I used to hate for the sun to go down.*

***

The sky highway became bumpy, causing the plane to bank and pitch. Nervous passengers clutched their armrests. Flight attendants continued loading their serving carts in the galley, bracing themselves against the bulkheads to steady themselves, utterly professional, as if turbulence was no big deal. Or like ducks on the pond, calm on top the water but paddling like hell.

The captain's calm voice broke the silence. "This is your captain. We have encountered some bumps in the road, and we are looking for a friendlier place to fly. Meanwhile, I have turned on the fasten seat belt sign. Please buckle up and remain seated. I have asked the flight attendants to take their seats."

Forrest didn't hear the message. His smile soaring thirty thousand feet where his reminisces were closer to heaven.

After passing through the turbulence, the rush of adrenaline, the groan of the engines, the gentle vibration, the dark interior, dotted by a few reading lights and hushed conversations, all became a potion for drowsiness and nodding heads.

The flight attendants resumed serving the passengers a full dinner of turkey, mashed potatoes and gravy, and a side of corn.

# 46

The flight attendant working first-class considered waking Mr. Nelthorpe but decided it was a long flight, and she'd take special care of him when he awoke. Besides, she figured if he had slept through the turbulence and the commotion, he must have needed the sleep. He looked as content as the Maharishi, oblivious to the airplane's pitch and roll, which had settled into a calm groove serenaded by the muffle of engines.

Long after serving the passengers, over six hours away from California's coast, near the halfway point to Australia, the passengers were sleeping, reading, or watching movies. Across the aisle from Forrest, Alexia slept, and her mother read the book, *The Help*.

First Class flight attendant, Roxane Ryan, was a charming middle-aged woman, perfectly suited for her job, admired by the flight crews. Stepping into the coach cabin, she motioned for one of her colleagues, CamilaRodriguez, to join her in the first-class galley.

When they were alone, in a hushed, urgent voice, she said, "The guy in 1B hasn't moved since we took off. I can't even tell if he's breathing. God, is he dead?"

"Let me take a look," Maria offered.

As casually as the alarm allowed, she walked past Forrest and glanced over to consider Roxane's concerns. On her way back, she leaned in and nudged his arm. He was smiling peacefully like a meditating monk. "Mr. Nelthorpe. Mr. Nelthorpe." When he didn't react, she nudged him again, harder. Again, there was no reaction. She calmly wrapped her hand around his wrist to see if she could feel a pulse. She quickly jerked her hand away and hastily returned to the galley.

Roxane waited for her. Taking a deep breath, "God, I think you're right. We need to notify the captain."

Turning her back to the passengers, Roxane, over the intercom in a low voice, explained the situation to the captain. Immediately, Captain Simone emerged from the cockpit and maneuvered the two flight attendants off to the side. "You say it's the man in 1B? What's his name?"

"Nelthorpe," Camila answered. "Forrest Nelthorpe. He didn't appear to be in any distress when he boarded. He was pleasant. Only had one glass of wine."

"Roxane, I need you to run interference. Distract the passengers across the aisle. We need to avoid alarming the other passengers. Some people are unnerved when they see the Captain out of his cave. Are there any open seats in first class?"

"The whole back row is open."

"If we need to, we'll move them to the back row. Also, check the manifest. See if there is a doctor on board."

As casually as a passenger taking a seat in First Class, the captain settled in next to Forrest. At the same time, a male passenger from coach entered First Class on his way to use the forward head. Camila intercepted him and asked him to use the coach head in her most pleasant voice, hoping to avoid a reaction, aware that sometimes passengers didn't always like when the riffraff in coach wasn't good enough to use the forward head. Roxane stood in the aisle as a lookout. The mother and small girl across the aisle were both sleeping.

Sitting in the seat next to Forrest, he gently shook him. Then harder. Next, he felt Forrest's forehead with the back of his hand. After trying to find a pulse, unsure, he looked around and placed his hand on his chest to feel for a heartbeat.

When he returned to the First Class galley area to regroup Roxane said, "We have a doctor in coach. Retired dermatologist."

"Close enough. Ask him to come up here. And, ask the family across the aisle to move to the seats in the back row."

Captain Simone disappeared into the cockpit to update the co-pilot, and when he returned, Camila was escorting an older man in his early eighties. He was distinguished looking, short in stature, with a bushy mustache that dripped over his upper lip. His long white hair flared out over his ears. Dr. Hill was traveling with his wife of sixty years. He looked more like a college professor, in his brown tweed sport coat and tortoiseshell glasses than a Mankato, Minnesota, dermatologist.

He sat next to Forrest and leaned in close. After a few minutes, he turned to Captain Simone. "Good news. He's alive." Turning to Roxane, "Was he drinking? Did he board drunk?"

"No. He was sober. He nursed a glass of wine."

"I can't rouse him. He needs medical assistance. Get some oxygen on him."

As Roxane and Dr. Hill watched over Forrest, unbeknownst to the passengers, the plane made a course correction as Captain Simone diverted the plane for an emergency stop. As they neared the point when the plane would slow and begin to make its descent, and become noticeable to the passengers, the captain announced, "We are making an emergency landing in Papeete, Tahiti. We have a passenger who needs medical attention. I am asking all passengers to remain in their seats while medical personnel board the plane and administer needed care. We are not planning a long delay and will proceed when the situation clears. All passengers will remain on board. Thank you."

Twenty minutes later, they landed at Faa'a International Airport in Papette. When the door opened, Hiro Otoo and Teva Faahotu, two uniformed members of the emergency team at The Centre Hospitalier de Polynésie Française rushed inside. Faces leaned into the aisles to catch a glimpse of what was happening.

Twenty-two minutes later, they arrived at Ta'aone Hospital. As they crashed through the hospital doors, the emergency room clerk directed them to a room. "Chambre cinq," she yelled out.

A lightweight cotton blanket covered Forrest, his mouth covered by an oxygen mask, Hiro Otoo held an IV drip. Fetia and Moana, the charge nurse, joined them as they rushed down the corridor. They situated the gurney and the two emergency techs took their position. Nurse Moana called out, "Un, deux, trois." Together they lifted him on to the emergency room bed.

Dr. Seruvatu entered as Nurse Fetia connected him to a monitor. Both Dr. Seruvatu and Nurse Fetia had studied in the states and spoke English. He graduated from UCLA, and she from Loma Linda

University, both in California. An IV drip snaked down to his forearm.

Stepping behind Forrest, he clapped loudly, then peeled Forrest's eyelids back and looked into his eyes. "Get me a fundoscope."

Dr. Seruvatu circled Forrest, felt his pulse again, and listened to his chest with a stethoscope. Next, he leaned close to smell his breath for alcohol, then began to evaluate his reactions by pinpricks to his feet and arms. He could see the patient was a man in his sixties. "American?"

"ID says he is from Minneapolis, en route to Australia. Forrest Nelthorpe," Nurse Fetia said.

"Nice name. Looks peaceful enough." Dr. Seruvatu could see he was in good physical condition, perfect weight for his height. Good muscle tone. "Call Dr. Mandara for a consult. This man appears to be in a coma or some kind of trance. Time could be urgent." Holding up Forrest's left hand, he showed her his diamond-studded wedding band. "This man is married, and it looks like true love." Smiling, "Have someone track down his wife."

# 47

While Dr. Mandara was en route to the hospital, Nurse Fetia and Dr. Seruvatu attended to Forrest. Nurse Fetia laid her hands on his arm. Seeing him lying there so peacefully but not in this world was puzzling. "He looks so peaceful. Like he is somewhere else."

"I can't explain it," Dr. Seruvatu answered. "Only God knows at this point."

Meanwhile, one of the administrative staff attempted to track down Mr. Nelthorpe's wife.

Manua, dressed in slacks and a short-sleeve white shirt, interrupted them. "We have a phone number for Mr. Nelthorpe's residence. Heikapu, is calling the number right now." Dr. Seruvatu quickly exited and made his way to the nurse's station.

Christina was passing through the kitchen on her way out. She had taken time off after the wedding. In a few days, she and Thomas were leaving for their honeymoon. She answered the phone on the third ring. "Hello, this is the Nelthorpe residence. She wouldn't normally answer the phone that way but she hadn't changed her phone number. It still felt like her father's home. Hello . . . ?" Christina repeated.

"Hello," Heikapu said. "Is this the Nelthorpe residence? In Minneapolis?"

Cautiously, Christiana answered. "Why, yes, it is. Who is this ?"

"Are you the wife of Forrest Nelthorpe?"

"Wife?"

"Is his wife available?"

"He doesn't have a wife. What do you want?"

"Are you a family member?"

"I'm Christina Nelthorpe . . . Bradley. I am his daughter. Now tell me who you are and what you want."

When Dr. Seruvatu arrived at the nurse's station, Heikapu handed him the phone. "I have the Nelthorpe residence."

"Hello, I'm Dr. Seruvatu. Who am I speaking to?"

"Christina Bradley . . . his daughter."

"Is his wife available?

"Why does everyone keep asking for his wife? She is deceased. She has been gone for a long time."

"I am sorry. I did not know. My apologies. He is wearing a wedding ring."

Christina drew a deep breath and gripped the phone. "I've never seen him wear a wedding ring. Why are you saying this?"

"I'm sorry to tell you . . . your father is in a coma. I am calling from Ta'aone Hospital in Tahiti. We do not yet know the source of his coma and are investigating. We need some permissions. Does he have a living will? I'm not suggesting . . . we need to be respectful of his wishes."

Christina gripped the phone and tried to catch her breath. Tears filled her eyes and began to pour down her cheeks. *He's in Tahiti. He's in a coma.*

Dr. Seruvatu could hear her crying. "I wish I knew more. We have just started to run tests. We have a specialist coming. He is a famous doctor. Your father is in a coma, and we don't know why. Do you understand? If there is something the doctor can do, we will need some permission."

Christina fought to regain control. "Yes. Do whatever you have to, to save his life."

"I can fax you some forms . . . ."

"No," Christina interrupted. "Don't do that. Do whatever you have to. Save his life. I will leave right now. I will be there as soon as I can."

As he hung up the phone Dr. Seruvatu heard Nurse Fetia scream out.

Rushing into the room, Dr. Seruvatu saw that Forrest's face had turned bright red like he was holding his breath. He began to shake. Dr. turned to nurse Fetia. "Note the time." They watched and waited. "We need the toxicology report stat."

Nurse Fetia looked to Dr. Seruvatu for additional orders.

"We do nothing. Watch that he doesn't rip out the line." After twenty seconds, the shaking abated. Still, he had a tortured look on his face.

"What happened?" Nurse Fetia asked.

"I don't know."

"It looked like he was in terror. Like he was having a nightmare."

***

Dr. Seruvatu went home to sleep about the same time Dr. Mandara arrived. He examined Forrest, reviewed all the tests, and called a medical expert friend in California. Dr. Mandara lived on another island, so he spent the night in the doctor's lounge.

When Chrissy arrived mid-morning, she rushed to his hospital room. She gasped when she entered the room, unable to step forward. A white sheet covered Forrest up to his neck. An IV bottle hung beside his bed, a monitor on a cart beside him, connected by wires running to his chest and arms. Oxygen tubing ran into his nasal passages. Forrest looked peaceful but lifeless. She looked at the monitor beside the bed and then to Forrest to observe his chest's rising and falling. She couldn't recall ever seeing him asleep, except bent over in his favorite leather library chair.

Dr. Mandara stepped beside her. "You are Christina."

Taking her by the arm, he guided her to an adjacent room. Christina turned and faced him. In his sixties, a whisper-thin, white-haired man, wearing small round silver-framed glasses and loose-fitting cotton pants under his white lab coat, and open sandals, he could have been mistaken for a man just coming off the beach. Holding her hands in his, in a soft prayerful voice, said, "I am sorry we have been unable to do anything for your father. He is resting comfortably."

A wall of tears gave way, dammed up from Minneapolis to Tahiti. She acknowledged him with a nod and a sob.

"I am Dr. Tapunui Mandara. I am taking care of your father. You talked to Dr. Seruvatu yesterday." A Harvard-trained neurologist, Dr. Mandara was a bit of legend on the islands, a descendant in a line of Tahitian physicians and priests. According to ancient Sanskrit legend about the god's search for immortality, Mandara was a sacred mountain from which flowed the waters of immortality.

"Your father remains unresponsive. We thought he was in a coma when he arrived. Since then, we have run every test we could, including an MRI brain scan. We are looking at everything. I even called a Harvard colleague. There doesn't appear to be any obvious causes or evidence of a coma. No evidence of trauma. He doesn't appear to have had a stroke. Basic blood tests don't suggest anything physiological. He's not diabetic, no infections or bites. No detectable toxins. We are stumped. I am not calling it a coma. It is more a dissociative state. More like a trance. So, I wanted to talk to you before you saw him."

Dr. Mandara patiently waited for her to collect herself. "Has anything like this ever occurred before in your family?"

"No, not that I'm aware."

"So, tell me about him. Is there anything you know that could cause him to check out like this?"

Shaking her head, searching her memory. "No. "He just retired."

"Was it traumatic for him?"

"No. For years I've heard him tell Flo and Luka he couldn't wait until retirement."

"Who is Luka?"

"I used to say he was his driver, but he's more a friend, a confidant."

"We may need to talk to him. How about your mom. I understand your mom is deceased?"

A puzzled look swept over Christina as she recalled the comment about her father wearing a wedding ring. "She died when I was a little girl. In a fire." Even as she heard her answer, she thought about the mysteries surrounding her father and how reluctant he had always been to discuss her mom, trying to make sense of even the smallest things. Her mother's death confused her, still.

Dr. Mandara studied her, wondering if there was more to the story.

"He never got over it. Dad loved her so."

"Is that why he has those scars? He was in the fire with her?"

She had never been asked about this even by Thomas. Now she needed to provide answers, answers to questions that had been percolating. "Probably. I guess he was. He was in a fire. He never got over losing her."

"How do you mean?"

"He began to drink."

Dr. Mandara interrupted, "Did he drink a lot?"

"I don't know. Dad didn't drink around me, but often at night when I was in bed. Sometimes, I could tell, drinks were sitting on his desk in the library or on the bar in the television room or kitchen counter. As I grew older and understood more about adult drinking, it was more obvious. I used to find him in the library curled up in his leather chair, a whiskey bottle on the stand next to him. I never wanted to wake him. Other than that, you wouldn't know anything was wrong . . . except . . . do you think his drinking had anything to do with this?"

"Not likely. Not directly anyway. His alcohol level is low. His liver is intact."

Dr. Mandara pressed her, "Except?"

"He was sad. Even when he seemed happy, I knew better. I heard him often tell Flo he was going to be with her. Flo always said not having her was killing him."

"Flo? Who is she? Is she his current wife? His friend?"

A smile flashed across Christina's face. "Oh, heavens, no. I wouldn't have minded it, her being his wife, but Dad never saw another woman. Flo was more my mother and his personal assistant. I never saw them together . . . she was loyal. I think he loved her in a special way."

"We talked to his physician back home, and he wasn't on any anti-depressants. Did he take any drugs you know of?"

"Not Dad. So, what can we do? Wait? How long? I need to see him."

"Give me a few more minutes. I can't say this is a coma. There's nothing to support it except his unresponsiveness. It's more like a depersonalization disorder, but it's hard to understand without a psychological profile. No, this is not something physiological. It's more a dissociative disorder. Not something you would necessarily be aware of, like a deep secret."

"That's him all right—deep secrets."

"When all the horses are accounted for, we start looking for zebras," Dr. Mandar said. "The number of people in this category is small, but derealization experiences have been reported by most of the general population, with varying degrees of intensity. Not usually in the deep end of the pool. Was he seeing any other doctors?"

Christina shrugged her shoulders. "I don't think so."

"It may be simply up to him. Science knows little in this area. Sometimes people choose to . . . check out. It is not uncommon, but there isn't much data."

# 48

Dr. Mandara's smile conveyed hope. "Let's go see him. Talk to him. Let him hear your voice. See if there is a response. Perhaps in time, something will trigger something in him."

Christina dabbed at her eyes. His white hair in this white room, covered with a white sheet, accentuated his red and craggy facial scars.

Throughout the afternoon, Chrissy stayed at his side, occasionally resting her head on the bed. He looked so peaceful. Powerless to understand what was happening, no matter how hard she tried, nothing in her learning, her experience, or what the doctor said provided any answers. Every thought led to a dead end. *What were his secrets? Was this about Mom? What was he like before the fire? What was she like? She tried to recall her mother's face, but she couldn't. She was too young for such memories. What happened?*

Chrissy sought answers to questions she wondered about before, stretching back to her childhood. *Was he with her right now? Dad always said she was his soul mate. She must have been a great woman to be so loved. Can a person will themselves to leave this earth to be in heaven with their soul mate? I remember he told me that how we lived our lives was the difference between Heaven and Hell. Forrest always told Chrissy how to live her life high on the stem. What did he mean?*

Dr. Mandara said this was beyond science. Her dad always said, keep an open mind when people use science for their arguments. Listen to your heart. What do humans know about science anyway? How primitive it is. Science has been wrong as often as it has been right. All you need to believe is we live in an age of forbidden science and of knowledge not yet attained. What are miracles anyway but merely real unexplained happenings?

At dinner time, a new nursing shift completed their transition and went about their routine duties. Several hours had passed since Christina's last conversation with both Dr. Seruvatu and Dr. Mandara. Nurses moved in and out, checking on him.

The hallway lights dimmed, and someone had turned the lights off in his room so only one light behind Forrest remained on. The hallway commotion of the changing shift, serving dinners, and delivering medications to the patients had subsided.

She pushed a chair beside his bed and laid her head on the bed and dozed off. She had traveled all night to get there and hadn't slept. When she awoke, Dr. Mandara and Nurse Fetia were standing on the other side of the bed. He tenderly stroked Forrest's shoulder.

"I know this is hard. The not knowing. The suddenness. When people give up or want to die, there is not much anyone can do. Could that be?"

As she considered his questions, she couldn't take her gaze off of her father. She expected him to open his eyes and smile. "I don't know. Sometimes I don't think I know him. He was so secretive. All I know is he was a great leader, and he poured all his love into me.

There wasn't room for anything else but raising me. He was so filled with love but so hollow. I never saw him happy around anyone else. If he's with my mother, he'll never come back." Christina began to weep softly. "He seems to be in a faraway place."

"What was your mother's name?"

Smiling through her tears, she answered, "Alexandra. Allie to Dad. My great grandfather was a history professor. Alexandra was the last empress of Russia. Dad called her his princess."

"Maybe he's with her right now."

"He'd like that. I guess . . . I guess I would too." Christina noticed Fetia's eyes were watering. "I think he is. Can you hear me, Daddy? Are you with Mom? Tell her I love her."

Dr. Mandara and his nurse left, and the hospital grew dark and quiet. Chrissy grew weary from staring at him and laid her head on the bed, and began to tenderly stroke his chest, feeling his heartbeat.

"Oh, please don't die," she pleaded. Through her tears, she cried out. "Can you hear me? Please."

"Allie."

At first, she thought it was a dream, then she heard it again, ever so softly. "Allie?"

Christina jumped to her feet and stood close to him. Forrest rolled his head to the side to see her. "Allie, is that you? Where are we? Allie, where are we?"

"No. It's me, Chrissy."

Forrest ripped his oxygen mask off. "Chrissy!" More loudly, "It's you."

She pushed the call button pinned to the side of his bed and tried to remain calm.

Forrest's gaze darted around the room and back to Chrissy. "I didn't think this would happen."

"What do you mean?"

Forrest looked away and then back to her. "I never imagined I would end up . . . where am I?"

"Tahiti."

"Tahiti?" A smile broke across his face. "Almost paradise."

Dr. Mandara and Nurse Fetia rushed into the room and examined him, looking into his eyes, testing his reflexes, and performing a basic neurologic exam. The nurse drew some blood. "Do you know where you are?"

"Paradise, I'm told."

Dr. Mandara smiled and looked to his nurse, "Note he has a sense of humor." Looking back to Forrest, he asked, "Do you know what happened?"

Forrest hesitated and rolled his head to the side. "I was dreaming, I guess."

"Dreaming?"

"I was with Allie."

"But you are here now."

Looking over to Chrissy, a curious look crossed Forrest's face, "With my daughter."

Dr. Mandara looked to Christina, "You can visit with your father. We will monitor him closely."

When Dr. Mandara and the nurse left the room, Forrest smiled at Chrissy and said, "I bet you came to ask me questions. Right?"

Christina laughed. "Finally. I had to come to Tahiti to get you to talk."

"I don't know what to say. I was with Allie. That's what I wanted, what I hoped. And now . . . I've gone over this in my mind a thousand times. So many times, I prepared myself to talk with you, but the time was never right. Sweetheart, life is so random. We all make mistakes in our lives, some small and some large ones, and they all can trigger events that can spin out of our control. Sometimes you don't do anything, somebody else does, and you get caught up in it, and it stays with you all your life. For some, it follows them to their grave, and for others, the problems drift into the atmosphere and, like a red balloon, poof, disappears. For me, it has followed me to this place."

Forrest looked to Chrissy to see if he was making sense to her. Her face was blank. She hung on every word, hoping for a breakthrough, praying for understanding.

"There was a lady . . . a lady in my company who was blackmailing me. Woody hired her into the company, and she turned out to be mentally disturbed. Beyond disturbed. She wanted a lot. More than I could give her. She stalked me. I learned people like her are more prevalent than any of us think. They can be fun people to be around, smart and successful, but they haven't got an ounce of empathy for anything or anybody. They're the kind of people who set cats on fire when they are young." Forrest's voice weakened. He stammered. "She set out to destroy me and become the CEO of the company." Choking on his words, "She ran your mom off the road and set fire to our cabin."

Chrissy gasped. "Oh, my God. Did she kill Mom? Does anyone know about this? There's a guy in prison for this, right?"

"Her name was Kim Merrymore."

Chrissy covered her mouth. "That's the woman. The woman in the crash. I saw it on the news at the airport. She died in a fiery crash on a winding road up by Monticello."

Forrest didn't change his expression and looked on passively.

"She was in a crash. I am sure of the name. It was her."

Chrissy studied him. Forrest's expression went blank. *What was he thinking? He doesn't seem surprised.* She was used to searching for answers in his silence. "Did you know about the crash?"

Forrest sighed, shaking his head, looking into the room for answers. Looking back to Chrissy, softly, he answered her. "Fiery death, like Allie's. She got what she deserved. Yes, that was the woman. When you get back, it'll be in all the papers, no doubt. The man in prison is innocent. They'll set him free. I am sorry for him."

"She set the fire and killed mom?"

"There is no doubt."

"Was I alive? Was I there? Was I in the fire?"

Forrest swallowed hard and tried to gather himself. "You were a baby. It was before you can remember anything."

"But I was there. In the fire?"

"Chrissy, I am so sorry." A torrent of tears gushed forth.

Chrissy couldn't recall ever seeing her dad cry like that.

"For so long, all I wanted was a cool drink of water," he said. "Always ahead of a mirage, just keep moving . . . I am so sorry. It was such a long ordeal. It's over." Forrest's tears were uncontrollable. Deep sobs shook him. "This was so unfair to you. What a way to be brought up—no mother, an alcoholic father. I tried so hard to be a good father."

Chrissy interrupted, "You were a great father. How could anyone want more?"

"I miss your mom so much. Every day I missed her, I saw you, your greens eyes. I always thought I was looking at her in your eyes. And now you are grown up, and you could be twins." Through his tears, Forrest struggled to finish. "I loved her so much. Our love was like a love no other, like loving a new soft puppy but all your life, the same feeling every day, forever."

Chrissy contemplated his words. "I love Thomas, too, but I never felt that way."

"Maybe in a thousand earth years, you will."

Chrissy leaned over his bed and rested her head on his chest. "Oh, Daddy, you were a great father. I remember the ABC song you used to sing to me. You always made me feel so important, so loved." She jerked her head up, startled like she had seen a ghost, and looked into his eyes. "You saved me in the fire, didn't you?"

Forrest broke off connection with Chrissy's gaze, rolled his head to the side, and began to shake.

"Didn't you?" Chrissy pressed him. "But you couldn't save mom."

Fighting to talk through his tears, Forrest emptied his heart. "Your mom was paralyzed. I tried to carry both of you. She told me to come back for her, but I couldn't. I tried." Rubbing his scars. "I promised her I'd come back for her, but the fire . . . Oh, Chrissy. I'm so sorry."

"Daddy, you are going home with me. I love you, Daddy. I'm going to take care of you like you did me." Tears began to run off her cheeks, not in a trickle but like a flowing river.

"Chrissy, you're so tired. We'll talk in the morning. You need to rest."

"I want to take you home. Promise me," she insisted. "I don't want to lose you."

"Chrissy. Go, get some rest. You look so tired."

Shrugging her shoulders, "I am. And, tired of crying." Shaking her head, "So tired. I don't think I have any more tears. Please promise me you'll come home with me."

Chrissy laid her head on the bed next to his. Several minutes passed before another word was spoken. Neither wanted to let go of the other. Rising, she said, "Okay. I'll rest and come back."

When she arrived at the door, she looked back and smiled.

Forrest smiled in return. "Your mom said she loves you too."

She looked at him curiously, turned, and left.

# 49

Join me in my nightfall dreams
Together again in moonbeam gleams
Then by day in puffy clouds
Of hopeless longing shrouds
Kiss my lips and hold me tight,
I will be with *you tonight.*

*Love makes us all poets.*

*I can't walk anymore. My life depends on a live-in caretaker, what life is left. For the longest time, I prayed for a miracle. Still, when I close my eyes, I'm with Allie, so I keep them closed for long periods.*

*When she promised we would be together again, I believed her with all my heart. Now the days pass slowly, time a paradox, life rushing between birthdays, but each day passes to the thunder of ticking seconds. Most of my days are spent alone. When the weather is good, we go outside by the fountain and in the snow season, bedside the fireplace in the library.*

*Maybe today will be the day.*

*Slumped in my two big wheels chair, I dream and hope. Candy, my live-in nurse, is available twenty-four hours a day. She is a heavy-set, middle-aged, tattooed blond woman, a committed spinster she tells me. She talks to me all the time, even though I don't respond. She tells me she's married to caring.*

*It's not often I look into a mirror. I can't remember the last time I saw myself, really saw myself, not the glancing image of the repulsive caricature I am, not who I am inside my head. The image in the mirror is not me. A shriveled sight, the scars on the side of my face and neck have turned purple, sag over my jaw, and blend into my wrinkled face and neck to present a grotesque image. I used to be embarrassed by the way I looked, but now it doesn't matter.*

*After I lost Allie, I was obsessed with being with her again, even made plans for the day Chrissy left home to be on her own. That was the pact Allie and I made. Before Chrissy's wedding, I made plans. I left my CEO position, sold my company, made generous contributions to charities, and gifted my Lake Minnetonka lake home to Chrissy and her new husband, Tom. I set up some trusts for people I loved who were at my side in my darkest hours. When Chrissy had her daughter, she named her Allie. Not Alexandra, Allie. She called Flo, Nana.*

*Chrissy and Thomas have been good to me through the years, although because I don't talk, they think I can't hear or think. I can. Since my second stroke, I am aware words take the long way from my brain to my mouth, and sometimes it's too late to let the words out, so they die on my tongue.*

*Now Luka is the only friend who visits. Originally, he was my driver, but he became a friend, my best friend, my brother. I love him with all my heart. When it was warm, we sat outside by the fountain and in the winter in the library in front of the fire. We enjoyed our times together. Sometimes, Luka had a beer or a glass of wine, but he wasn't much of a drinker. I was but now I don't. I always thought he didn't drink so he could watch out for me.*

*Sometimes, Flo would join us, but she was uncomfortable with the long silence periods. He was always looking out for me in ways the world would never know. He was the keeper of my secrets and me of his. Most of all, we shared a secret we both would take to our graves.*

*Not long ago, Flo passed away quickly, taken by a six-month cancer. One day she was caring for me then she went to the hospital and never came back. Florine Lasalle was my house manager, and for a long time, my personal assistant and mother to Christina, my everything, then she just vanished. Like magic.*

*Flo was always there for me. She lived along a narrow cobblestone path beyond the swimming pool and patio. We grew old together, our hairs whitened, and skin wrinkled as we faced the best and the worst of my years. I didn't go to her funeral. Chrissy never saw me shed a tear over her passing. But when I was alone, I cried. I bawled without uttering a sound.*

*I miss the times she read me books from her library. She didn't seem to care whether I was listening. Even though my eyes were closed, she knew I was taking it all in on some level. She always picked the best stories. The last book she read to me was Heart Earth by Ivan Doig. Having grown up in northern Minnesota, I was never much of a city boy. I loved stories about the country life and the landscapes folds where your mind wanders between cloud breaks, the rising and falling of the days, and cascading sunsets with a full moon at your shoulder.*

*I had read the book before. My head drooped, drooling, and my eyes closed for long periods easily misinterpreted that my mind was gone. But Flo knew the book was one of my favorites. It was a story about the author's mom, who passed on long before her time. It was a companion prequel to Ivan Doig's, This House of Sky, which, in western Shakespearean prose, expressed the author's love for his father and mother.*

*Toward the end of the book, Flo's reading slowed. She stammered a little and fought back tears as she recalled memories of her mother and father, the loss of her husband, and the sadness we shared with Allie's passing.*

*She paused. I knew she was watching me as she reached the end of her reading.*

*Dreams give us lift; she had known that ever since Moss Agate.*

*The trick is to bear up after the weight of life comes back.*

*It was hard coming back home with Chrissy. I wanted to continue my journey even after my failed attempt to be with Allie.*

*I remember daylight was waning, but we were close to the end of the book, so Flo pressed on:*

*"Nobody got over her."*

*Flo let out a deep sigh and reached out for my hand. I could feel the warmth of her touch by memory. She sighed and began to read again.*

*"And I can see at last, the curtain of time which fell prematurely on us, that I am another one for who my mother's existence did not end when her life happened to."*

*The sound of Flo's voice drifted away. Water tumbling over the fountain rocks consumed the silence. My eyes were closed. It was always the same image of being with Allie and pleading for the time we would be together again. I thought we would be together before now. God knows I tried.*

*Skeptics don't believe love can be forever, that Allie was waiting for me to join her, that miracles happen every day. I believe we have always been together with all my heart, and we will continue throughout eternity.*

*When I close my eyes, I am with Allie. I think of our days together, when we met, our first kiss, the miracle cabin, that evening on the lake. We didn't know we had arrived at the pinnacle of our lives, and change could come quickly as a day turns to night. How could we have known? How could anyone?*

*It was in the late fall and our last trip to the cabin for the season. Allie was starting to show, carrying our little Chrissy. As if spring had arrived again, the woodlands were blooming like flowers in colors of carmine and pumpkin spice, and weeping Tamarack had turned a rusty hue.*

*Late in the afternoon, we had taken the canoe halfway down the lake. The sunburned faces of summer boaters had left the lake to return to their city homes, the shoreline cabins were dark, the water was still, and the encroaching night caressed the remaining daylight.*

*We stopped and listened to a pair of loons sing out in a haunting tremolo, a joyful celebration of the good life. In the distance, an Osprey dipped toward the water. A Moose waded into the shallows nearby, and a minute later, we spied a calf standing one step away from invisibility at the edge of the forest. We held our breaths. Turning toward each other, our gazes embraced, and in the sudden stillness, we knew we were at that moment—life would never be better than that moment. The wind shifted to the north, and we knew it was time to return to the cabin.*

***

In the night, Forrest's wish came true. He found Allie again, lying on their Ten Mile Lake dock, smiling up to him, waiting for him to open his eyes. Aristotle was with her. Forrest was wearing a Twins ball cap, Hawaiian swim trunks, Allie a yellow two-piece swimming suit, and her long brown hair pulled back in a ponytail tied with a yellow ribbon. Two loons swam close to the dock. Together they watched white puffy clouds drift by. One of the clouds was shaped like Mickey Mouse.

# Other Books by Richard McMaster

***Voyage of Life***. The Voyage of Lifestory is told as the Robert Cole *Voyage of Life* paintings are described: *Childhood, Youth, Manhood, and Old Age*. The paintings are a metaphor for Sean's life. In early manhood he thinks MADDY, his one true love, has left him for another man and spends his life wondering what happened.

***The Other Half***. Twelve days before Christmas LUKE loses his job and his wife is called away to care for her dying mother. Left alone at Christmas time, of the major traumatic life events—being fired from a job, fearing divorce, plotting murder, the death of a family member and jail time, any one of which can threaten your very existence—he faces them all.

***Aaron's War***. Aaron's War is about a young soldier who can't kill, overwhelmed by the horrors of war, conflicted by religion and ravaged by memories, makes the painful choice to leave his wife and child. Later, when he confronts the German soldier who spared his life, he faces a life decision that could take him back home.

**2018 runner up fiction book of the year Arizona Author's Association**

*A Love Divided by Time*. FORREST AND ALLIE believed they found love in a previous life and being born again was a game of hide and seek to find each other in plain sight, seeking their better halves, united and whole. When tragedy strikes, Forrest makes a pact to find her killer, raise their daughter, and find peace by joining her in the ever after.

**2019 finalist unpublished book of the year of the Arizona Author's Association.**

**The Attic.** The attic is an emotional story about facing adversity and overcoming loss. When BYRON KELLY's wife dies, he faces assault charges and a lawsuit, and flees to Chicago and assumes a new identity. When Byron Kelly becomes a whistleblower on the run from the FBI he hides out in the attic of a dying old man, HENRY STEELE. Byron cares for the old man and learns he is estranged from his daughter over the death of her mother, his wife, because of family secrets he has kept from her.

For information on novels by this author go to:
www.Richard-McMaster.com